"Come here," Harding said once they were under way. "Take the tiller. You may as well start learning right off."

"Yes, sir," Art said, taking the tiller in his own hands. He could feel the surge of the water and the control he had over the boat.

"You're doing a good job," Harding said, sitting down on a bale of cloth and lighting his pipe. He took a few puffs while he studied Art. "Run away from home, did you?"

"No, I . . ." Art started. Then he decided that it was time to be honest with the man who had helped him. "Yes, sir," he said sheepishly. "I ran away."

"Trouble at home?"

"No. I just wanted to . . ." He let the sentence trail off, and Harding laughed.

"You wanted to see the creature, didn't you?"

"See the creature?"

"That's just a saying, son. It's a saying for folks like us."

"Like us?"

"You and me. There are some folks who are born, live, and die and never get more'n ten miles away from home in any direction. Then there's folks that's always wondering what's on the other side of the next hill. And when they get over that hill, why, damn me if they don't feel like they got to go on to the next one and the next one, and the next one after that. They're always hopin' they'll find somethin' out there, some sort of creature they ain't never seen before. I know it's that way with me."

Art smiled. "Yes, sir," he said. "I'd say it's that way with me too."

BOOK YOUR PLACE ON OUR WEBSITE AND MAKE THE READING CONNECTION!

We've created a customized website just for our very special readers, where you can get the inside scoop on everything that's going on with Zebra, Pinnacle and Kensington books.

When you come online, you'll have the exciting opportunity to:

- View covers of upcoming books
- Read sample chapters
- Learn about our future publishing schedule (listed by publication month *and author*)
- Find out when your favorite authors will be visiting a city near you
- Search for and order backlist books from our online catalog
- Check out author bios and background information
- Send e-mail to your favorite authors
- Meet the Kensington staff online
- Join us in weekly chats with authors, readers and other guests
- Get writing guidelines
- AND MUCH MORE!

Visit our website at
http://www.kensingtonbooks.com

THE FIRST MOUNTAIN MAN: PREACHER

William W. Johnstone

PINNACLE BOOKS
Kensington Publishing Corp.
http://www.kensingtonbooks.com

PINNACLE BOOKS are published by

Kensington Publishing Corp.
850 Third Avenue
New York, NY 10022

Copyright © 2002 by William W. Johnstone

All rights reserved. No part of this book may be reproduced in any form or by any means without the prior written consent of the Publisher, excepting brief quotes used in reviews.

If you purchased this book without a cover, you should be aware that this book is stolen property. It was reported as "unsold and destroyed" to the Publisher and neither the Author nor the Publisher has received any payment for this "stripped book."

All Kensington Titles, Imprints, and Distributed Lines are available at special quantity discounts for bulk purchases for sales promotions, premiums, fund-raising, and educational or institutional use. Special book excerpts or customized printings can also be created to fit specific needs. For details, write or phone the office of the Kensington special sales manager: Kensington Publishing Corp., 850 Third Avenue, New York, NY 10022, attn: Special Sales Department, Phone: 1-800-221-2647.

Pinnacle and the P logo Reg. U.S. Pat. & TM Off.

First Printing: January 2002
10 9 8 7

Printed in the United States of America

He was a man known far and wide. A mountain man who could out-cuss, out-dance, out-sing, ride farther and faster than any of his contemporaries. He was a legendary figure of the West before it became a West civilized with towns and trains and sheriffs and telegraph wires.

But before he became the stuff of legend, he was a run-away youth, known only as Art. This is Art's story, as sung in Indian councils, told around campfires, embellished in saloons, immortalized in dime novels, and remembered by those historians who, nearly two hundred years later, will record events in the life of a man called Preacher.

One

1813, Ohio

Leaving his brother sleeping in the bed behind him, the boy stepped out of the bedroom and into the upstairs hallway. He moved down to the end of the hall to his parents' bedroom, where he stood just outside their door for a moment listening to his pa's heavy snoring.

His pa's snores were loud because he slept hard. He worked hard too, eking out a living for his family by laboring from dawn to dusk on a farm that was more rock than dirt, and took more than it gave.

His ma was in there too, though her rhythmic breathing could scarcely be heard over her husband's snores. She was always the last to go to bed and the first to get up. It was nearly two hours before dawn now, but Art knew that his mother would be rolling out of bed in less than an hour, starting another of the endless procession of backbreaking days that were the borders of her life.

"Ma, Pa, I want you both to know that I ain't leavin' 'cause of nothin' either of you have done," the boy said quietly. "You been good to me and there ain't no way I can ever pay you back for all that you done for me, or let you know how much I love you. But the truth is, I got me a hankerin' to get on with my life and I reckon twelve years is long enough to wait."

From there the boy, who had been christened Arthur, but was called Art, moved down to his sisters' room. He went into their room and saw them sleeping together in the bed his father had made for them. A silver splash of moonlight fell through the window, illuminating their faces. One was sucking her thumb, a habit she practiced even in her sleep; the other was clutching a corncob doll. The sheet had slipped down, so Art pulled it back up, covering their shoulders. The two girls, eight and nine, snuggled down into the sheet, but didn't awaken.

"I reckon I'm going to miss seeing you two girls grow up," Art said. "But I'll always keep you in my mind, along with Ma and Pa and my brother."

His good-byes having been said, Art picked up the pillowcase in which he had put a second shirt, another pair of pants, three biscuits, and an apple, and started toward the head of the stairs.

Although he had been planning this adventure for a couple of months, he didn't make the decision to actually leave until three days ago. On that day he stood on a bluff and watched a flatboat drift down the Ohio River, which flowed past the family farm. There was a family on the flatboat, holding on tightly to the little pile of canvas-covered goods that represented all their worldly possessions. One of the boat's passengers, a boy about Art's age, waved. Other than the wave, there had been nothing unusual about that particular boat. It was one of many similar vessels that passed by the farm every week.

To anyone else, seeing an entire family uprooted and looking for a new place to live, traveling the river with only those possessions they could carry on the boat with them, might have been a pitiful sight. But to Art, it was an adventure that stirred his soul, and he wished more than anything that he could be with them.

Art was nearly to the bottom of the stairs when the sudden chiming of the Eli Terry clock startled him. Gasping, he nearly dropped his sack, but recovered in time. He smiled sheepishly at his reaction. The beautifully decorated clock, which sat on the mantel over the fireplace, was the family's most prized possession. His mother had once told him, with great pride, that someday the clock would be his. Art reckoned, now, that it would go to his brother. His brother always put more store to the clock than he did anyway.

Recovering his poise, Art took a piece of paper from his pocket, and put it on the mantel beside the clock. It was addressed to "Ma and Pa."

At first he hadn't planned to tell anyone in his family that he was leaving. He was just going to go, and when his folks woke up for the next day's chores, they would find him gone. But at the last minute he thought his parents might rest a little easier if they knew he had left on his own, and had not been stolen in the middle of the night.

Art had enough schooling to enable him to read and write a little. He wasn't that good at it, but he was good enough to leave a note.

Ma and Pa
    Don't look for me for I have went away. I am near a man now and I want to be on my own. Love, your son, Arthur.

With the note in place, Art opened the front door quietly and stepped out onto the porch. It was still dark outside, and the farm was a cacophony of sound: frogs on the pond, singing insects clinging to the tall grass, and the whisper of the night wind through a nearby stand of elm trees.

Once he was out of the house and off the porch, Art moved quickly down the path that led to the river. When he reached the bluff, he turned and looked back. The house loomed large in the moonlight, a huge dark slab against the dull gray of the night. The window to his parents' bedroom was gleaming softly in the moonlight. It looked like a tear-glistened eye, a symbol that wasn't lost on Art. A lump came to his throat, his eyes stung, and for a moment, he actually considered abandoning his departure plans. But then he squared his shoulders.

"No," he said aloud. "I ain't goin' to stand here and cry like a baby. I said I'm a'goin', and by damn I'm goin'."

He turned away from the house.

"Sorry about sayin' 'damn,' Ma, but I reckon if I'm goin' to be a man, I'm goin' to have to start talkin' like a man."

Art left the beaten path, then picked his way through the brush down the side of the bluff to the river's edge. To the casual observer, there was nothing there, but when Art started pulling branches aside, he uncovered a small skiff.

He had found the boat earlier in the year during the spring runoff. No doubt it had broken from its moorings somewhere when the river was at freshet stage, though it was impossible to ascertain where it had come from. Art didn't exactly steal the boat, but he did hide it, even from his father. And he assured himself that if someone had come looking for the boat, he would have disclosed its location. But, as no search materialized—at least none of which he was aware—he got to keep the boat.

The boat provided him with a golden opportunity, and it wasn't until it came into his possession that he seriously began considering running away from home. He was leaving, not because of any abuse, but because of pure wanderlust.

If he put into the current now, some two hours before dawn, he would be six miles downriver by sunrise. By sundown he would be forty miles away. Throwing his sack into the bottom of the boat, he pulled it out of its hiding place, pushed it into the water at the river's edge, got into it, then paddled out to midstream and pointed downriver.

Under way now, he looked back toward the bank and saw that he was moving at a fairly good clip. It wasn't until that moment that he realized this might well be the last time he would ever set eyes on the land of his birth. That realization did not weaken his resolve.

Art had an oar, but as the current was swift and steady, no rowing was required to establish locomotion. Rather, he used the oar as a tiller to keep the boat centered in the river.

The boat moved downstream much more swiftly than he would have thought. By midafternoon he was already farther from home than he had ever been in his life.

He ate a biscuit.

He watched the sun set from the middle of the river. The sun flamed a wide, fan-shaped bank of clouds, turning them into a brilliant orange-gold. The river itself took on a light, translucent blue, as pretty as he had ever seen it. He began looking for a good place to put in, and saw a fallen tree lying half in and half out at the water's edge. He rowed over to the tree, tied his boat to it, and used its branches to hide the boat from view. Only then did he allow himself to eat the second of his three biscuits. His meal consumed . . . what there was of it . . . he stretched out in the bottom of the boat and went to sleep.

Two days later, his biscuits and apple gone, he was feeling pretty hungry when he saw several boats gathered beneath a high bluff. Halfway up the bluff was a large cave, and a hand-lettered sign explained that this was "Eby's River Trading Post." Even from the boat, he could hear loud conversation, laughter, and the music of fiddles and a jug. He could also smell the enticing aroma of roasting meat.

Art had no money, but he was mighty hungry, so he paddled ashore, hoping to be able to trade a little work for food. He tied the boat up to an exposed tree root, then walked up the path toward the mouth of the cave.

A few wide boards, supported by upright wooden barrels,

formed a counter that stretched across the front of the cave. Behind it, in the cave itself, were several shelves and boxes and barrels of goods, from whiskey, to clothing, to flour, bacon, beans, and 'taters. A red-faced, rather plump man was manning the counter and when Art walked up, the man came toward him.

"What can I do for you, sonny?"

"You have food here?"

The man laughed, then pointed back into the cave. Two women were cooking over an open fire.

"What's the matter with you, boy, that you can't smell it?" the man asked.

"I can smell it," Art replied. On his empty stomach, the smell of cooking food was about to drive him mad.

"Sonny, you ask anybody up and down the whole Ohio, an' they'll tell you that Eby's got near 'bout anything you could want," the man went on. "We got roast pork, chicken, rabbit, squirrel, and possum. We got fried dove, catfish, and carp. We got biscuits, cornbread, beans, 'taters, and gravy. You go back down and tell your ma she don't have to cook no supper tonight 'cause we got anything she might want right here. Yes, sir, for ten cents you can feast like a king."

"Are you Mr. Eby?"

"Mr. Eby?" The man chuckled. "Don't many folks call me mister," he said. "But yeah, I'm Eby. Now, you goin' to run down and tell your ma what I said?"

"My ma's not here.

"Well, who is here? Your pa?"

Art shook his head. "Ain't nobody here but me."

"You mean a boy like you is out here, travelin' on his own, with no family?"

Art pulled himself up to full height. He was tall for a twelve-year-old, and strong from at least three years of doing a man's work.

"By damn, I'm near to full-growed," Art announced resolutely. "I reckon I can travel without a family if I want to."

He thought the use of the phrase "by damn" was particularly effective.

Eby held up his hand. "Whoa, boy, don't be takin' no offense to my palaverin'. Your dime's as good as the next fella's, I reckon. What'll you have?"

"I'd love some pork and beans," Art said.

"Why, sure, boy, just show me your dime and I'll serve it right up to you."

Art cleared his throat and ran his hand through his hair. "Uh, well, that's just it, mister. I ain't got no dime. I ain't got no money a'tall."

"You ain't got no money?"

"No, sir."

"Well, now, if you ain't got no money, would you mind tellin' me just how the Sam Hill you was a' plannin' on eatin'?"

"I thought maybe I could work some for it," Art said.

Eby shook his head. "Boy, I got no need for someone to work for me. I got me two women back there, as you can see. They all the workers I need, and they don' cost me nothin', one of 'em bein' my wife and the other'n bein' her sister."

"Do you know of anyone who needs any work done?" Art asked. "I'm a good worker, I'm strong, I been carryin' my own load for the better part of three years now."

"This here ain't no hirin' hall," Eby said gruffly. "If you got a dime, I'll give you some supper. If you ain't got no money, then get the hell out of here and don't be takin' up space."

"Give the boy somethin' to eat," a tall, bearded man said.

"I ain't givin' him nothin' iffen he don't pay for it."

The tall man produced a dime, slapping it down on the counter with a loud snap. "Here's your goddamn dime. Now give the boy some vittles!" he ordered.

"No, sir," Art said, shaking his head, holding his hand

out toward the tall, bearded man, and walking away. "I thank you kindly, sir. But I don't aim to take no charity."

"Who said anything about charity?" the man replied. "I've got a flatboat down here, loaded with goods that I'm takin' to the Louisiana Territory. If you're willin' to work for your keep, I'll take you on."

Art smiled broadly. "Yes, sir!" he said. He turned back toward the counter. "I'll have me that pork and some beans now," he said. "And maybe some 'taters."

Scowling, Eby went back to the cooking fire, spooned up some beans and potatoes, cut off some pork, and put it on a tin plate. He brought the plate and a spoon back to the counter.

"Thanks," Art said.

"Seems to me like there ought to be a biscuit go with that," the man who had bought the supper said.

Eby reached under a cloth and pulled out a biscuit, then set it beside the plate.

"The name's Harding," Art's benefactor said. "Pete Harding. What's yours?"

"Art."

"Art? That's all?"

Art thought for a moment. Harding seemed to be a nice man; certainly he had bought a meal and was promising employment. But Art was planning on making a clean break from his past, and he didn't want anything that would make that connection, including a last name.

"Art's all the name I use," he said.

Harding laughed. "If that's good enough for you, then I reckon it's good enough for me. How'd you get here anyway? Did you walk?"

"No, sir. I come by boat," Art said.

"Well, after you eat your supper, come on down and help me get loaded up. Then, if you're a mind to go with me, why, I reckon you can tie your boat on behind. Or else, leave it here."

"You got a boat you want to leave here, I'll keep it for you till you get back," Eby said. "Won't charge you but a dollar to keep it for a whole month."

Harding laughed. "Yeah, in a pig's eye you will," he said. He stroked his beard and looked at Art. "Boy, you don't have any money at all?"

"No, sir."

"Well, if that boat don't mean nothin' personal to you, why don't you just sell it? That way you can go on down-river with me, and have a little money besides."

"Sell the boat? Why, yes, I reckon I could," Art said. The boat had served its purpose, getting him away from home. Now he truly was on his own, and any money the boat brought would have to be good.

"All right, Eby. What'll you give the boy for the boat?"

"Fifty cents."

"It's worth five dollars," Harding said.

"Not to me, it ain't."

"As many people as you got comin' through here, you could give the boy five dollars for the boat, then turn right around and sell it within a week to someone else for seven dollars."

"I'll give the boy three dollars."

"Four," Harding said.

"All right, four dollars."

Harding looked at Art. "What do you think, son? It's your boat, and your decision."

"Four dollars?" Art said. "I've never had that much money in my life. Yes, I'll sell it."

"Give the boy four dollars," Harding said.

"Where's the boat?"

"I'll take you to it," Art said.

"We'll take you to it," Harding corrected. Then he looked at Art. "After you make the transaction, we've got work to do."

"Yes, sir!" Art said.

* * *

Harding had unloaded his goods there, in order to do some business with the folks who had tied up at the trading post. It took no more than half an hour to get them loaded back onto his boat. It was a flatboat, nearly as wide as it was long, with a small cabin at mid-deck. A long tiller, which could also be used to propel the boat, stuck out from behind the boat. Every available square inch of the boat was covered with cargo: bales of cloth, pots, pans, various kinds of tools, barrel staves, hoops, and three cases of Bibles.

When the boat was loaded, Harding invited Art to step aboard.

"It's time for us to get a'goin'," he said.

"We're going to run the river at night?" Art asked.

Harding shook his head. "No, we'll put in a couple miles downstream," he said. "It'll be safer than staying here with the river pirates."

"River pirates?"

Harding's searching look covered both sides of the river, into the rocks and behind the trees.

"They like to hang around river stops, like trading posts and the like," he said. "That way they can get a good look at what the boats are carrying, and if they see anything they like, they'll go cross-country till they can find a place to set up an ambush. What with the river meanderin' back and forth, it's easy enough for them to get ahead of a boat."

"You mean there might be pirates here right now?"

"Truth to tell, boy, I wouldn't put it past Eby himself. I've always suspected him, but I've never been able to prove it. If I ever got proof, I'd get some of the other boatmen together and we'd clean this place out."

Harding cast off the line, then using the tiller, worked the boat out into the center of the river. He pointed it downstream and, as had been the case with Art's skiff, the current provided all the propulsion they needed. The only difference was that the flatboat didn't travel quite as fast as the skiff.

"Come here," Harding said once they were under way.

Art stepped to the rear of the boat.

"Take the tiller," Harding said. "You may as well start learning right off."

"Yes, sir," Art said, taking the tiller in his own hands. He could feel the surge of the water, and the control he had over the boat. It was similar to what he experienced with the skiff, though as the flatboat was bigger, the tiller longer and with more surface area, he felt a much greater pull.

"You're doing a good job," Harding said, sitting down on a bale of cloth. Reaching down into his pocket, he pulled out a pipe, filled it with tobacco, then using a flintlock and steel mechanism, managed to get his pipe lit. A few minutes later, he was puffing contentedly.

"How far do we go before we put in?" Art asked.

Harding laughed. "You tired already?"

"No, sir!" Art replied, his face stinging in embarrassment. "I just meant, well, I just wondered, that's all."

"Not much longer," Harding said easily. He took a few more puffs while he studied Art. "Run away from home, did you?"

"No, I . . ." Art started; then he decided that it was time to be honest with the man who had helped him. "Yes, sir," he said sheepishly. "I ran away."

"Trouble at home?"

"No. I just wanted to . . ." He let the sentence trail off, and Harding laughed.

"You wanted to see the creature, didn't you?"

"See the creature?"

"That's just a saying, son. It's a saying for folks like us."

"Like us?"

"You and me. There are some folks who are born, live, and die and never get more'n ten miles away from home in any direction. Then there's folks that's always wondering what's on the other side of the next hill. And when they get over that hill, why, damn me if they don't feel like they got to go on to the next one and the next one, and the next one after that. They're always hopin' they'll find somethin' out there, some sort of creature they ain't never seen before. I know it's that way with me."

Art smiled. "Yes, sir," he said. "I'd say it's that way with me too."

"Pull in over there," Harding said. "We'll camp here, tonight."

Two

"Get up, boy!" a gruff voice ordered.

Art was jerked awake when someone grabbed him and pulled him up from the bale of cloth he was using for a bed.

It was still dark, but in the ambient light of the moon, Art could see that two men were holding Harding. One of the men had the point of his knife sticking into Harding's neck, far enough that a little trickle of blood was streaming down. One flick of the hand, Art knew, and Harding would bleed his life away in seconds.

The third man, the one who had so abruptly awakened Art, was now holding Art's arm twisted behind him. He put pressure on the arm and Art winced in pain, but he didn't cry out.

"What'll we do with the kid?" the one who held Art asked.

"Knock him in the head and throw him overboard," the man with the knife replied.

Art's captor was holding a club, and he raised it over Art's head in order to accomplish the task.

"No, wait! Eby told me he give the boy four dollars for that boat. Check his pockets, he ain't had no chance to spend it yet."

"That right, boy?" his captor asked, smiling at Art. Two of his teeth were missing and his breath was foul. "You got four dollars on you?"

The man started to put his hand in Art's pocket, but in order to do so, he had to loosen his grip. That was all that was needed, for as soon as the grip was relaxed, Art twisted away and jumped into the river beside the boat.

"Goddamnit, Percy, you let him get away!"

"Couldn't help it, Deekus. The little sumbitch was slick as a greased hog."

This close to the bank, the river was only about chest-deep, but it was dark, and Art moved up under the curve of the boat keel so he couldn't be seen by those on board. His heart was racing. These men must be some of the river pirates Harding had told him about. And the fact that they had mentioned Eby's name seemed to prove Harding's theory about Eby's involvement with the pirates.

"What'll we do with Harding?" Percy asked.

"Well, we know he's got some money, 'cause Eby seen 'im doin' a lot of business back at the trading post," Deekus replied.

"That right, Harding? You got yourself a poke hid some'ers on this here boat?"

"If I did, I wouldn't tell you, you sorry sack of shit."

"Oh, I think you'll tell us," Deekus said. "Break one of his fingers, Clyde."

Even from his place of hiding, down in the water, Art could hear the bone pop as Clyde broke one of Harding's fingers. Harding gasped in pain, but he didn't cry out.

"Harding, we know you got the money hid on the boat, and you know that we're a' goin' to find it. All we're askin' is that you make it easier on us, and we'll make it easier on you."

"Yeah," Percy added with a demonic giggle. "We'll be real nice to you. We'll kill you fast, instead of slow."

"Go to hell," Harding said. His refusal was followed by

the sound of another snapping bone, and another gasp of pain.

"You got ten fingers and ten toes," Deekus said. "And ole' Clyde there, he's the kind of fella that likes to make other folks hurt. So, you can tell us now, or you can just let Clyde bust you up, one bone at a time, until you do."

Carefully, and quietly, Art pulled himself back onto the boat, boarding it at the bow. Harding and the three men who were working him over were back at the stern.

Art had no idea why he was doing this. Every impulse and nerve in his body was screaming at him to run. The night was dark enough, and the woods by the riverbank were thick enough that he could easily get away from them. And yet, here he was, crawling back onto the boat.

Keeping low, and staying behind the bales of cargo, Art slipped into the mid-deck cabin from the front end. He knew exactly what he was looking for, because he had seen them early that afternoon.

It was considerably darker inside the cabin than it was on the deck of the boat. Art couldn't see six inches in front of his face, so he had to do everything by feel. On the other hand, there was some advantage to that, because even if the pirates were looking right at him, they wouldn't be able to see him.

Art's fingers closed over what he was looking for—two fully charged, primed, and loaded fifty-caliber pistols. Picking them up, he eased both hammers back quietly, then moved to the stern door of the little cabin. He was less than ten feet away from the pirates, but they couldn't see him.

"He ain't goin' tell us nothin', Deekus," Percy complained.

"I reckon you're right," Deekus said. "We may as well kill 'im now, and get it over with."

Deekus drew back his knife, ready to plunge it into Harding's chest. It was at that exact moment that Art fired. The gun roared and bucked in his hand, while the muzzle flash lit up the deck like a bolt of lightning. For one instant in time, all action was frozen and Art could almost believe he was looking at a drawing. In a harsh white-and-black tableau, he could see Deekus's expression of shock and pain as he looked down at the gaping hole in his chest, the surprise on Clyde's face, and the fear in Percy's eyes.

"What the hell?" Percy shouted.

Only Harding was jolted into action. Dropping to one knee, he grabbed Deekus's knife, then, with a quick underhand flip of the wrist, threw the knife at Clyde. The knife buried itself in the pirate's neck and, with a gurgling sound, Clyde reached up to pull it out, too late, for it had already severed his jugular.

Only seconds before, Percy had been one of three river armed men, easily in command of the situation. Now he was the only one left, and he realized that his position had suddenly become very perilous. With a roar of anger and desperation, he raised his own knife and started toward Harding.

Because Harding had thrown the knife at Clyde, he was unarmed. Still on one knee on the deck, Harding rolled to his right, just barely managing to avoid Percy's lunge.

"Mr. Harding!" Art shouted. "Here!" He thrust the other pistol toward Harding. Harding grabbed it, then spun toward Percy, who was just now recovering from his failed lunge.

Percy turned back toward Harding, then realized too late that Harding was no longer unarmed. Harding pulled the trigger, and Art watched as the impact of the heavy ball knocked Percy backward, over the boat rail. He hit the water with a splash, then floated away, leaving a thick, black stream of blood in the water behind him.

Harding checked the two men who were still on board. He leaned down over Deekus.

"Is he . . . is he dead?" Art asked from the shadows of the cabin.

"Dead as a doornail," Harding replied. "You did a job on him, boy."

"Oh," Art said rather pensively.

Harding dragged both Percy and Clyde to the edge of his boat. "Get the hell off my boat, you bastards!" he said angrily as he pushed them over. They fell into the water with a little splash.

Harding stood there for a long moment, looking down at the three floating bodies. He spat down at them.

It was not until then that Art came out of the cabin. He too looked down at the dead pirates.

"Are we just going to leave them here?" Art finally asked.

"Hell, yes, we're going to leave them here," Harding responded. "You don't think I'm going to take the time to dig graves for those sons of bitches, do you?"

"No, sir, I guess not."

"Let the alligator-garfish feed on their sorry carcasses. I just wish they weren't quite dead yet, so they could feel it."

"Yes, sir," Art said.

Harding looked up at the sky. "It'll be getting light soon," he said. "We may as well get under way. Untie the forward line."

Art picked his way to the bow, then untied the line that held them secure to an overhanging branch. Harding poled them away from the bank, then out into the river. After they reached midstream, the current took over and, once more, they moved rapidly down the river.

"Take the tiller, boy," Harding said. "I've got to tend to this hand."

Art watched as Harding pulled on both his fingers, grimacing in pain as he straightened them out. After that he rummaged through the little pile of firewood until he found a stick just the right size. He put the stick alongside his two fingers, then called Art over.

"Take some of that rawhide cord there and bind these fingers to this here splint."

Art started to do what Harding said, but as soon as he began wrapping the rawhide around the badly swollen fingers, Harding winced in pain. Art stopped.

"Don't stop, boy, else I'll have a couple of useless hooks here, instead of fingers," Harding said. "And do it pretty tight. It's goin' to hurt a mite, but I'll be the one hurtin', not you."

"Yes, sir," Art said. He wrapped the cord around the two fingers.

"Not so tight that it cuts off the blood," Harding cautioned.

Art nodded, then finished the task, cutting off the rawhide and tying it secure. Harding held his hand out and looked at it.

"Doubt there's a doctor this close to St. Louis who could've done a better job," he said. "I'm proud of you, boy."

"Glad I could help."

Art went back to the tiller. By now the sky had turned a dove-gray, and streaks of pink slashed through the eastern sky. Harding got a fire going, then disappeared into the cabin. He came out a moment later with a pot, which he placed over the fire. After a few minutes, the rich aroma of brewing coffee permeated the boat.

"Coffee comes so dear that I don't generally drink it, 'cept on Sundays," Harding said. "But I reckon this occasion is special enough for us to have some this mornin'."

"What's the occasion?" Art asked.

"Well, you saved my life," Harding said. "Now, that might not be all that much of an occasion to some folks, but it sure is to me."

"I didn't do much."

"The hell you say," Harding said. "Once you went over the side of the boat and into the water, you could've kept on going and they would've never found you. But you came back. And you saved my life."

"I . . . I wish I hadn't had to . . ." Art let the sentence hang.

"Kill a man?" Harding asked.

Art nodded.

"First time you ever had to do it?"

Art nodded again.

"Well, of course it is, you bein' no older'n you are. How old are you, Art?"

"I'm, uh, sixteen," Art said.

Harding just looked at him.

"All right, I'm thirteen. Well, nearly so anyway," Art insisted.

"Nearly thirteen. So that means what? That you're twelve?"

"Yes, sir," Art admitted sheepishly.

Harding poured two cups of coffee, and handed one to Art. Art took a swallow, then frowned a little at its bitter taste.

"You're used to having milk and sugar in your coffee?"

"Milk, sometimes a little syrup or honey," Art said.

"Well, you'd best get used to having it black. You see, you can purt' near always have coffee with you. You can't always have milk or sugar."

Art took another swallow. "It's good," he said.

Harding laughed. "You're going to do fine, boy. And don't worry none 'bout that no-count son of a bitch you killed. His kind always die young. If you hadn't killed him, someone else would have."

"I just wish it hadn't been me."

"Listen to me, boy," Harding insisted. "He may have been the first one you've killed, but he won't be the last one you're going to have to kill. Not by a long shot. Not if you are going to survive out here. You've got to realize that, and not dwell none on it. Maybe you are only twelve years old by the calendar, but today, you showed me you're a man."

"Because I killed someone?"

"No. Any fool can kill. But you came back to help me, when you could've easy gotten away. There's lots more things that go into making a man than the number of years someone has lived. Live long enough, and the years will come to ever'one. The other things—honor, duty, and knowin' how to do what's right—don't come to ever'one, but they done come to you. Let nobody tell you different, Art. You're a man now. And I'm glad to call you my friend."

Harding stuck out his hand. Art started to shake it, remembered the broken fingers, pulled back, then realized that the broken fingers were on Harding's left hand. Smiling, he gave Harding a good, strong grip.

Harding explained to Art that they were no longer on the Ohio River, but were now on the Mississippi. The Mississippi was broader, and the current stronger than it was on the Ohio, and the boat moved a lot faster. One of the first things Art noticed was the number of felled trees. During his trip down the Ohio he had seen maybe as many as a hundred downed trees, but here, there were literally thousands of trees on the ground.

"I've never seen such a thing," Art said in awe.

Harding chuckled. "Well, boy, you left home to see the wonders of the world. This is one of them."

"But how can this be? Was there such a wind that it could blow this many down?"

"It wasn't the wind that did it. It was the trembling earth."

"Trembling earth?"

"Shakers. Some folks call 'em earthquakes. What happens is, the ground just starts to shaking something awful, shaking so bad a fella can't even stand up."

"You seen such a thing?"

"Yep, it happened a couple of years ago," Harding said. "Trees was fallin', and the earth was opening up, sulphur commenced spewing into the air. All the shakin' and tremblin' made the Mississippi River flow backward. And it pushed it right out of its channel for a bit, to form a new lake."

"I would sure like to see somethin' like that."

Harding laughed out loud. "Well, when we get to New Madrid, don't tell any of them folks that. I reckon they've seen enough of it over the last couple of years."

"Is that where we're goin'? New Madrid?"

"Yep. It's in the Missouri Territory."

"What's there?"

"New Madrid is a good marketplace," Harding said. "Folks buy there, then take it up to St. Louis, or on down to New Orleans. I plan to sell everything I got on this here boat. Then I'm going to sell the boat. Then, after a couple of days of raisin' hell and havin' a good time, I'll buy myself a horse, ride back to Ohio, get me another boatload of goods, come down here to do the same thing all over again."

"You're going back to Ohio?"

"Sure am. That's where I can get goods the cheapest. The trick in this or any business is to buy cheap and sell high," Harding said with a laugh. "What about you? You're sure welcome to come along with me. You can be my partner if you want to."

"I . . ." Art started, but with a wave of his hand, Harding interrupted him.

"I know, you don't have to say it. You're anxious to see the creature."

Smiling, Art nodded. "I reckon I am," he said.

"Well, I can't say as I blame you. And as long as you're plannin' on seein' the creature, why, I figure New Madrid is as good a location as any to start."

* * *

New Madrid was a booming town of nearly three thousand people, spread out along the west bank of the Mississippi River. There were nearly one hundred flatboats and scores of skiffs tied up along the riverbank, and less than one hundred feet from the river's edge on a street called Waters Street, nearly as many wagons, carts, horses, and mules.

The wooden structures of the town were built right up against each other: leather-good stores, trading posts, cafes, and taverns. Art realized that, like the trees, the earthquake must have also destroyed New Madrid. That was the only way he could explain the fresh-lumber appearance of all the buildings. Even now, half-a-dozen new buildings were going up, but whether they were a sign of the town's growth and progress, or merely the reconstruction of destroyed buildings, he didn't know.

In addition to the sound of hammering and sawing coming from those buildings under construction, the air also rang with the clanging of steel on steel, emanating from the blacksmith shop. These sounds of commerce were clear evidence of the vibrant new community. Waters and Mill Streets, the two streets that ran parallel with the river, were crowded with people, visitors as well as permanent residents.

It didn't take Harding long to sell his goods. Once his task was accomplished, he came back to Art, holding a handful of money. He counted out ten dollars in silver, and handed it Art.

"What's this for?" Art asked.

"Your wages," Harding said. "You earned them."

"But I was only with you for a couple of weeks," Art said. "You fed me, and gave me transportation. You don't need to pay me as well."

Harding laughed. "Son, you're going to have to learn

your own value. Anytime you sell your services to someone, sell them for as much as you can get. If you are going to argue, argue for more, not less."

"Yes, sir."

"Besides, whether you did ten dollars worth of labor isn't the question. You saved my life, and that's certainly worth ten dollars to me. Now, do you want the money or not?"

"I want the money," Art said.

"I thought you might come around," Harding said. "Now, since you will soon be going to go your way and I'm going mine, what do you say we go to a dram shop and have a beer?"

"A beer? Well, I . . ."

"Hell's bells, boy! Are you going to tell me you don't like beer?"

"I don't know," Art admitted. "I've never had a beer."

Harding laughed. "You've never had a beer?"

"No, sir. My mom didn't hold with drinkin'. Not even beer."

"What do you think about it?"

"I've never give it much thought, one way or the other."

"Then it's time you did give it some thought," Harding said. "You've got some catchin' up to do. Come on, it'll be a pleasure for me to buy you your first beer."

The sign in front of the building read WATSON'S DRAM SHOP. Inside the saloon was a potbellied stove that, though cold now, still had the smell of smoke about it from its winter use. A rough-hewn bar ran across one end of the single room, while half-a-dozen tables completed the furnishings. The room was illuminated by bars of sunlight, shining in through the windows and open door. Flies buzzed about the room, especially drawn to those places where there was evidence of spilt beer.

"Mr. Harding, good to see you back in New Madrid

again," a man behind the bar said. He was wearing a stained apron over his clothes, and a green top hat over a shock of red hair.

"Hello, Mr. Watson. I hope you haven't sold all of your beer."

"I just got a new shipment down from St. Louis," Watson answered, taking a glass down from the shelf, then holding it under the spigot of a barrel of beer. "What about the boy?" he asked.

"Don't let his looks and age fool you," Harding replied. "Art's as good a man as I've ever come across. I reckon he'll have beer too." He looked over at Art. "That right?"

"Yes, sir. I'll have a beer," Art replied, watching as the mug filled with a golden fluid, topped by a large head of white foam.

"Here you go, boy," Watson said, sliding the first mug over to him.

Art raised the glass to his lips and took a swallow. He had never tasted beer before and had no idea what to expect. It was unusual, but not unpleasant.

"Here's to you, Art," Harding said, holding his own beer out toward Art. For a moment, Art didn't understand what he was doing, but when Harding tapped his mug against Art's, he realized it was some sort of ritual, so he followed along.

Art had that beer, then another.

"Let's go," Harding said, suddenly getting up from the table.

"Where are we going?"

"There's a certain etiquette to spendin' money in a town like New Mardrid, and part of it is that you spread your money around. This is my favorite place. I spend all my money with Watson, then he's liable to start takin' me for granted, while all the other places will be resentful. Do you see what I mean?"

"I guess so," Art replied.

"Besides, we all have our own way of looking for the creature," Harding added with a twinkle in his eye. "I've always been of the opinion that it might be in the next dram shop."

Art followed Harding out the door, then up the boardwalk toward the next drinking establishment.

A wagon rolled by on the street. Driving the wagon was a tall, rawboned man, dressed in black. He had beady eyes, high cheekbones, a hooked nose, and a prominent chin. A short, stout, very plain-looking woman was sitting on the bench beside him. The wagon had bows and canvas, but the canvas was rolled back at least two bows. As a result, Art could see the third occupant of the wagon, a girl about his own age. She was sitting on the floor with her back leaning against the wagon side opposite from Art. As a result, when he glanced toward her, he saw that she was looking directly at him. For a moment their gazes held; then, embarrassed at being the recipient of such scrutiny, Art looked away.

"Ah, here we go," Harding said. "Let's pay a visit to Mr. Cooper."

Cooper's saloon was almost an exact copy of Watson's, with a bar and a few tables and chairs. However, there was a card game in progress here, and Harding joined it.

Cardplaying was another of the vices his mother had warned him against. But as beer drinking was proving to be a rather pleasant experience, Art decided he would investigate cardplaying as well. So, drinking yet another beer, he leaned against the wall and watched the card game.

As he stood leaning against the wall, Art happened to see a "pick and switch" operation lift a man's wallet. The victim was a middle-aged man who was standing at the bar, drinking his beer while carrying on a conversation with another man. A nimble-fingered pickpocket deftly slipped the victim's billfold from his back pocket. At that moment, a big, black-bearded man came in through the door, and Art watched as the pickpocket passed the pilfered wallet off to the man who had just come in.

The entire operation was so quick and smooth that the victim never felt a thing. No one else in the saloon saw it happen, and if Art had not been in the exact spot at the exact time he was there, he wouldn't have seen it either. The accomplice walked directly to the table where Harding and three others were playing cards.

"May I join you, gentlemen?" Blackbeard asked.

"Sure, have a seat," Harding offered congenially. "Your money is as good as anyone else's. What do you say about that, Art? Isn't his money as good as anyone else's?" Harding asked, teasing his young partner.

"It would be, I suppose, if it really was his money. Trouble is, it isn't," Art said easily. "He stole it."

Three

Art's matter-of-fact comment brought to a halt all conversation in the saloon.

"What did you just say, boy?" Blackbeard asked with an angry growl.

"I said it isn't your money."

"What the hell do you mean by that?" Blackbeard sputtered.

"Yes, Art, what do you mean?" Harding asked.

Art looked over toward the bar. Nearly everyone in the place had heard his remark, and now all were looking toward him with intense interest.

"This man," Art said, pointing to Blackbeard, "has this man's poke." He pointed to the middle-aged man who was standing at the bar. It wasn't until that moment that the man standing at the bar checked his pocket.

"What the hell? My poke *is* missing!" he said.

"I don't know what this boy is talking about!" Blackbeard said. "Hell, I just this minute come in here. I haven't even been close to the bar."

"He's right," another man said. "I seen him come in."

"If somebody took that man's money, it wasn't me," Blackbeard said.

"Oh, you didn't take it," Art said.

"Boy, you ain't makin' a hell of a lot of sense," Cooper said. Cooper was the man who owned the place. He was also working the bar. "First you accuse Riley there of takin' McPherson's poke; now you say he didn't take it."

"I said he *has* the poke," Art said. "I didn't say he took it." Art pointed to the original pickpocket, who was now at the far end of the bar, trying to stay out of sight. "That's the man who took it. He picked the man's pocket, then gave it to Mr. Riley when he came in."

"By God! I don't care if you are just a pup," Riley said. "A fella doesn't go around accusin' another fella of some- thin' lessen he can prove it."

"I can describe my purse," the man at the bar said. "It's made of pigskin and it's sewed together with red yarn. My wife made it for me."

"Well, this seems like a simple enough problem to solve," Harding said. He looked at Riley. "Why don't you just empty your pockets on the table? If you don't have it, then we'll just go on about our business."

"That sounds reasonable," one of the others in the saloon said.

"Yeah, if you didn't take it, just empty your pockets and be done with it."

"To hell with that. I ain't goin' to empty my pockets just 'cause of some snot-nosed boy's lie."

Harding looked over at Art. "You're sure about this, are you, Art?"

"I'm sure," Art said.

"Empty your pockets," Harding said. This time his tone was less congenial.

"Wait a minute! You are going to take this boy's word over mine?"

Harding scratched his cheek. "Yeah, I reckon I am," he answered easily. "See, here's the thing, Riley. I don't know you from Adam's off-mule. But I do know this boy and he's already proved himself to me. So if truth be known, I reckon I'd take his word over that of my own mama. Now, either empty your pockets on the table, or by God I'm going to grab you by the ankles, turn you upside down, and empty them for you."

"The only thing you are going to empty is your guts," Riley said, suddenly pulling a knife.

"Look out!" someone shouted.

"He's got a knife!" another yelled.

"Yeah, I sort of figured that out," Harding said.

There was a scrape of chairs and a scuffling of feet as everyone else backed away to give the two belligerents room. Riley held his knife out in front of him, moving it back and forth slowly, like the head of a threatening snake.

Harding pulled his own knife; then the two men stepped away from the table to do battle. They raised up onto the balls of their feet, then crouched forward slightly at the waist. Each man had his right arm extended, holding his knife in an upturned palm. Slowly, they moved around each other, as if engaged in some macabre dance. The points of the knives moved back and forth, slowly, hypnotically.

Art watched them. The fight with the river pirates had been deadly, but it had also been quick and spontaneous. This was the first time he had ever seen two men fight face-to-face, each with the grim determination to kill the other. Although he had a vested interest in the outcome—for surely if Riley killed Harding, he would then turn on Art— yet he was able to watch it without fear. He was certain that the day would come when he would find himself in this same situation. Some inborn sense of survival told him to watch closely, and to learn, not only from the victor, but also from the vanquished.

"You ever seen one of them big catfish they pull out of the river?" Riley asked. "You see the way they flop around when they're gutted? That's how it's going to be with you. I'm going to gut you, then I'm goin' to watch you flop around."

Riley made a quick, slashing motion with his knife, but Harding jumped out of the way. Mistaking Harding's reflexive action as a sign of fear, Riley gave a bellow of defiance, and moved in for the kill, lunging forward.

It was a fatal mistake.

Harding easily sidestepped the lunge, then taking advantage of Riley's awkward and unbalanced position, counterthrust with his own knife. Because Riley was off balance, he was unable to respond quickly enough to cover his exposed side. He grunted once as Harding's knife plunged into his flesh.

The blade slipped in easily between the fourth and fifth ribs. Harding held it there for a moment, then stepped up to Riley and twisted the blade, cutting-edge up. As Riley fell, the knife ripped him open. Harding stepped back from his adversary as Riley hit the floor, belly-down. Almost instantly, a pool of blood began spreading beneath him.

"Boy," Cooper said to Art. It wasn't until that moment that Art and the others in the saloon realized that Cooper was holding a double-barreled shotgun, and had been throughout the fight. "You look through Riley's pockets there. For your sake, and for the sake of your friend there, you had better come up with McPherson's purse. 'Cause if you don't, I reckon we might have to hang the both of you for murder."

"Wait a minute!" Harding complained. "How can you call this murder?" He pointed to Riley's body. "You saw that he drew the knife first. Hell, everyone saw it."

"Seems to me like he didn't have much of a choice," Cooper said. "You all but called him a thief. If he wasn't the thief, then he had ever' right to defend his honor."

Art looked at Harding.

"Go ahead, Art," Harding said easily. "If you say Riley has McPherson's wallet, then I've got no doubt but that he does."

At that moment Riley's accomplice, the man who originally made the pick, started to leave the saloon.

"Hold it right there, Carter," Cooper called out to him.

"If the boy's right, if he finds the wallet, then you're goin' to be the one we'll be askin' questions."

"Wait a minute!" Carter said. "What if he does find McPherson's purse on Riley? That don't prove I had anything to do with it. It just means that Riley took it."

"Huh-uh," Cooper said. "Everyone agreed that Riley had just come in through the door and didn't come nowhere near the bar. That means if he has McPherson's wallet, the only way he could have it is if you give it to him."

Art knelt beside Riley's body. He hesitated for a moment.

"Go ahead, boy. Look for it," Cooper said.

Nodding, Art took a deep breath, then stuck his hand in one of the back pockets.

Nothing.

The other back pocket produced the same result. Art tried to turn Riley over, but Riley was a big man and his inert weight made turning him difficult. Harding started to help him.

"No!" Cooper shouted, and he pulled back the hammer on one of the two barrels. "Let the boy do it alone. If he finds that purse, I don't want nobody claimin' that, somehow, you sneaked it to him."

"All right," Harding said, backing away.

Straining with all his might, Art finally got the body turned over onto its back. Riley's eyes were still open, and they gave the appearance of staring right at Art. Gasping, Art pulled back slightly.

"He ain't goin' to hurt you none, boy. He's dead," Cooper said. "Get on with it."

Art searched Riley's front pants pockets without success, then reached into one of the man's jacket pockets. He came away empty-handed. Now, there was only one pocket left.

"This is it, boy," Cooper said. "If it ain't in that pocket, then you done got a man killed for nothin'. And don't think it'll go easy on you just 'cause you're young."

"It's in there," Art said resolutely.

But it wasn't. He stuck his hand all the way down and felt the entire pocket. When he pulled his hand out, it was empty.

"Haw!" Carter said. "I reckon this proves the boy was lyin'."

Art's stomach tumbled in fear. Almost in desperation, he put his hand back in Riley's jacket pocket, and this time, he felt something. Grabbing it, he realized that whatever he was feeling wasn't actually in the pocket, but was behind a layer of cloth. Something was sewn into the lining of the jacket.

"I think I've found it!" Art said.

"Pull it out. Let us see it," Cooper said.

"It's behind . . ." Art started to say, then seeing Riley's knife, he picked it up and used it to rend the fabric. After that, it was easy to wrap his hands around the wallet.

"Glory be!" McPherson said. "That's my purse!"

"Damn your hide, boy!" Carter shouted from the edge of the bar. As Art looked toward the one who had let out the bellow, he saw that Carter was pointing a pistol at him.

Carter fired, just as Art leaped to one side. The huge-caliber ball dug a big, splintered hole in the wide-plank floor. Though the bullet itself didn't strike Art, he was sprayed in the face by the splinters that were ejected when the bullet passed through the floor.

On top of the roar of Carter's pistol, came a second, even louder blast. This was from Cooper's shotgun, and Art saw Carter's chest and face turn into instant ground sausage. Carter pitched backward, dead before he even hit the floor.

"Free beer to anyone who helps drag that trash out of here," Cooper said as he stood there holding the still-smoking gun.

The offer of free beer was all the inducement necessary. Instantly, it seemed, half-a-dozen men sprang forward. It took them but a moment to drag the two bodies out into the alley behind the dram shop. Leaving them there, they hurried back inside for their reward.

Although neither Art nor Harding joined the detail in dragging the bodies out, they didn't lack for beer. McPherson, whose poke Art had saved, bought a round for each of them.

After the round furnished by McPherson, Harding suggested that it might be better if they moved on. As a result, Art, who by now had drunk five beers, was a little unsteady on his feet as he followed him outside.

"Does this sort of thing happen often?" Art asked.

"What sort of thing?"

"What sort of thing?" Art repeated, surprised by the question. He nodded toward the bar they had just left. "The knife fight. I mean, that man was trying to kill you."

"Yeah, he was," Harding answered easily. "That's why I killed him."

"I've never seen anything like that before."

"The hell you say. What about the business down on the river?"

"That wasn't the same thing," Art said. "The fight on the river happened real quick. This . . . I don't know . . . this sort of unfolded real slow. One minute everyone was having a nice time, and the next minute you and that man Riley were fighting."

"Have you thought about what caused us to fight?"

"You said he wanted to kill you."

Harding chuckled. "I mean, have you thought about why he wanted to kill me?"

"I guess because . . ." Art paused.

"Because I asked him to empty his pockets," Harding said. "And the reason I asked him to do that was because you had just accused him of stealing."

"Oh!" Art said. "Then *I* was the cause."

Harding chuckled again. "No, not really. Riley and Carter brought it on themselves. Stealing is not the safest way to make a living out here. If someone plans to make his livelihood that way, then he damn well better be prepared to face the consequences. And in this case, the consequences were pretty severe."

"Yeah, I guess they were," Art said rather pensively.

Harding reached over and rubbed his hand through Art's hair. "Look, Art, it's like I told you back on the boat when you killed that son of a bitch who was trying to kill me. Life is hard out here. Look around you, and you'll see an eagle killing a mouse, a snake killing a frog, and a fox killing a rabbit. If you aren't ready to face up to that, then you may as well go on back home to your mama and papa. Do you understand?"

"Yes, sir, I reckon I do," Art said.

"Good."

"But I don't reckon it's ever goin' to be somethin' I will enjoy doin'. Killin' someone, I mean."

"Son, I pray to God that you never do get to where you enjoy it. There's a difference between doin' somethin' that you have to do to survive, and doin' it for the pure, evil pleasure of it. And when you stop to think about it, it's those who do take pleasure from it who are going to wind up giving you the most trouble."

"Yes, sir," Art said.

"Well, that's enough teaching for now. I've saved the best for last. Come on, I want you to see the Blue Star."

The Blue Star dram shop was decidedly more attractive than the other saloons had been. Where the others had been thrown together with unpainted, ripsawed, raw lumber, the Blue Star was a carefully finished building. The outside was painted white, and trimmed in red. It was also a two-story building with a false front that made it look even taller from the street.

"Doesn't look like this building suffered any from the earthquake," Art said.

"Oh, but it did. It went down, just like the others did.

But whereas everyone else has only halfway built their buildings, Mr. Bellefontaine decided he would return the Blue Star to its original state, complete with paint and all the furnishings. The other bar owners were a little put out with him, and if truth be known, I think most of them are sort of privately hoping that the earthquakes come again to sort of even things out for them. Come on, let's go in. If you think it looks nice from out here, wait until you see the inside."

The inside lived up to Harding's promise. Instead of rough-hewn lumber, the bar was finished mahogany, and behind the bar was a large, gilt-edged mirror. Scores and scores of elaborately shaped and colored bottles stood on the counter in front of the mirror, their number doubled by the reflection. At the back of the room, a finished staircase climbed up to a balcony that overlooked the ground floor. Though he couldn't see it all, he knew that the balcony went as deep as the saloon itself, so there had to be rooms upstairs as well. The interior of the bar was lit, not by un-filtered sunlight, as had been the case with the others, but by a brightly shining chandelier. As a result the windows were closed, and no flies were crawling around on the cus-tomers' tables. Even these tables, Art noticed, were made of finished wood.

"Oh, my," Art said, looking around.

"Impressive, huh?" Harding asked. "My friend, there is not another dram shop like this on the Mississippi, not from St. Louis to New Orleans. And I ought to know, for I have been in just about every one of them."

"It is beautiful," Art said. "I don't think I've ever seen anything like it."

"You can see now why I saved this for last."

As soon as they chose a table, a woman came over to join them.

"And, as an added attraction, the Blue Star has something that none of the other dram shops have," Harding added, smiling at the approaching woman. "It has women. Art, meet Lily."

"Well, Harding, I hear you've had a busy night," Lily said by way of greeting.

"You mean you've already heard?"

"Word of a killing gets around fast. Even if it is some no-count like Moe Riley, who needed killing."

"You knew him?"

"All the girls knew him," Lily said. "And there won't be any of us shedding any tears over the likes of him."

Art had never seen a woman who looked like Lily. There were dark markings around her eyes, her lips were as red as ripe cherries, and her cheeks nearly so. The top of her dress was cut very low, and it gapped open so that Art could actually see the swell of the tops of her breasts. He couldn't stop staring at her.

Bellefontaine brought three beers to the table. Art didn't remember ordering, but he picked up the beer and began drinking it. Whereas the taste had been somewhat foreign to him when he began the evening's drinking spree, he now found that he liked it. He drank nearly half the mug before he set it down. As he looked at Lily's breasts again, they seemed to be floating in front of him. His head was spinning, and he felt very peculiar.

"Do you like what you see, Art?" Lily asked, looking directly at Art.

"Yesh, ma'am," Art said. His tongue was thick and he found that he couldn't make it work as easily as he normally could. He pulled his tongue out of his mouth, felt it with his thumb and forefinger, then looked down at it, trying to see it.

Lily laughed. "I'll say this for your boy, Harding. He's a polite one, calling me ma'am."

"He's not my boy. He is my friend and business partner."

"Business partner, is he? He's a fine-looking young boy,

I'll give you that. But isn't he a little young to be a business partner?"

"Well, he *was* my partner," Harding said. "And he still could be if he wanted to, but he wants to see the creature."

"Yesh, shee the creasure," Art repeated.

"Uh-huh," Lily said. "Well, it ain't 'the creature' he's been lookin' at since he come in here." She stared right at Art and grinned broadly. He was still trying to see his tongue. "Ain't that right, sonny?"

"Whash right?" Art asked, his speech still slurred.

"I just told your friend here that I don't believe you been lookin' at the creature tonight. I think you've been lookin' somewhere else." She grabbed Art by the back of his head, then pulled his face down onto her breasts. He could feel the warm smooth skin against his face, and he reacted quickly, pulling away.

All the other patrons in the tavern had a good laugh at Art's expense.

"I . . . I'm shorry," Art said, blushing in embarrassment.

"Hell, sonny, don't be sorry," Lily said with a whooping laugh. "If I didn't want men to see my titties, I wouldn't wear clothes like this."

Art had not only never seen a woman who looked like this, he had never heard one talk like this.

"You're embarrassing him, Lily," Harding said.

"I'm not embarrassing him. I'm giving him an education," Lily said. "Here, Art, as long as we are at it, have yourself a good look." She unbuttoned two more buttons, then opened her bodice, exposing her breasts all the way to the nipples. "Do you like what you see?"

Again, there was reaction from the others in the tavern. Lily didn't stop at exposing herself to Art. She opened her blouse wide, then turned toward the others in the tavern, curtsying formally as they whistled, cheered, and beat their hands on the tops of the tables.

She turned back toward Art. "Well, we know what they

think about them, but what about you? Do you like my titties?"

"I think your titties are very nice," he finally said.

Lily whooped again. "Nice," she said. "I have to tell you, sonny, nice is not a word folks use much around Lily Howard. I do appreciate it, though."

"Are you a painted woman?" Art asked.

"A painted woman? Well, yes, I reckon I am."

"Come on," Harding said, taking Lily by the arm. "You've got a room upstairs, don't you?"

"Right at the head of the stairs, honey," Lily replied. "As if you didn't know that. You've been there enough times."

This time the laughter was at Harding's expense.

"Well, so I have," Harding admitted. "But what do you say we go again? I think Art has seen as much of 'the creature' as he needs to see."

"I could get Sally to join us. We could teach the boy a thing or two, we could," Lily offered.

"The boy has grown a lot since he came to me," Harding said. "But I don't think he's ready to be that grown just yet."

"Okay, honey, whatever you say," Lily replied. She put her hands on his shoulders, leaned against him so that the spill of her breasts mashed against his chest, then looked up at him.

"Here, watch that. Else we'll be startin' right here."

Smiling, Lily took Harding by the hand and led him to the foot of the stairs.

Harding looked back toward his young friend. "Art, I'll be back in a little while," he said. "In the meantime, why don't you get something to eat? I think it might do you good."

As Art watched them climb the stairs, it was almost as if he was watching himself watch them leave. He had never felt such a peculiar sense of detachment from his own body.

"Another beer, sonny?" Bellefontaine asked.

"What? Oh, uh, no, thank you," Art replied. "I think I'd rather have something to eat, if you've got it."

"I got bacon, eggs, taters right here, if that's to your likin'."

"That'll be fine," Art said. He stood up, almost too quickly, and had to grab the edge of the table to steady himself.

"You all right, boy? You look a little unsteady on your get-along there," Bellefontaine said.

"I'm all right. I think I'll jush step out back to the privy," he slurred. "I'll be right back."

"Take your time, sonny. Wouldn't want you to wet your pants," Bellefontaine said, laughing loud at his own joke.

"I told the boy I wouldn't want him to wet his pants," Art heard Bellefontaine telling someone as he stepped out into the alley.

It was quite dark outside, and Art wondered how long he and Harding had been drinking the beer. He wasn't surprised by the dark. He had watched it get progressively darker after each beer, because he'd found it necessary to visit the privy after each one. He had never peed as often as he had been peeing since he arrived in New Madrid. He wondered if something was wrong with him. Using the privy, then feeling much better, he turned to go back into the tavern to have his supper.

Suddenly he felt a blow to the back of his head! He saw stars, his ears rang, then he felt himself falling. After that, everything went black.

Four

Harding awakened to the aroma of coffee. When he opened his eyes, he saw Lily sitting on the edge of the bed, holding a cup of coffee.

"Uhmm," he said. "Is that for me?"

Smiling, Lily handed it to him. "I'll just bet you don't get service like this from all your other women."

"What other women?" Harding asked, receiving the cup from her, then taking a welcome swallow of the brew. "You're the only woman for me, Lily. Hell, you know that."

Lily laughed out loud. "You are full of it, Mr. Pete Harding," she said. "I know at least three other women right here in New Madrid you have bedded."

"Well, yes, but I had to pay them for it."

"Here, now, what are you trying to do? Cheat a poor working girl out of her money? Of course you had to pay them for it . . . just like you are going to pay me."

"Oh, Lily, now I am really hurt," Harding said. "And here I thought you invited me to your place out of love."

"Compassion, maybe, but not love," Lily teased. "Besides, this is what I do. I'm a . . . what did the boy call me? A painted lady?"

"Oh, shit!" Harding said, sitting up quickly. "Art."

"What about him?"

"I just left him sitting there last night."

"I'm sure he'll be all right. He looked like a pretty resourceful young man to me."

"He's very resourceful," Harding said. "And about the finest person I've ever run into, regardless of his age. But he was also drunk."

Lily laughed again. "He damn sure was. Cute too."

"The thing is, he's never been drunk before. I think I'd better go down and try to find him."

Harding swung his legs over the edge of the bed. As soon as he did so, Lily hiked up her nightgown and straddled him.

"Wherever he is, he has waited this long," she said. "Don't you think he could wait just a little longer? This one is free."

Feeling himself reacting quickly to her, Harding lay back down. "He could wait just a little longer," he said.

Art felt the sun warming his face, but that was the only thing about him that felt good. He had a tremendous headache, and he was very nauseous. He was lying down, and even though he had not yet opened his eyes, he knew he was lying on sun-dried wood, because he could smell it. He was also in motion. He could feel that, as well as hear the creak and groan of turning wagon wheels, and the steady clopping sound of hooves.

The last thing he remembered was leaving the tavern to go to the privy. What was he doing *here?* For that matter, where exactly *was* here?

Art opened his eyes. It was a mistake. The sun was glaring and the moment he opened his eyes, two bolts of pain shot through him.

"He's awake," a girl's voice said.

Putting his hand over his eyes, Art opened them again. Now that he was shielding his eyes from the intense sunlight, it wasn't as painful to open them. Peering through the separations between his fingers, he looked at the girl who had spoken. She appeared to be about his age, with long, dark curls hanging down and with vivid amber eyes staring intently at him. There was something familiar about her and for a moment, he couldn't figure out what it was. Then he remembered. She was the girl he had seen in the passing wagon yesterday afternoon.

Was it yesterday afternoon? Somehow it seemed much longer ago than that.

"Who are you?" Art asked.

"My name is Jennie."

"Whoa, team," a man's voice said. The wagon stopped. "Boy?" the same voice called. "You all right, boy?"

Art sat up and as he did so, his head spun and nausea swept over him.

"I've got to throw up," he said, leaning over the edge of the wagon. He threw up until he had nothing left, which didn't take long as his stomach was nearly empty.

When he was finished, he looked back into the wagon. Besides the girl who had introduced herself as Jennie, there was a man and a woman in the wagon. Both of them were staring at him as if he had just turned green.

"I'm sorry about that," he said.

"Had a bit too much to drink last night, did you?" the man asked.

"Yes, sir," Art said. He felt the back of his head. There was a bump there that was very tender to the touch. "At least, I reckon I did." He felt another wave of nausea, and once more he leaned over the edge of the wagon. Although he didn't think he had anything left to throw up, he managed a little. Mostly, though, it was a painful retching.

"I'm sorry," he said again.

"That's all right; anytime you got to throw up, you just do it," the man driving the wagon said. "My name is Younger. Lucas Younger. I own this here wagon. This is my wife, Bess. What's your name?"

"Art."

"Art what?"

"Just Art. I ain't got no last name."

"Why, Art, honey, that can't be right," Bess Younger complained. "Ever'one has to have a last name."

"I ain't got one," Art said resolutely.

"Don't bother the boy none, Bess," Younger said. "If he don't want to give us his last name, he don't have ta'."

Art looked around outside the wagon. They were on a road of some sort, now passing through swampland. On either side of the road he could see stands of cypress trees, their knees sticking up from standing pools of water. "Where are we?" he asked. "What am I doing here?"

"You sure ask a lot of questions," Younger replied.

"Last thing I remember is orderin' my supper. But I don't remember eating it."

"From the way you looked when we found you, you didn't eat your supper. You drank it," Younger said.

"Oh . . ." Art groaned. He put his hand to his head. "I did. I drank beer. I drank a lot of beer." He looked up again sharply. "What do you mean, when you found me?"

"Just what I said, sonny. Me, the wife, and the girl there found you. You was lying out in the road leavin' New Madrid. The wife thought you was dead, but soon as I got down and looked at you, I know'd you wasn't dead."

"You say you found me on the road leaving New Madrid?"

"Sure did."

"My money!" Art said. He stuck his hands in his pockets, but they came out empty.

"Boy, if you had any money on you, somebody took it offen you a'fore we come along," Younger said. "I hope you don't think we took it."

"No," Art said. "No, I don't think you would take my money, then take care of me like this."

"Glad you know that."

"Where are we now?" Art asked.

"Oh, we're some north of New Madrid, headin' on up

to St. Louie. This here road we're on is called the El Camino Real. That means The King's Road."

"We saved back a biscuit for your breakfast if you're hungry," Bess said.

At first thought, the idea of eating something made Art feel even more queasy. But he was hungry, and he reasoned that, maybe if he ate, he would feel better.

"Thank you," he said. "I'd like that."

"Jennie, get him that biscuit."

"Yes, ma'am," Jennie said. She fumbled around in some cloth, then unwrapped a biscuit and handed it to Art. He thanked her, then ate it, hoping it would stay down.

It did stay down, and before long he was feeling considerably better.

"Right after you left, the boy went out the back door to the privy," Bellefontaine replied to Harding's question. "He never come back in. When you find him, tell him he owes me for the supper he ordered."

"How much?"

"Fifteen cents ought to do it."

Harding put fifteen cents on the counter, then pointed toward the back door. "You say he went through there?"

"Yep. Ain't no use in lookin' back there, though. I got to worryin' some about him, seein' as how he didn't come back, so I went out there to have a look around myself. He wasn't nowhere to be found."

Despite Bellefontaine's assurance that there was nothing to be seen out back, Harding went outside to have a look around. Art was nowhere to be seen.

After satisfying himself that Art wasn't behind the Blue Star, Harding checked all the boardinghouses in town. Art hadn't stayed in any of them. Then he checked the other taverns, and even checked with all the whores on the possibility that Art might have decided to give one of them a try. Nobody had seen him. He decided it was time to talk to the sheriff.

The sheriff was in his office, feet propped up on a table, hands laced behind his head. A visitor to the office was sitting on a stool near the cold stove, paring an apple. One long peel dangled from the apple, and from the careful way he was working it, it was obvious he was going to try and do it in one, continuous peel.

"Sheriff Tate, I'm Pete Harding."

"Hell, Harding, I know who you are," the sheriff answered. "After the show you put on last night, I reckon ever'one in town knows who you are.

"Damn!" the apple peeler suddenly said. Looking toward him, Harding saw that the peel had broken.

"Ha!" Sheriff Tate said. "That's a nickel you owe me."

"I could'a done it if he hadn't come in," the apple peeler said. "Him walkin' on the floor like he done jarred it so's that it broke."

"You're full of shit, Sanders," the sheriff said. "It would'a broke whether Harding come in here or not. Pay your nickel."

Sanders took a nickel from his pocket and slapped it down on the sheriff's desk. Then, looking at Harding with obvious disapproval, he left the office.

"Now," Sheriff Tate said, putting the nickel away. "What do you need, Harding? If it's about last night, don't worry about it. Enough folks have given statements about what happened that there ain't even goin' to be an inquiry."

"It's not about last night," Harding said. "Well, yes, I guess it is, in a way. I come in here with a boy named Art. He was working on the boat with me. The thing is, I've lost him."

"What do you mean, you lost him?"

"I left him at the Blue Star for a while when I left to, uh, conduct some business."

Sheriff Tate laughed. "Conduct business? You mean going off with one of the whores, don't you?"

"Yes," Harding admitted. "And when I came back . . . this morning . . . the boy was gone."

"Well, hell, Harding, you didn't expect him to sit there the whole night, did you?"

"No. But I've checked with every place he could possibly be. I've checked all the boardinghouses, taverns, even the other whores. Nobody has seen him."

"You think something happened to him?"

"I'm a little worried about him, yes. He drank quite a bit of beer last night. I'm pretty sure he had never had one before. Nobody's reported anything to you, have they?"

"You mean like a body?"

"Yeah," Harding said with a sigh. "That's exactly what I mean."

"Far as I know, we only got two bodies in this town right now," Sheriff Tate. "Riley and Carter. And I reckon you know about them."

"What about the river? What if someone threw a body in the river?"

"Unless they went to the trouble of weighing the body down, it'll come back up within an hour," Sheriff Tate said. "And what with the bend in the river, it pretty near always stays right here. You think maybe, him bein' drunk and all, he might'a fallen in the river?"

"I don't know," Harding replied. "I hope not."

"Well, I'll keep my eyes open and if I see anything, I'll let you know."

"That's just it, I won't be around after today. I've bought myself a horse and I'm ridin' back up to Ohio to put together another load of goods. I just thought I'd see what I could find out before I left."

"You got 'ny reason to suspect foul play?"

"No."

"Was he plannin' on goin' back to Ohio with you?"

"No," Harding said again. "He said he would be going on from here."

"Well, there you go then. Most likely, that's what happened to him. We had a couple of wagons pull out of here early this morning, bound for St. Louis. Could be he went out with one of them."

"That's probably what happened," Harding said. "Sorry to have been a bother to you."

"Ah, don't worry about it. I'm sure he's all right, but like I said, I'll keep my eyes open."

"Thanks," Harding said.

It was midafternoon by the time Harding rode out of town. He headed north, intending to cross the river just above the juncture of the Ohio and Mississippi. That way, he would only have to cross once.

"Art, I don't know where you got off to, but I'd feel better if I knew for sure that you were all right," he said, speaking aloud to himself.

There were nearly three dozen other wagons parked where they made camp that night. Although few of the wagons were traveling together, and some in fact were even going in opposite directions, it was quite common for wagons traveling alone on the frontier to join with other travelers at night in a temporary wagon park. And not only wagons, but travelers on horseback as well, for at least a dozen single men had staked out their horses and thrown their bedrolls down within the confines of the wagon camp.

Such an arrangement not only granted company and the opportunity for some trade, it also provided the safety of numbers against attack from hostile Indians or marauding highwaymen. Younger asked Art if he would mind doing a few chores.

"I'll be more than glad to. It's little enough to pay you back for your kindness."

"I was just doin' my Christian duty," Lucas replied. "But if you're up to workin' for your keep, first thing I want you to do is help me get this tarp up." Younger began untying the canvas on one side of the wagon, and indicated that Art should do the same thing on the other.

Art untied his side, then he and Younger unrolled the canvas, stretching it across the wagon bows so that the wagon was covered. After that, Lucas did something that Art thought was rather strange. He tied a red streamer to the back of the wagon.

"There, that'll do just fine," Tryeen said.

"What's the red flag for?" Art asked.

"Never you mind about that," Lucas replied. "You just take the team down to water. Then, when you come back, check with the Missus. I 'spect she'll have some chores she'll be a'wantin' you to do for her."

"Yes, sir, I'll be glad to do anything she wants," Art said.

Art took the team down to water. When he returned, Bess gave him a bucket and had him get some water for cooking. Then she had him gather wood for the fire.

Looking around the camp, Art saw Younger going over to the area occupied by the men who were traveling alone, mostly those who had ridden in on horseback. He had no idea what he was saying to them, but some of them were visibly animated by the conversation, for they began moving around in a rather lively fashion, while looking back toward the Younger wagon. After visiting with them for a few minutes, Younger returned to the wagon. "Jennie," he called. "You've got some business to take care of, girl. Get on up here."

It wasn't until then that Art realized he hadn't seen Jennie since they made camp.

"Jennie, get up here now," Younger called, a little more forcefully than before. "You know what you have to do."

Jennie crawled out from under the little tent that had been made by dropping canvas down around the edge of the wagon. Art gasped in surprise when he saw her. Jennie no longer looked like a little girl. She looked much more like a woman, and not just any woman, but like a painted woman, the way Lily had looked at the tavern back in New Madrid.

Younger spoke directly to Art. "Boy, I'll thank you to stay out of the wagon now until after Jennie is finished with her business."

"Finished with her business? What business?" Art asked.

"Business that ain't none of your business," Lucas replied with a hoarse laugh. "Now, just you mind what I say. Stay out of the back of the wagon. The missus will keep you busy enough."

"Yes, sir," Art replied.

"Jennie, you ready in there?"

"I'm ready," Jennie's muffled voice replied.

Suddenly, and unexpectedly, Younger let out a yell.

"Yee haw! Yee haw! Yee haw! Sporting gentlemen!" he shouted at the top of his voice. *"Now is your time! If you are after a little fun, you can get it here! Yee haw! Yee haw! Yee haw!"*

Nearly a dozen men of all ages and sizes began moving toward the wagon, most from the area where the riders were encamped, but a few from some of the other wagons as well. Art watched them approach, wondering what this was all about.

The men stood in a line behind the wagon. The first in line handed some money to Younger, then climbed up into the wagon. Because of the canvas sheet that was covering the wagon, Art couldn't see what was going on inside.

After a few minutes, the first man came out, adjusting his trousers. Some of the other men said something to him and he answered, then several of them laughed. Because Art was standing near the fire that had been built several feet in front the wagon, he was too far away to hear what was being said.

"Mrs. Younger, what's going on back there?" Art asked. "What's Jennie doing in the wagon with all those men?"

Bess Younger looked uneasy. "I got no part with that business," she said in a clearly agitated voice. "And neither do you."

"But Jennie's in there," Art said.

"I told you, you got no business worryin' about that. So you just don't pay it no never mind," Bess said.

"I know I ain't got no business. I was just curious, that's all."

"Don't be curious," Bess said. "Sometimes, what you don't know don't hurt you. You'll be wantin' to sleep with us tonight?"

"I aim to, yes. That is, if you and Mr. Younger don't mind."

"We don't mind. We figured you'd be goin' on to St. Louis with us. I just thought you ought to know that we ain't got no extra blankets for you to make your bedroll. But I reckon if you want to, you can sleep up on the wagon seat. There's a buffalo robe up there that you can wrap up in if it gets too cool."

"Yes, ma'am, thank you, ma'am," Art said.

Art ran errands for Bess Younger until long after dark, gathering wood for the breakfast fire the next morning, and even rolling out dough for tomorrow's bread. All the while men from all over the camp continued to make their way to stand in line at the back of the wagon. When Art finally finished all his chores and climbed up onto the seat to go to sleep, there were still men waiting in line at the back of the wagon. But because a tarpaulin drop separated the wagon seat from the bed of the wagon, he was still unable to see what was going on.

He was asleep when he heard Jennie and Lucas Younger

talking. By the position of the stars and moon, he figured it to be after midnight.

"We done pretty good tonight," Lucas was saying. "Near 'bout ten dollars we took in."

"Please," Jennie said. "Please don't make me do this no more. I don't like it."

"We all got to do things we don't like," Younger said. "Besides, you got nothin' to complain about, girl. You could be workin' in the fields, pickin' cotton with the niggers. Would you rather be doing that?"

"Yes, sir. I'd rather be doing that."

"That's just 'cause you're crazy," he said gruffly. "Now crawl into your little nest under the wagon and get to bed. I don't want to hear no more 'bout this."

The little canvas-enclosed area where Jennie had pitched her bedroll was beneath the forward part of the wagon, just under Art. As a result, she was no more than two feet from him, separated only by the bottom of the wagon. Art could hear her rustling about as she got ready for bed. He started to call out to her, but something held him back. Instead, he just lay as quietly as he could.

Then, later, when all the rustling around had stopped and everything was still, he heard Jennie crying. She was being quiet about it, stifling her sobs as best she could, but there was no mistaking what he heard. Jennie was crying.

Why was she crying? Art wondered. What was it Younger was making her do in the back of that wagon?

"Ten dollars, Bess," Art had heard Younger telling his wife just before they went to sleep. "We made us ten dollars here tonight."

"I can't help but think that it is Satan's money," Bess replied in a troubled voice.

"The hell it is," Younger said. "It's *my* money." He laughed at his own joke.

Five

They had been on the trail for the better part of four hours the next morning. Jennie was sitting in the back of the wagon, dozing sometimes, other times just looking off into the woods alongside the road. Bess was driving the team; Younger and Art were walking alongside the wagon to make it easier on the mules.

A couple of times Art tried to do something to cheer Jennie up, popping up suddenly beside her, or throwing little dirt clods at her. The only time he managed to get through to her was when he turned upside down and walked on his hands for a few yards. When he was upright again, he thought he saw her smile.

But the smile, as hard-won as it was, was short-lived. It was no time at all before Jennie was morose again. Art didn't think he had ever seen anyone looking as sad as Jennie did, and he wished he could do something to make her feel better.

That opportunity presented itself about midafternoon. Looking over into a little clump of grass, Art happened to see a tiny bunny. Reaching down, he picked it up and held it. The rabbit was so small that it barely filled the palm of his hand. It was furry and soft, and he could feel it trembling in fear as he held it.

Jennie! he thought. This was bound to cheer her up.

He trotted back to the wagon, holding the rabbit in such

a way that it was obvious to Jennie, even as he approached, that he had something.

"Look what I found," he said, though he still hadn't showed her what he was holding.

"What is it? What do you have?" Jennie asked.

"Huh-uh, you'll have to guess."

"Oh, now, I'm not good at guessing. Please tell me what it is."

"I'll do better than that," Art said. "I'll give it you. It's yours to keep." He held the little rabbit out toward her.

"Oohhh!!" Jennie squealed in delight as she held the wriggling little piece of fur in her hands. "Oh, thank you! He is so pretty."

Jennie's face lit up brighter than it had been at any time since Art first saw her. She held the little rabbit to her cheek. "What's his name?" she asked.

"Oh, that's not for me to say. He belongs to you now. You'll have to name him," Art said.

"I think I'll call him . . ."

That was as far as she got. Unnoticed by either one of them, Younger had walked quickly up to the wagon. Reaching over the edge of the wagon, he grabbed the little rabbit, then turned and threw it as far as he could.

"Mr. Younger no!" Jennie screamed, while Art watched the little bunny flying through the air, kicking ineffectively. It fell hard, several feet away, bounced once, then remained perfectly still.

"I told you, I don't hold with that kind of business," Younger said. "Keepin' rabbits 'n such as pets is for babies and chil'run. You're a woman, full-growed now, and it's time you started actin' like one."

"Yes, sir," Jennie said contritely.

"And you," Younger continued, turning toward Art. "Next time you bring in a rabbit, it better be big enough to make into a stew."

"Yes, sir," Art said, mimicking Jennie's response.

Younger moved on up toward the head of the team. He reached out to grab the harness of the off-mule, using it to help pull him along.

Art looked up at Jennie and saw that tears were sliding down her cheeks. He had hoped to cheer her up, but wound up making things worse. He felt very bad about it.

"I'm sorry about the rabbit," he said quietly.

"It's all right. You couldn't do nothin' about it," she answered with a sniff.

"Why do you call your pa Mr. Younger?"

Jennie looked at Art in shock. "He ain't my pa," she said.

"Oh, I see. He's your step-pa then? He married your ma, is that it?"

Jennie shook her head. "Mrs. Younger ain't my ma."

"They ain't your ma and pa?"

"No. They're my owners."

"Owners? What do you mean, owners?"

"I'm their slave girl. I thought you knowed that."

"No, I didn't know that," Art said. "Fact is, I don't know as I've ever knowed a white slave girl."

"I ain't exactly white," Jennie said quietly.

"You're not?"

"I'm Creole. My grandma was black."

"But how can you be their slave? You don't do no work for 'em," Art said. "I mean . . . no offense meant, but I ain't never seen you do nothin' like get water or firewood, or help out Mrs. Younger with the cookin'."

"No," Jennie said quietly. "But gathering firewood, or helping in the kitchen, ain't the only way of workin'. There's other ways . . . ways that"—she stopped talking for a moment—"ways that I won't trouble you with."

"You mean, like what you was doin' with all them men last night?"

Jennie cut a quick glance toward him. The expression on

her face was one of total mortification. "You . . . you seen what I was doin'?"

"No, I didn't really see nothin' more'n a bunch of men linin' up at the back of the wagon. Even when I went to bed, I couldn't see what was goin' on on the other side of the tarp."

"Do you . . . do you know what I was doing in there?"

Art shook his head. "Not really," he said. "I got me an idea that you was doin' what painted ladies do. Onliest thing is, I don't rightly know what that is."

Jennie looked at him in surprise for a moment; then her face changed and she laughed.

"What is it? What's so funny?" Art asked.

"You are," she said. "You are still just a boy after all."

"I ain't no boy," Art said resolutely. "I done killed me a man. I reckon that's made me man enough."

The smile left Jennie's face and she put her hand on his shoulder. "I reckon it does at that," she said.

"You don't like doin' what Younger is makin' you do, do you?"

"No. I hate it," Jennie said resolutely. "It's—it's the worst thing you can imagine."

"Then why don't you leave?"

"I can't. I belong to 'em. Besides, iffen I left, where would I go? What would I do? I'd starve to death if I didn't have someone lookin' out for me."

"I don't know," Art said. "But seems to me like anything would be better than this."

"What about you? Are you going to stay with the Youngers?"

"Only as long as it takes to get to St. Louis," Art replied. "Then I'll go out on my own."

"Have you ever been to St. Louis?" Jennie asked.

"No, have you?"

Jennie shook her head. "No, I haven't. Mr. Younger says it's a big and fearsome place, though."

"I'll bet you could find a way to get on there," Art said. "I'll bet you could find work, the kind of work that wouldn't make you have to paint yourself up and be with men."

"I'd be afraid. If I try to get away, Mr. Younger will send the slave catchers after me."

"Slave catchers? What are slave catchers?"

"They are fearsome men who hunt down runaway slaves. They are paid to find the runaways, and bring 'em back to their masters. They say that the slave hunters always find who they are lookin' for. And most of the time they give 'em a whippin' before they bring 'em back. I ain't never been whipped."

"I can see where a colored runaway might be easy to find. But you don't look colored. How would they find you? Don't be afraid. I'll help you get away."

"How would you do that?"

"Easy," Art said with more confidence than he felt. "I aim to leave the Youngers soon's we get to St. Louis. When I go, I'll just take you with me, that's all. You bein' white and all, you could pass for my sister. No one's goin' to take you for a runaway. Why, I'll bet you could find a job real easy."

"Maybe I could get on with someone looking after their children," Jennie suggested. "I'm real good at looking after children. You really will help me?"

"Yes," Art replied. He spat in the palm of his hand, then held it out toward Jennie.

"What . . . what is that?" Jennie asked, recoiling from his proffered hand.

"It's a spit promise," Art said. "That's about the most solemn promise there is.

Smiling, Jennie spat in her hand as well, then reached out to take Art's hand in hers. They shook on the deal.

Half an hour later they stopped to give the team a rest. Younger peed right by the side of the road, making no effort to conceal himself from the women. Buttoning up his trousers, he came back up to the wagon.

"Art, they's a cow down there," he said. He reached down into the wagon and pulled out a piece of rope. "I want you to go down there and get her, and bring her back up here. Tie her off to the back of the wagon."

"You mean just go get her?" Art asked in surprise. "How can I do that? Doesn't she belong to anyone?"

"Yes. She belongs to me," Younger said.

"But how can that be? I thought you said you hadn't been up this way before."

"The cow belongs to me because I say she does," Younger said irritably. "Now, go get her like I said."

"I'd rather not," Art said. "I'm afraid that would be stealing and I don't want to steal from anyone."

"It's not stealing," Younger insisted. "Look, the cow is just standing out there. If she belonged to someone, don't you think she would be in a barn somewhere? Or at least in a pen. Now, go get her like I said."

Art thought about it. On the one hand, he felt a sense of obligation to Younger for taking him in. On the other, he was sure that the cow didn't belong to Younger, so taking it would be stealing. It was clear, however, that if he didn't go get the cow, Younger would, so the end result would be the same. And if Art was being ordered to take the cow, then he didn't think it would be the same thing as him stealing.

"All right," he said, taking the rope. "I'll get her."

"Good lad," Younger said. "You're going to work out just fine."

They hadn't gone more than a mile beyond that when two horsemen overtook them. Both riders were carrying rifles and they rode up alongside the wagon, demanding that it stop. One of the riders was about Younger's age; the other looked to be little older than Art. Art was sure they were father and son.

"Something I can do for you gentlemen?" Younger asked.

"Hell, yes, there's something you can do, mister," the older of the two riders said. He pointed to the cow. "You can untie our cow from the back of your wagon."

"This is your cow?"

"You're damn right this is our cow."

"Art, untie that cow right now," Younger ordered. "Give it back to the rightful owners."

"Yes, sir," Art said, walking back toward the cow.

"I'm sorry about that," Younger said to the two men.

"What I'd like to know is, what are you doing with our cow in the first place?"

"I can see how it might look a little suspicious," Younger said. He pointed to Art. "But the boy there had the cow with him when we picked him up on the road."

"You say the boy had the cow?"

"He did. He said he had a hankerin' to go to St. Louis, and he offered me the cow in exchange for my wife and me to take him there."

Art heard Younger's lie, but he made no attempt to dispute it.

"If you was a mite older, boy, you'd be hanging from yonder tree," the older rider said as Art passed the end of the cow's lead rope up to him.

"He's near as old as I am, Pa," the younger rider said. "Seems to me like that's old enough to hang."

The older man shook his head. "No. I don't take to hangin' boys." He pointed his rifle at Art. "But hear this, boy. If I ever see you in these parts again, I'll like as not shoot you. I figure the earlier you can stop a thief, the less grief other folks will be getting from him."

"I don't think the boy meant to steal the cow, mister," Younger said. "He told us he found it walkin' down the road. think he thought the cow had just wandered off."

"Uh-huh. You say you just picked him up, did you?"

"Yes, sir, my wife and I did. Figured it would be a Christian kindness to take him in."

"Well, you'd better watch that he don't steal ever'thing you got and leave you in the middle of the night," the older of the two riders said gruffly. "Come on, son. Let's get Nellie back into the barn."

The riders left then, at as fast a trot as the cow would allow. Art waited until they were well out of earshot before he spoke.

"Mr. Younger, it wasn't right, you telling those men I stole that cow."

"I didn't tell them you stole it, I told them you found it," Younger said. "Besides, you saw how they were. If they had thought I took it, they would've hung me. Would you have wanted that on your conscience?"

"No, I reckon not," Art replied. It didn't occur to him to tell Younger that his conscience would have been clear since he had opposed taking the cow in the first place.

"I guess we'll just have to be more careful next time, won't we?"

Art didn't answer.

"Let's step up the pace a little," Younger said, running his finger around his neck collar. "This place don't sit well with me."

Six

When they stopped that night to make camp, there were no other wagons around. Younger griped a bit about the fact that nobody else was there.

"You'd think for sure there'd be some travelers here," he complained. "They's a goodly supply of wood, grass, and water. The land is flat, makin' for easy campin'. Seems to me like it's the perfect place to stop, only ain't nary a traveler in sight."

Jennie didn't say a word, but Art knew that she was happy they were alone. That meant she didn't have to entertain any men.

After supper, Younger asked Art to come with him to look for some dewberries. "I seen me some back a ways, so there's likely to be more around here some'ers. Iffen we can gather us up a mess of berries, I'll have the missus make a dewberry pie. I reckon both of you young'uns would like that."

Art thought of the blackberry pies and cobblers his mother used to make, and his stomach growled. It had been quite a while now since he had anything like that.

"Yes, sir, I'd like it a lot," he said.

"Well, then let's get to lookin'," Younger ordered.

The two left the campsite, Younger carrying a shovel with him, while Art had two empty buckets. Younger indicated that they should go out into the woods, so they left the wagon trail. To Art fell the job of breaking through the brush, while Younger had the somewhat easier task of following along behind.

They were nearly half a mile deep into the woods when Art saw several of the fruit-laden bushes. "There are some over there," Art said, pointing, already tasting the dewberry pie.

"No, them's too little to make a good pie," Younger said. "Let's walk on down a little farther and see what we can find. The bigger and fatter the berry, the sweeter it is. And the sweeter the berry, the better the pie."

"Little? If you think those berries are little, they must grow awful big here. Those are about as big as any I've ever seen," Art said.

"Don't be smart-mouthin' your elders, boy," Younger said.

Art was surprised by Younger's vitriolic response.

"Sorry, didn't mean nothin' by it," he said.

"Uh-huh. And I suppose you didn't mean nothin' by tryin' to talk Jennie into runnin' away with you when you got to St. Louis either."

Art didn't answer.

"You prob'ly thought I didn't hear what you was sayin' to her. But I got ears like an old hound dog and I heard ever' word."

"It ain't right, what you're makin' her do," Art said. "She don't like it, and I don't think it's right."

"You don't think it's right, do you?"

"No, sir. Not even a little bit," Art said resolutely.

"Well, let me tell you somethin', boy. It ain't none of your business what I do with her. That girl belongs to me, bought and paid for."

"I don't hold with no kind of slavery either. Black or white," Art said.

"Yeah, well, what you think don't matter. And you already showed me that you ain't goin' to be worth a damn when it comes to takin' advantage of the lay of the land, so to speak. Iffen you had acted quicker when I told you to take that cow, like as not we would've been long gone before them folks discovered what happened. What you almost done was get me hung."

"That ain't right, Mr. Younger, and you know it," Art said. "In the first place, even if I had gotten that cow the first time you told me, they would have still caught up with us. And in the second place, what you done wasn't right. I don't hold with stealing, and those men were right to be mad."

"So what you are telling me is, you're planning on traveling with us, but you don't plan to help out along the way. Is that right?"

"Not if helping out means stealing."

"Uh-huh. I sort of thought that," Younger said. "That's why I aim to leave you here for the buzzards to pick over your bones."

During the entire conversation, Younger had been walking just behind Art. Now these words, coming from behind him as they were, had a chilling effect, and Art turned.

"What do you mean, leaving me here for the buzzards to pick over my bones?" he asked.

Younger answered Art by swinging his shovel at him. Art threw up his arm at the last minute, but it did little to ward off the blow. He felt a sharp pain in his arm, then a smashing blow to the side of his head.

Younger looked down on Art's still form.

"I should'a left you lyin' alongside the privy back there in New Madrid. But you had near fourteen dollars on you and I figured anybody as young as you, with that much money, must be a pretty enterprisin' fella. Too bad you turned out like you done. A young boy like you would'a been pretty good at stealin' and such. We could'a made out pretty well along the trail, if you'd'a had enough sense to listen to me. But some folks are just too hardheaded to listen."

Younger began digging a grave then. He started it with every intention of making the grave six feet deep, but after a few minutes he got tired of digging. He looked at the hole he had dug, then at Art's still form. Figuring it was deep enough, he rolled Art's body over into the hole, and started covering him with dirt.

It began to rain . . . just a few drops at first, then the rain came harder, and harder still.

"Shit!" Younger swore loudly. He looked down at Art's body. It was only half covered with dirt from the waist down. "Shit, shit, shit!" He sighed. "Well, don't blame me for leavin' you for the wolves and sech," he said. "I was goin' to bury you proper, but I ain't goin' to stay out in no downpour to do it."

Picking up the two empty buckets and throwing the shovel over his shoulder, Younger started back toward the wagon. He didn't look back at the melancholy sight behind him.

The rain continued to fall, drumming into the trees, sifting down through the limbs, and causing little rivulets to run and form pools on the ground below.

When he felt the rain on his face, Art reached for a blanket to pull over his head. He thought he and Pa had fixed the leak in the roof, but it must've come back. Reaching for the blanket, he got nothing but a handful of leaves.

Leaves?

What were leaves doing in his bed?

When Art opened his eyes, he saw, not the roof over his bedroom, but the low-bending limb of a nearby tree. Because of the darkness, that was all he could see. He felt a weight on the bottom half of his body and, sitting up, saw that he was covered with dirt.

Suddenly it all came back to him. Younger had tried to kill him . . . in fact, Younger thought he *had* killed him, and left him half-buried in the woods. He didn't know why Younger had only half-buried him, but he was grateful that he had, for if Younger had finished the job, he would surely be dead by now.

Pulling himself out of the grave, Art fought the dizziness for a few minutes until he felt good enough to walk. Then he started back toward the wagon. He wasn't entirely sure what he was going to do when he got there. Younger did have a rifle, after all, while Art had no weapon of any kind. But he would do something, even if it was no more than stealing Jennie away from him and setting her free.

But Art learned rather quickly that it wasn't going to be as easy getting back to the wagon as he thought it would be. In the first place, he could still feel the pain of the blow from the shovel. And that pain, coupled with the dizziness it caused, compounded by the pitch-black darkness, made it difficult for him to retrace their path. In addition, it was raining, and dark, and he was in totally unfamiliar territory.

Somewhere along the way he became completely disoriented. He walked for two or three miles before he realized that if he had been going in the right direction, he would have been to the wagon long before now.

Frustrated, and now nauseous, both from the blow on the head and the physical exertion, he saw a large, flat rock protruding from the side of a little hill. Crawling under the rock, he lifted his knees to his chin, wrapping his arms around his legs in an unsuccessful attempt to stay warm and dry. He was cold, wet, tired, and miserable.

He thought of his home, back in Ohio. The entire family would be asleep now, warm, snug, and dry in bed, under cover, while rain beat down upon the roof and against the windows. He had always liked the sound of rain at night;

he liked the idea of being inside, in a warm, dry bed, while it was cold and wet outside.

Outside.

Where he was right now.

Art felt a choking in his throat, a stinging of the eyes, and warm drops of water joining the cold rain, sliding down his cheeks. They were tears, and he was crying.

Damn it, he was crying!

"No!" he shouted, shaking his fist at the heavens. "No! I am not going to cry like a two-year-old baby! I put myself here, and whatever it takes to survive, I'll do. If I have to steal, then as God is my witness, I will steal! And if I have to kill again, I'll kill again, but by all that's holy, I will survive!"

"Where's Art?" Jennie asked when Younger returned to the wagon alone.

"It ain't none of your concern where he is."

"Where is he?" Bess Younger asked, looking over Younger's shoulder back into the woods.

"If you must know, the sonofabitch ran away," Younger said. "That's the thanks you get for trying to help someone."

"Why would he do that?" Bess asked. "I thought he was anxious to go to St. Louis."

"You tell me why he would do that," Younger replied. "We've been providing him with three good meals a day, a place to sleep at night, and a safe way of travel. So how does he repay us? By running off like a thief in the night." Younger put the two buckets and the shovel into the wagon. "Well, let's get goin'. What with the rain and all, I'd like to find us a better place to stay."

"What?" Bess asked in surprise. "I thought we were going to stay the night here. The team has already been unhitched and I've started rolling out the dough for tomorrow. Besides, you said yourself this was a good place to stay."

"Yeah, well, I must've been wrong," Younger said. "There ain't nobody else here; they must know somethin' we don't know. If you ask me, this may be a floodplain. Could be that with a good rain, there could come a flood and we'd find ourselves underwater come mornin'. You wouldn't want that, would you?"

"No," Bess agreed.

"Then do what you got to do to get ready to go. I'll hitch the team up."

Jennie helped Bess tidy up the wagon as Younger hitched up the team. When she moved the buckets and shovel, she noticed something on the end of the shovel blade. She examined it closer, then she gasped.

"What is it?" Bess asked.

"Miz Younger, they's blood on the shovel," Jennie said. "Oh, Lord, it's Art's blood, ain't it? Mr. Younger done killed Art."

"Hush you mouth, girl," Bess said sharply. "He didn't do no such thing."

"Then whose blood is that?"

Bess picked up a rag and wiped off the stain, then held up the rag for a closer examination. "Hmmph," she said. "It's not blood at all. It's nothing more than the stain of a few berries."

"Are you sure?"

"You're not questioning me, are you, girl?"

"No, ma'am, I reckon not."

"You just finish tidying up and don't worry your mind anymore about that boy. Truth to tell, he's prob'ly better off on his own. Looked to me like him 'n Mr. Younger was goin' to get cross-wise with each other one of these days."

"Yes, ma'am," Jennie said.

* * *

As the wagon rolled through the night and the rain, Jennie sat in the right, rear corner, trying to stay dry and warm. If Art really did run away, it would be the best thing for him. But was that really what had happened? And was worry about a flood the real reason for pulling out in the dark? As long as she had been with the Youngers, they had never moved on in the dark.

She was also concerned about the stain on the shovel. Mrs. Younger had insisted that it was nothing but a berry stain, but it looked too red for that. On the other hand, Mrs. Younger wasn't an evil woman. She was actually kind to Jennie, and it was obvious that she didn't approve of what Younger made her do. From time to time Jennie had overheard them arguing, with Mrs. Younger begging him to stop forcing Jennie to be with men. Her entreaties had always fallen on deaf ears, but the very fact that she had championed Jennie's case improved her standing in Jennie's eyes.

Maybe Mrs. Younger was right. Maybe it was just berry stain. Jennie didn't know if God would listen to prayers from a sinner like her, but she prayed, fervently, that Art hadn't been killed.

Seven

Finding Younger was easy. The rain had left the trail soft, and Younger's wagon wheels cut ruts that were easy to follow. Nevertheless, it was nightfall of the following day before Art came upon a small encampment area filled with travelers. Nearly ten wagons and as many riders were gathered together for the night.

Moving up closer to the campground, Art used the light of a dozen fires to study the wagons. Then he saw what he was looking for: a canvas-covered wagon marked by a red streamer. Though it was sitting aside from the others, it wasn't isolated, for several men were queued up behind the wagon, just as before. Younger was standing at the back, collecting money from the men who were just arriving, then directing them to the end of the line. Mrs. Younger was in front of the wagon, sitting on the tongue, staring into the fire. Art knew she didn't approve of all this, but he also didn't believe she tried hard enough to prevent it.

Lying on his belly under a bush, Art fought mosquitoes and insects while he watched long into the night. Finally the last man who had entered the wagon came crawling out. After exchanging a few words with Younger, the man drifted away, disappearing into a night that was now lit only by the moon, since most of the fires had burned down to a few glowing coals.

"All right, Jennie, girl, that there was the last 'un," Art

heard Younger call. "You can come on down now. Bess? Bess, come on out now."

It wasn't until then that Art realized that Mrs. Younger had gone to bed in Jennie's little nest beneath the wagon. He watched as Mrs. Younger and Jennie traded places, Mrs. Younger climbing up into the wagon, while Jennie crawled into the little canvas-drop area underneath. Younger climbed into the wagon behind his wife; then all movement stopped.

Art stayed where he was, waiting at least another hour, until he was absolutely certain everyone in the camp was asleep. Then he made his move, starting toward the wagon. The moon was so bright that he decided not to cross the opening upright, but to crawl on all fours until he reached the right front wheel. There he stopped and waited a few minutes longer, just to make sure no one had seen him. Not until he knew with absolute certainty that he was alone did he call out.

"Jennie," he whispered.

No answer.

"Jennie. It's me, Art!"

A small stirring came from behind the canvas. "Art?" Jennie replied.

Above him, inside the wagon, Art heard Younger groan and move.

"Shh!" Art cautioned.

The canvas parted and Jennie stuck her head out. "I saw blood on the shovel and I was afraid you were dead!" she said. "But Mr. Younger said you ran away, and I guess he was right."

"He was only partly right," Art said. "And you were almost right." He put his hand to the back of his head. "The blood on his shovel was mine. He tried to kill me with it, and must've thought that he had."

"What are you doing here?" Jennie asked.

"I came to get you."

"No, I can't go. I told you, I belong to Younger. I'm his slave."

"Even if you are his slave, he doesn't have the right to treat you like this. Especially with what he makes you do. Come on, I'm going to take you out of here."

"Where will we go? What will we do?" Jennie asked.

"I don't rightly know," Art admitted. "I haven't figured that part out yet, but anything has to be better than this."

Jennie crawled out from under the little shelter. "Wait," she said. "What about my things?"

"You're wearing your clothes. What else do you need?"

Jennie looked back toward the little tent. Art was right. She didn't need anything else.

"Let's go," she said.

Holding his finger up to his lips as a caution to be quiet, Art led her down into the woods.

"Hey! Come back here!"

Younger's sudden and unexpected call startled them.

"Run!" Art shouted, and the two of them ran into the woods. They ran for several minutes before Art said they could stop running. They stood there then, leaning against a tree, gasping for breath.

Jennie started to say something, but Art held up his hand, signaling her to be quiet. He listened for a long moment before he was satisfied that Younger wasn't coming after them.

"All right, you don't have to be so quiet now," he said. "He's not coming."

"Oh!" Jennie squealed happily. She threw her arms around Art in a spontaneous embrace. "Oh, you are wonderful!"

"Yeah, well, no call for you to do all that," Art said uneasily, backing away from her embrace.

"I know, it's just that I'm free," she said. "I'm free!"

* * *

Younger wasn't sure what woke him up. It wasn't any-thing he heard as much as it was something he felt. He sat up quickly.

"What is it?" Bess asked.

"Nothin'," he said gruffly. "Go back to sleep."

He started to lie down again, then decided that as long as he was awake, he might as well get out of the wagon and take a leak. He had just reached the ground when he saw, by the light of the moon, two people moving toward the edge of the woods. He didn't have to look twice to identify them. They were Jennie and Art.

How could it be Art? He was certain he had killed him.

"What is it?" Bess called down from the wagon. "What's going on?"

"Give me my rifle."

"What?"

"My rifle, goddamnit! Give it to me!" Younger shouted.

By now the commotion had awakened some people in adjacent wagons.

"What is it, Indians?" someone asked.

"Indians?" another repeated.

"Indians!" a third shouted, giving the alarm.

Younger took the rifle from Bess and aimed it toward the woods. He didn't even have a real target now, for they had disappeared in the trees. He was so angry that all he wanted to do was shoot and hope he hit one of them. And he didn't care which one it was.

He pulled the trigger, but heard only the snap of the hammer striking the pan. When he reached up to pull the hammer back, his thumb felt the powder in the pan and he realized that it was still damp from last night's rain. He hadn't bothered to clean his gun and replace the powder.

"Damn you, boy!" he shouted. "Damn you!"

By now, half-a-dozen other armed men had raced to the scene.

"Where are the Indians?" one of them asked.

"Indians?" Younger replied, confused by the question. "What Indians are you talking about?"

"The Indians you saw!"

"I didn't see no Indians."

"Then what the hell were you just trying to shoot at?"

"My slave girl got stole from me," Younger said. "I was trying to shoot the son of a bitch what stole her."

"You talking about the little girl you was whoring?" one of the others asked.

"Yes."

"By God, if I'd'a known that, I'd'a never got out of bed. I'll be damned if I'll help you get back a slave girl you ain't doin' nothin' with but whoring."

Grumbling, the others started back toward their wagons. The self-appointed spokesman of the group turned back toward Younger.

"Mister, I don't think decent folks want your company anymore. It might be better if you would leave camp before breakfast in the morning."

"Why would I want to do that?" Younger asked.

"Because if you don't, we may just tie you to a tree and give you a good whipping."

Like New Madrid, Tywappiti was a river town, consisting of two streets that ran parallel with the river, intersected by three streets than ran perpendicular. All the buildings were of brick construction, a residual benefit of the fact that Tywappiti's main industry was brick-making.

Younger was still griping about losing Jennie when he pulled into town.

"If you ask me, I'm just as glad she's gone," Bess said. "What you was makin' that girl do wasn't Christian."

"She's a colored girl. It ain't the same with colored girls," Younger insisted. "Why, they's some farms that breeds 'em like breedin' animals. Leastwise, I wasn't doin' that."

"She isn't colored."

"Her grandma is pure-blood African, and that means she's a fourth colored. Even someone who is one-eighth is the same as colored," Younger said. He stopped the wagon in front of a general store. "Anyhow, you been a'wantin' to get into a town so's you could buy a few things, ain't you? Well, here we are. And we got money for you to buy because of what I was doin' with that girl. So don't you go puttin' me down because of it."

While Bess was in the general store, Younger went into the saloon. As it happened, a couple of men who had been his customers a week or so earlier were in there as well.

"Younger!" one of them called. "Come, have a drink with us!"

Nodding, Younger joined them. "Whiskey," he told the barkeep.

"Hey, I'm glad to see you've made it as far as Tywappiti. You goin' to be settin' up business here? 'Cause if you are, I plan to pay that little ole' girl of your'n a visit."

"What girl is that?" one of the others in the saloon asked.

"He's got him a Creole girl, prettiest little thing you ever seed," the first man explained.

"She's gone," Younger said.

"Gone? You mean you sold her?"

Younger shook his head. "No, she got stole from me."

"Well, hell, that ain't no problem. We got us some slave chasers in this town can find anyone."

"Problem is, she don't look colored. She could pass for white, folks would never find her."

"Ain't that many places around here she could go. Believe me, if she can be found, Boyd Jensen can find her."

"How much will it cost me?"

"Sometimes it don't cost nothin'. Sometimes he just buys the slaves before he goes lookin' for 'em. Course, he gets 'em at a bargain rate. Then, once he finds 'em, he makes his money when he sells 'em."

When Younger drove his wagon north out of Tywappiti later that day, he was much less agitated about the loss of Jennie. Bess commented on it.

"I'm glad to see you ain't mad anymore."

"Yeah," he said. "Well, you can't stay mad forever."

Younger reached his hand around and felt the fat purse in his pocket. He was 250 dollars richer than he had been when they rode into town, the result of a deal he made with Boyd Jensen. He planned to keep that little transaction secret from his wife. No sense in letting her know of his windfall. And no sense in letting her know how he had handled the situation with Art. He had come up with a brilliant solution. It was not only satisfying, it was profitable.

Art and Jennie were exhausted and starving. In the six days since they left, they had eaten nothing but berries. They had found a patch of mushrooms, but Art knew that some mushrooms were poison, and he didn't want to take a chance on getting the wrong kind. Thus it was that when the three riders came upon them, Art would have been unable to resist them, even if he had known their purpose.

Though he had no idea of the immediate danger they posed to him, their very appearance was somewhat alarming. All three were rough-looking men, bearded and dirty with ragged looking clothes. But it wasn't the state of their clothes that caught Art's attention. It was the pistols stuck in their belts and rifles protruding from saddle sheaves.

The leader of the group had narrow, gray eyes, a three-corner puff of a scar on his forehead, and terrible-looking, twisted, yellow teeth.

"Well, now, lookie here," he said. "You folks must be Art and Jennie."

Art was about to deny it, thinking it couldn't be a good sign that these men knew who they were. But before he could deny it, Jennie gave them away.

"How do you know our names?" she asked.

Art groaned inwardly.

The leader of the group chuckled. "Well, missy, we know your names because you are both slaves, and we are slave hunters by profession. Anytime we go after runaway slaves, we purt' near always know their names."

"I'm no slave!" Art said sharply.

"You got papers to prove that you ain't?"

"Papers? No, I'm white! Why would I have to have papers provin' I'm not a slave?"

" 'Cause I got papers provin' that you are," the leader of the group said. He pulled a paper from his pocket, then opened it up and began to read. "Bill of sale from Lucas Younger to Boyd Jensen." He looked up and smiled,."Boyd Jensen, that's me."

He continued reading. "Two white-skinned slaves, a Creole girl, Jennie, age fourteen, and a high-yella boy named Art, age thirteen." He folded the paper and put it back in his pocket. "Jennie and Art," he said, pointing to the two. "A Creole girl and a high-yella boy. White-skinned slaves, that's you. You did belong to Lucas Younger, but I bought you, so now you both belong to me."

Pulling his pistol, Jensen pointed it directly at Art. "Now, you ain't goin' to give your new owner any trouble, are you, boy?"

"No," Art said.

Jensen cocked his pistol, and the metallic click of the hammer coming back made a chilling sound. "Didn't think you was. Boys, put 'em in shackles."

The other two riders climbed down from their horses, each of them carrying a length of chain and shackles. One of them went over to Jennie, who stuck her hands out without question. Obviously, she had been through this before. Art left his hands by his side.

"Stick your hands out here, boy," one of the two men said gruffly. He grabbed Art's wrist, clamped one of the shackles on it, then brought the other one up to secure it as well.

With Art and Jennie secured, one of the men passed a chain around the shackles, connecting them to each other, and ultimately to the saddle of one of the horses.

"You chil'run keep up now," Jensen said as his two cohorts mounted their horses. "Don't give me no trouble and I'll be good to you. I won't go too fast." With everyone mounted, they started down the road. Although Jensen kept his promise not to go too fast, it still required a very brisk walk for Art and Jennie to maintain the pace. By nightfall, Art was exhausted, and he couldn't help but wonder how Jennie could possibly keep up.

Eight

As Jensen and the others rode into town pulling Art and Jennie along behind them, several of the town s citizens turned out to look them over in curiosity. By now both Art and Jennie were so tired and dispirited that they were barely aware of the fact that they were the center of attention of just about everyone in town.

They stopped in front of one of the larger buildings. A sign on front of the building read:

Tywappiti Traders' Market
Buyers and Sellers Welcome
Auctions Every Saturday
Tools, Machinery, Slaves

"Keep an eye on 'em, " Jensen said as he dismounted.

Jennie shuffled over to sit down on the edge of the wooden porch.

"Get up, you," one of the men said, jerking hard on the chain. As the chain was looped around in a way to be attached to both of them, Art tried to spare Jennie by taking up the energy of the jerk, but he couldn't. Jennie was pulled off the porch, and landed, facedown, in the dirt in front of the trade market.

"Haw!" the one who jerked the chain said. "D'you see that, Pauley?"

"Leave 'er be, Dolan," Pauley said. "Let 'er sit down."

"You gone soft on her, have you?" Dolan asked. "You ain't a'thinkin' ole' Boyd's gonna let you sample this girl, are you? 'Cause I tell you true, he ain't goin' to do it. He aims to get as much as he can out of her, and he figures if any of us mess with her, she won't bring as much."

"Let 'er sit down," Pauley said again. "Let both of 'em sit down."

"Sit," Dolan said, making a motion with his hand.

Art helped Jennie up; then they both sat on the edge of the porch. A moment later Jensen came back out of the building with another man.

"See what I told you, Sheriff? They both as white as you or me," Jensen said. "But I got papers says they're slaves, the both of them."

"Sheriff?" Art said, perking up. "Are you the sheriff?"

"I am."

Art held up his hands. "Turn us loose, Sheriff. We aren't slaves."

"You got any papers says you aren't?" the sheriff asked.

"No, I don't have any papers," Art answered. "Why should I? People don't go around carrying papers saying they aren't slaves."

"Them that was slaves at one time do," the sheriff replied. He looked at Jennie. "What's your name, girl?"

"Jennie."

"Jennie what?"

"I don't know as I got a last name," Jennie replied.

"And you?"

"Art."

Jensen handed the sheriff a piece of paper and the sheriff looked at it, then nodded. "According to this, a Creole female named Jennie and a young, male high-yella named Art were the property of one Lucas Younger. That property was transferred by a bill of sale to Boyd Jensen. I'm Boyd Jensen."

"Wait a minute! I never belonged to Younger," Art said.

"I've never belonged to anyone! In fact, Younger tried to kill me. Look at the back of my head. That's where he hit me with a shovel."

"True enough, Sheriff," Jensen said. "Mr. Younger explained how this young buck went after his wife and he had to hit him with a shovel to stop him. He said he knocked him out, then went to get some water to throw on him to bring him to, but by the time he got back, the boy was gone. Then that night, the girl was gone too, so he figured the boy come back for her. He sold 'em to me at a bargain, seein' as how I was goin' to have to run 'em down."

The sheriff stroked his chin as he studied the two. Finally, he nodded. "Take 'em inside. Tell Ancel I said if he wants to buy 'em, it's up to him."

"Sheriff, you're making a big mistake!" Art insisted. "I'm not a slave!"

"You ain't, huh? Then how come you ain't got a last name?"

"I'll tell you my last name. It's . . ."

The sheriff held up his hand, interrupting Art. "Never mind, boy. You could make up a last name, wouldn't mean anything now."

"Come on inside, you two," Jensen said. "I want you to meet Ancel. He's a slave trader. If you think I was unfriendly, you ain't seen nothin' till you see Ancel. Best you do every thing he tells you to do."

Ancel was a very overweight man with a round face, bulbous nose, heavily lidded eyes, and a thin mouth. He handed over a sum of money to Boyd Jensen.

Jensen counted the money, then put it in his pocket. He smiled at Art and Jennie. "I want to thank you two for runnin' off like you done. It made me a handsome profit."

Ancel turned to a man who was standing nearby. "Take

their shackles off, Frank, then take 'em on into the back and get 'em cleaned up," he said. "I'll be along directly."

Frank, who was a large, muscular man, put the club he was carrying under one arm. Then, getting the key from Jensen, he removed the shackles and gave the devices, plus the key, back to Jensen.

Art began rubbing his wrists, gratified that, after several days of wearing the restraints, he was finally free of them.

"Back there," Frank growled, pointing to a door.

There were two barred cells on the other side of the door. One of the cells was filled with black men, the other with black women. All were naked.

"Take your clothes off," Frank said. "Both of you."

Jennie began complying without question, but Art hesitated.

"I'm not going to take off my clothes," he said defiantly.

The muscular man hit him with the club at the juncture of the neck and shoulder. He inflicted the blow with an easy snap of the wrist, seemingly putting no power at all in it, yet the effect was devastating. Art felt a numbing pain run up his neck, then out his shoulder to his arm, and finally into his stomach, causing a nausea so severe that he thought, for a moment, that he was going to throw up.

"Take off your clothes," Frank said again. He did not increase the tone of his voice, but repeated it in the same cold, dispassionate way he had used earlier. Oddly, it was much more frightening than it would have been had he shouted the words.

Art looked over at Jennie, who by now was naked. It was the first time he had ever seen a naked woman and, though Jennie was still quite young, her small, but well-formed breasts and the little patch of pubic hair showed that she was indeed a woman. He had long been curious about seeing a woman nude, but his current state of despair and humiliation robbed him of any sense of satisfying that curiosity.

Jennie made no effort to cover her nakedness, but stood there as if totally detached from herself. Art decided that the best way to survive this was to be as much like Jennie as he could be. Making his mind a complete blank, he took off all his clothes.

"You two get over here," Buck said, pointing to a wooden platform. When they complied, two men came in carrying buckets of water. One man threw a bucket of water onto Art; the other threw a bucket onto Jennie. Each was given a piece of soap.

"Scrub yourselves down," Buck ordered.

Following Jennie's lead, Art did as he was instructed. Then, when they were both covered with soap, the second bucket of water was thrown onto them. Not until then were they taken to their respective cells. The door slammed behind Art with a loud clang. Though he wasn't the only one naked, he was the only one white. The others in the cell stared at him with as much curiosity as had been displayed earlier by those on the street.

A young boy, no older than Art, came up to him, then ran his finger along Art's skin. After that, he stared into Art's eyes.

"Your eyes be blue," he finally said.

"Yes."

"Ain't never seen no colored boy with blue eyes before."

"I'm not colored, I'm white," Art said.

"What you doin' in here then?"

"I don't know," Art said.

"I tell you why he's here," one of the others said. "He been passin', that's why he's here. He's a high-yella that's been passin' hisself off as white, but he got caught."

"I am white," Art said.

"Not as long as you in here, you ain't," one of the men said. "Don't make no difference what color skin you wearin'. When you in here, you as black as the blackest one of us."

Half an hour later a basket of cornbread and a bucket of molasses were shoved through the bars. The others swarmed around the food, but Art hung back. The boy who had commented on his blue eyes brought him a piece of cornbread with a dab of molasses.

"You better eat," the boy said. "This here be the only food we get today."

It wasn't until that moment that Art realized he was hungry. He took the piece of cornbread. "Thanks," he said.

The young black boy smiled broadly. "I be Toby," he said. "Who you be?"

"Art."

"Me'n you be tight," Toby said.

It took Art a moment to figure out what Toby meant; then he realized that Toby was offering to be his friend. Despite the misery of his condition, this unreserved offer of friendship warmed him, and he smiled at his new friend.

"Yes," Art said. "We're tight."

Bruce Eby had been doing very well in Ohio, until he was forced to flee to save his neck. For nearly three years he had run Eby's River Trading Post in a cave alongside the Ohio River. It was a place where he sold to travelers goods he had stolen from other travelers.

He was successful for as long as his operation was secret, and the operation was secret as long as the river pirates who worked for him left no witnesses. Normally they were pretty good about that. They would swoop down on the flatboats, be they commercial or immigrant, kill everyone on board, then steal everything of value and bring it back to Eby.

But his men got careless. They attacked a family that was traveling in two boats. They didn't realize this when they attacked the first boat, and before they knew what was happening, the second boat was upon them. There were six men in the family, all armed, and for the first time, the river pirates found themselves outnumbered. Two were killed, and two got away.

They thought their getaway was complete, certain that the immigrants, grateful for their escape, would continue their journey. But they thought wrong, for one of the immigrants remembered seeing the pirates at Eby's Trading Post. Tying their boats to the bank, they came back down river to the cave, where they found Eby and the two surviving pirates engaged in a serious conversation. That was all the evidence they needed, and that night they attacked.

Eby managed to escape, but his remaining two men were killed, as were his wife and sister-in-law. He didn't mourn his wife, a half-Indian that he had bought, and her half sister was full-blooded Indian. But he did regret losing what had been a lucrative business.

He was in Missouri Territory now, trying to decide what to do next, when he happened upon the slave auction in Tywappiti. He had no real need of slaves, but he thought he would hang around and watch the auction anyway, because the sight of human beings being traded like cattle intrigued him. He actually got a perverse sort of pleasure from watching a wrenching family separation.

When they brought the female slaves out for auction, he was stunned to see that one of them was white. When he inquired about her, he learned that she was a Creole. And as she had never done much physical labor, no one expected her to bring very much money.

"I heard tell that the last man who owned her sold her services as a whore," one of the spectators commented.

"That's a hell of a thing," another said. "It's one thing to own slaves to do labor. That's in the Bible. But a man ought to treat his slaves decent, and turnin' a young woman into a whore, be she black or white, is a sin."

As it turned out, most of the men at the slave auction shared that same opinion, for when the bidding began, the girl known only as Jennie received only a few, halfhearted bids. Eby was able to buy her at a very cheap price.

Even as the male slaves were being brought out for their own auction, Eby had the girl tied to his horse. She was walking alongside him as he headed north to Cape Girardeau.

Jennie looked back, hoping to see Art, but Eby gave a jerk on the rope, and she had to turn back quickly to avoid falling down.

"Keep up, girl," Eby ordered. "Or by God I'll drag you all the way to Cape Girardeau."

By the time they led Art and the other men out of their cell and up to the sale block where they stood, nude, the women's sale had already taken place. The sales of the men and women were purposely separate because there were some family members who were being separated and the officials didn't want any difficulty.

It was a lively auction, with spirited bidding being done on several of the slaves, especially some of the bigger, more muscular ones. The auction was brought to a premature end, however, when a man named Matthews made a bid on all the remaining slaves. Art and Toby were in that lot, and as soon as the bidding was over, Matthews came up to auction block to pay for and claim his property.

"You boys go over there to the wagon and find you something to put on," Matthews said to the group of slaves he had just bought.

Art looked hard at Matthews, hoping to be able to get his attention, to explain to him that he wasn't supposed to be here.

"Art, don' do that. Don' never be caught lookin' into a white man's eyes," Toby warned. "They don' like that."

"I was trying to get him to look at me so I could say something to him."

Toby shook his head vigorously. "That be a good way to get yourself a whuppin'." Toby studied his new friend for a long moment. "You tellin' the truth, ain't you?" he finally said. "You ain't no high-yella passin'. You really be white."

"Yes, I'm really white. That's why I want to talk to Mr. Matthews."

"That ain't goin' do you no good," Toby said. "I believe you, but the white folks ain' goin' to. They done sell you for a slave, so that mean you be a slave, no matter what."

"Damn it, can't they look at me and tell?" Art asked, exasperated by the situation.

"Boy, they look at you, all they think is maybe a white man crawled in your mama's bed one night. You look white, but it don't matter what your skin say. All that matters is what The Man say, and right now, The Man say you ain't white."

Matthews owned a brick kiln, and for the next six weeks Art, Toby, and the other slaves who were purchased, made bricks, watched over at all times by an armed guard. They were given a biscuit and coffee for breakfast, cornbread and greens for their supper. On Sunday they were given meat, generally fried salt pork.

Art did whatever it took to survive, learning from Toby how to avoid any direct contact with the guards, and how to be "not there."

"What does that mean, to be not there?" Art asked when Toby first suggested it as a means of survival. "How can you not be there?"

"It mean don't be there to The Man," Toby said.

"I don't understand."

"They's a horse tied to the pole that turn the mud grinder," Toby said. "What color he be?"

"He's, uh . . ." Art stopped to consider the question, then he smiled. "I don't know what color he is," he admitted.

Toby laughed. "That 'cause he ain't no horse, he a mule. And you didn't even know that, 'cause you ain't never see him."

"Sure I have, I see him every day," Art replied. "We walk right by him when we come to work."

"You walk by him, but you don't see him," Toby insisted. "That ole' mule, he be in his world, you be in your world, and the white man? He be in his world. What you do is, you just stay in your world and that way you not be there in his world. You not be in his world, he don' give you no trouble."

Over the next several days Art thought about what Toby had told him about "not being there," and was amazed at how accurate Toby's observations had been. Even the guards whose duty it was to watch them would often look right by them as if they weren't there.

It wasn't only Toby who understood this peculiar tactic. The other slaves knew it as well, and they could carry on a conversation among themselves, talking about white men in general or one in particular, right in front of them, and not be overheard. Or if they were, not be understood, simply because the whites felt that nothing the blacks could say or do would have any impact upon their own lives.

They did this by giving nicknames to all the guards and overseers. Matthews was "Ole Mistah Moon," because he had a very round, almost pasty-white face. One of the guards, who had a constant swarm of flies buzzing around a beard matted with expectorated tobacco juice, was called "Blowfly." Others were "Rabbit," "Snake," and "Weasel."

Often one of the slaves would break into song, using a familiar tune but substituting their own lines and using the nicknames of the guards. One slave would do one verse, another would follow with a second verse, a third with a third verse, and so on for several verses. By the end of the song nearly every guard, overseer, or white man of any importance would have been the subject of the most degrading comments, right under their noses.

> Ole Mistah Moon go chasin' him a coon,
> Oh yay, oh yay,
> But the coon so fast Mistah
> Moon fall on his ass,
> Oh, de oh-yah-yay.

The trick, Art learned, was to enjoy the song without laughing. Laughter was not expected under the conditions in which the slaves worked, and if one laughed, it would break through the wall that separated the slaves' world from the masters'.

Then, one hot day when the work was particularly hard, the two water buckets were emptied faster than normal. Blowfly pointed to them. "Pick those up and come with me," he ordered Art.

Blowfly started toward the river with Art following along behind. When they got to the river's edge, Art filled one of the buckets with water, then set it aside. As he started to fill the other bucket, he saw Blowfly peeing in the first one.

"What are you doing?" Art asked. "That's our drinking water."

"Hell, white man's piss will just make it taste better," Blowfly said, buttoning his pants up again.

Art felt a rage bubbling up inside him like boiling water. He was holding the second bucket in his hand, and before he realized what he was doing, he swung the bucket at Blowfly, smashing it down hard on the guard's head. Blowfly's eyes rolled back in their sockets and he went down. Art kicked over the remaining bucket, then started running.

He had run half a mile without stopping before he realized he should have picked up Blowfly's rifle.

But it was too late now. It was too late for anything but to keep running. If they caught him now he would, at best, be tied to the whipping post for striking a guard and running away. At worst, he could be hanged. He didn't know if Blowfly was alive or dead, but he had hit him as hard as he could.

He was at least a mile away before he heard the dogs. They had found Blowfly, and now they were coming after him.

Looking out into the river, Art saw a log floating down with the current. Without giving it a second thought, he dived into the water and started swimming toward the middle. He knew from his experience on the flatboat with Harding that the river was full of rip currents and whirlpools. It was an exceptionally dangerous river to swim in, but he had no choice.

The log was coming downriver faster than he realized, and he saw it go by before he reached the center of the stream. He was forced to swim hard downstream in order to catch up to it. Finally he reached it, then grabbed hold and hung there, panting from the exertion.

He could hear the dogs quite clearly now, and when he looked back he saw them gathered at the riverbank where he had gone in. A couple of the dogs jumped into the water, paddled out a short way, then with a few high-pitched barks of fright, swam back to shore and clambered back onto the bank.

"Where'd he go?"

The voice sounded clear, carried to him by the flat surface of the river.

"I hope the son of a bitch drowned," another said.

Art drew a deep breath and, while still hanging onto the log, ducked his head underwater. He stayed underwater for as long as he could, and when he raised up again, he saw that a fallen tree was blocking his view of the men, which meant that it was also blocking their view of him.

He was free. That was a condition he had taken for granted all his life, but never would he take it for granted again.

Nine

He had no idea where he was. He thought he might still be in Missouri Territory, at least, because he was still on the western side of the Mississippi River, but exactly where in Missouri, he couldn't say. It had been nearly a week since he had escaped. Since then he had survived on nuts, berries, and honey.

During his wanderings he had seen a lot of game: rabbits, squirrels, birds, even deer. But as he had no weapon of any kind, not even a knife, he had to watch in frustration as a veritable feast showed itself while remaining agonizingly out of reach.

Then he was awakened one morning by the unmistakable aroma of cooking meat. When he opened his eyes he saw a rabbit, cooking on a spit, over an open fire.

How had this gotten here? He certainly wasn't responsible. He hadn't even managed to make a fire yet, let alone kill, clean, and cook a rabbit. And yet, here it was. Was he dreaming?

Art went over to look more closely at the rabbit. The aromas of its cooking made him salivate and caused his stomach to growl in hunger. The smell was real and when he touched it, he knew he wasn't dreaming.

Moving quickly, as if frightened that it might go away, Art pulled the rabbit off the skewer, then began eating ravenously, pulling the animal apart with his hands and teeth, not even waiting for it to cool. When all the meat was gone, he broke open the bones and sucked out the marrow.

Not until he was finished eating, with a satisfying fullness in his stomach, did he begin to wonder once more where it could have come from. That question was answered when he heard a sound behind him. Turning quickly, he saw four Indians standing there.

One of the Indians made a motion toward his mouth with his hands, then pointed at the rabbit bones. Then moved his jaws, as if eating.

"Oh, damn! I ate your breakfast, didn't I? I'm sorry," Art said. "I was so hungry, I didn't know."

The Indian pointed to the bones, then to himself, then to Art. The meaning of the sign was unambiguous. He was indicating that he had given the rabbit to Art.

"You gave this to me?" Art asked. He repeated the Indian's sign, but in reverse.

"Uhnn," the Indian grunted, though he nodded yes.

"I, uh, have nothing to give to you," Art said. He made a motion toward himself and his ragged clothing, intuitively signaling that he was nearly destitute.

The Indian indicated that Art should go with them. They turned and started to walk away, but Art remained behind, not sure if he should go or not.

The Indian turned toward him once more, again indicating that Art should accompany them.

"Well, it was a good rabbit," Art said. "And I sure don't seem to be doing that well feeding myself. Besides, if you wanted to kill me, I reckon you would have done so by now. And I don't think you would have fed me first."

It was clear that the Indians had no idea what Art was saying. In fact, Art knew they wouldn't understand; it was just a way of talking out loud without actually talking to himself.

"All right, I'll go," Art said, following them.

With a grunt, the Indian turned and they began walking.

Although he had been somewhat re-energized by his meal, Art was still unable to keep up with the Indians. As a result, the Indians had to stop several times to wait for him. Finally, they came over a low ridge and Art saw, on the banks of a small river, an Indian village consisting of several wigwams, domed structures made of saplings, twigs, and woven grass. Men and women of the village looked up curiously; then the children and several dogs ran out to meet them. The dogs barked, while the children laughed and shouted back and forth to each other in excitement. One young boy, braver than the others, picked up a stick and ran up to Art. Art thought the boy was going to hit him. Instead, he just touched him, then, with a loud whoop, ran back to boast of his accomplishment to the others.

The four Indians led Art to the center of the little village, where an old man was standing in front of one of the lodges. The Indians who brought Art into the village spoke to the old man, who nodded, then turned to Art.

"You are English?" the old man asked.

"Yes," Art replied, though he wasn't sure he understood the question. Was he being asked if he was English, or if he spoke English?

"It is good that you are English," the old man said. "I am Keytano of the Shawnee. The Shawnee are allies with the English in their war with the white men who have come to take our land."

Art knew there a war was going on between the United States and England, but he hadn't paid much attention to it. Now he understood Keytano's question, and he was glad that he had answered as he had. If he had answered that he was American, they might have considered him an enemy.

"I'm glad you speak English," Art said.

"Yes, I speak English very good. I am friend to the English people. How are you called?"

"My name is Arthur," Art said. He wasn't sure why he

used the more formal version of his name. Somehow, he just believed that was the right response.

"Where is your home, Arthur?" Keytano's pronunciation made the name sound like Artoor.

Art didn't want to say he was from Ohio. He remembered a big battle with the Shawnee at Tippecanoe a few years earlier. The chief of the Shawnee, Tecumseh, was not at Tippecanoe, but he did fight at the Battle of Thames, and there he was killed. Some of Art's family's Ohio neighbors had been a part of the force that fought against Tecumseh.

"I have no home," he said. At the moment, it was a statement he could make truthfully.

"You are lost, Artoor?"

"Yes." This answer was even more truthful.

Keytano smiled broadly. "Now you are not lost. Now you have a home. You will become Shawnee."

Art thought of his present situation. He had the distinct impression he wasn't being invited to become Shawnee, he was being told to do so. If he refused the invitation now, he would in all likelihood insult them.

"I will be happy to stay with you," Art said.

And why not? he thought. At least with the Indians, he wasn't going to starve to death. And he might even learn a thing or two that he could put to good use.

"It is good," Keytano said. He shouted something, and a younger man appeared. "This is Techanka. Techanka is my son," Keytano said. "You will be the son of my son."

Techanka said something to Art.

"Do you speak English?" Art asked.

Keytano said something, and Techanka hit Art with an open-palm slap.

Surprised by the sudden show of hostility, Art jumped back and put his hand to his face.

"Artoor, from this day forth, you will speak in our tongue."

"But I don't know your tongue," Art said.

Techanka hit Art again.

"If you do not learn quickly, Artoor, you will be hit many times," Keytano said.

Art started to say something else, then realized that every time he spoke in English he was going to be hit. He caught the words before they left his tongue. It was obvious, however, that they were waiting for him to say something . . . anything . . . in their language. Then he smiled, and pointed at Techanka.

"Techanka," Art said.

Techanka smiled broadly and pointed to himself, nodding yes. "Techanka," he said.

Art pointed toward the old man. "Keytano."

Again, Techanka smiled and nodded his head. "Keytano," he repeated.

Art pointed to himself. "Ar . . ." He paused for a moment, then decided to use Keytano's pronunciation. "Artoor," he said.

This time Techanka raised his hands to the others, signaling them to speak as well. "Artoor!" they said in unison. Then, each in turn came up to Art, pointed to him, called him Artoor, then pointed to themselves and spoke their own name. One of those who introduced himself was a boy about his same age and size. He was Tolian, and Art learned that same day that Tolian was Techanka's son, and now his stepbrother.

The river was placid, though with a powerful enough current to keep him moving at a good clip. It was nearly dusk and the sun, low in the west, caused the river to shimmer in a pale blue, with highlights of reflected gold. If Pete Harding could find some way to save time in a leather pouch and call it up again, this would be one of the moments he would save.

Harding worked the tiller to keep the boat in midstream,

thus taking maximum advantage of the current. This boat wasn't quite as large as the one he had brought down when Art was with him. That was good, though, because then he'd had Art to help him. He was alone for this trip.

Harding missed Art, and he found himself thinking about the boy often, wondering where he was and hoping he was getting along well. A lot about Art reminded him of himself when he was younger. He too had left home at an early age, though in his case it was not by choice.

Harding was only fourteen years old when both his parents and his younger sister contracted pneumonia and died during a New York blizzard. Harding had been snowed in and unable to go for help. The ground was too hard to bury them, so Harding moved them to the barn and wrapped them in a tarpaulin. While the frozen bodies of his parents waited in the barn for the spring thaw, Harding spent the time just trying to survive.

When neighbors came to call that spring, they were shocked to find the fourteen-year-old boy living alone. He had had to cut his own firewood, had hunted and cooked his own food, and had even fought off an attack by a starving, frenzied pack of wolves.

Well-meaning people put Harding in an orphanage, but within six months he ran away and went to Ohio, where he hired on as a deckhand on an Ohio River keelboat. In that position he learned the rivers—the Ohio, the Tennessee, and later the Mississippi. When he felt he was ready, he went out on his own, buying his own flatboat and cargo, taking it downriver where he would sell his goods, then buying a horse for the ride back. Once back, he would sell the horse, buy a new flatboat and more cargo, and start all over again.

He had been on the rivers for ten years now, both as a hand and as his own man, and he knew not only the rivers, but the other men who plied them. There were several places along the rivers where the boats would tie up for the night, often in groups of five or six boats. Those were good times too, for at the "tie-ups" the boatman would play cards, tell stories, and share their food.

One such tie-up was at a place called Fox Point. Here, where the river had carved a natural basin at the river's edge, the bank was a wide, flat beach. Seeing it ahead, Harding noticed that three other boats had already put in for the night, and he began working his tiller, angling toward the landing.

A couple of boatmen saw him coming and, waving, they walked down to the edge of the water.

"Pete! You old river rat. You got 'ny whiskey? We done purt' nigh drunk all our'n," one of the men yelled, waving at Pete. He held out his hand, signaling for Harding to throw him a line, and when Harding did, he pulled the boat ashore, making the landing a lot easier.

"Hell, Caleb, I've never seen you when you hadn't drunk all your whiskey," Harding said as he stepped ashore. Not until his boat was made secure did he shake hands with Caleb and the others. Counting Harding, there were now seven boatmen ashore. A fire was already burning, and over the fire hung a black kettle.

Seeing that the men had opted for a community stew, Harding dug through his provisions, came up with a potato, an onion, a couple of carrots, and some salt pork.

"Better let me handle that," one of the others said, taking the viands from Harding. "I've got a good stew going here and I ain't goin' to let you ruin it."

"Ole Hank there thinks he's the only one can cook," one of the other men said.

"Well, now, he is a mighty fine cook," Caleb said. "Fact is, if he was a mite prettier, I'd marry him."

The others laughed.

The food was good, the tobacco mellow, and the whiskey smooth. The men were enjoying the long, lingering twilight when suddenly an arrow plunged deep into Caleb's chest.

Caleb looked down at the arrow as if he couldn't believe

it was there; then, with an expression that was a combination of shock and pain, he looked up at the others.

"Fellas, I . . ." he began, then fell forward.

"To your guns, men!" Harding shouted, running toward his boat where he had two pistols and a rifle.

By now arrows were whistling all around them, sticking in the ground alongside, and plunking into the boats and splashing in the water. Two other men were hit; one went down with an arrow in his back, while Hank took one in the leg.

Harding reached his weapons first. Turning back toward the woods, he saw half-a-dozen Indians charging toward them, all with raised tomahawks. He shot the first one with his rifle, then raised one pistol and held it until the next Indian came into range. He fired again and that Indian went down as well.

By now some of the other boatmen had reached their weapons and they too began returning fire. One more boatman was killed, but at least four more Indians went down. Realizing they had lost the advantage of surprise, the remaining Indians turned and scurried back into the woods.

"Hurrah, boys! We've turned them away!" Hank shouted.

"Yeah, but they'll be back, and there are only four of us left," one of the others said.

"We had better reload quickly," Harding suggested. "Get the guns from the fellas who were killed. We'll be needing every one of them."

Scurrying around quickly, the remaining four men gathered up all the other weapons, loaded them, and waited for the Indians to return.

Instead of Indians, however, there came a thunderous boom. Immediately thereafter, a cannonball burst in their midst. A second cannonball smashed into one of the boats.

"Cannons?" Harding said in surprise. "The Indians are using cannons?"

"Indians my eye!" Hank said, pointing. "Lessen they've

taken to wearin' them fancy red coats, it ain't Indians that's attackin' us."

Looking in the direction Hank pointed, Harding saw that two field artillery pieces had been rolled out of the woods. Manning the artillery pieces were soldiers in uniform. The most prominent feature of each uniform was its red jacket.

The cannons fired a second time. Hurling toward the boatmen out of the twilight came a cloud of chain shot. Hank and the other two boatmen were cut down in the terrible carnage the chain shot created. Harding was the only one left.

By now, mercifully, the twilight had faded to the point of near-darkness. Staying on his belly, but always keeping a wary eye on the wood line from which the Indians had emerged, Harding abandoned his weapons and wriggled backward, down to the water's edge. He slipped down into the water quietly, and dog-paddled away from the shore, swimming all the way out to the middle of the stream. Once there, he took advantage of the current to swim downriver as hard and as fast as he could.

Behind him, he heard the whoops and shouts of the Indians. When he was far enough away, he crossed the river and came out on the other side. There, wet, cold, and exhausted, he looked back. The Indians were unloading the boats; then, as each boat was emptied, it was set to the torch. By the light of the burning boats he could see the Indians dancing in glee while a group of uniformed British soldiers stood by, looking on.

Harding knew that America was at war with the British, but as far as he was concerned, the war was the business of politicians and soldiers.

"Damn you British bastards," Harding said. "You've just made this war my business."

Ten

Running hard down the path, Art skidded to a stop, then looked toward the center circle of the village. There he saw his goal—a vest, decorated with red-dyed porcupine quills, hanging from an arm at the top of a thirty-foot pole. He had only to reach that pole, climb it, and grab the vest to claim his prize. However, seven other contestants had the same objective in mind.

It was six months now since Art had joined the Shawnee, and he was participating in a weeklong festival that gave thanks for the warmth of the sun, the nourishment of the rain, and the supply of fish and game by which the village fed itself. The most significant part of the festival, however, was the Counting Out ceremony, a rite of passage in which boys became men.

Part of the passage to manhood was the young men's participation in the games. The winner of the games won a handsome vest. The desirability of the vest was not just due to its attractiveness, though the village's most skilled weaver and decorator was always chosen to make it. The real value of the vest was based upon its symbolism, for whoever won it would be an honored member of the community from that point forward. For the rest of his life, he would bring the vest out and display it proudly at special events, and would be treated with great deference by the others in the village.

There were eight candidates for manhood today, each one

beginning at individually assigned starting points outside the village. From there, they had to successfully negotiate numerous obstacles before reaching the outskirts of the village itself. The preliminary obstacles consisted of temporary constructions such as moats to be crossed, tunnels to be crawled through, walls to be scaled, and ropes to be climbed. With the completion of the first part of the circuit, the difficulty increased dramatically; for from that moment on, the contestants would not only face the course obstacles, they would have to compete against each other as well. And anything that prevented one's opponent from reaching his goal, short of inflicting serious bodily injury, was considered fair.

From the onset the men, women, and younger children of the village had gathered to shout encouragement to the eight participants. The last leg of the circuit was shared by all the contestants, so nearly everyone from the village had gathered to cheer their favorites on.

Art was warmed to hear his own name called as he started toward the pole, where hung the prize.

"Artoor! Artoor! Artoor!" several shouted in excitement as Art, who was now in the lead, prepared to cover the final one hundred yards.

Art was nearly exhausted by the ordeal, but he smiled and waved to acknowledge the cheers of the crowd.

"Tolian! Tolian! Tolian!" the crowd began to chant.

Art looked back over his shoulder and saw that Tolian had just completed the first part of the contest and he too was on the final leg. Though Art would have preferred to be far in front of everyone, he was glad that the one closest to him was Tolian, for he and his stepbrother had become best friends over the last six months. It didn't surprise him to see Tolian so close, however, for the two had been competitors from the very beginning. Their rivalry was good-natured, though, and each would go to the aid of the other in a moment, should that ever be required.

By now three other contestants were in view, so that five of the eight who had started were still in the hunt. One of the remaining participants was Metacoma, a young man who had long been Tolian's rival and enemy. Art had tried to befriend everyone, but because he was Tolian's brother, a position accorded as much validity as if they had actually been born brothers, Metacoma now considered Art his enemy as well.

Suddenly a wall of fire flared up in front of Art, igniting so quickly and with such ferocity that he could feel the blast of heat. It was a planned obstacle, ignited by one of the village elders, but Art had been paying such close attention to those running up behind him that he was not looking ahead, and he nearly ran headlong into the flames.

Gasps and squeals of surprise and excitement erupted from the spectators, and they drew closer to see how the contestants were going to overcome this most spectacular of all the hurdles.

The fire served the purpose of stopping Art long enough for the others to catch up. For a few seconds the five young men stood there, contemplating the latest in the long series of challenges they had encountered.

"Ho!" one of the other young men shouted to his rivals. "Would you have a small fire stop you? Cower, if you wish. I will claim the prize."

The young man backed up a few feet, then ran toward the fire. He leapt through it, but even before he disappeared, Art saw his clothes catch on fire. He could hear the young man screaming in pain from the other side, where someone quickly threw him to the ground, rolling him over to extinguish the flames. The young man's approach had clearly failed.

"Artoor! Come!" Tolian shouted.

"What is it?" Art asked.

"We can help each other, if you will trust me," Tolian said.

"You want me to trust you?"

"My brother, have I given you cause not to trust me?" Tolian asked.

Art laughed. "Only every time we have competed," he replied.

"Well, that is true," Tolian agreed. "But you must trust me now. Either we work together, or the prize will go to another."

"What would you have me do?" Art asked.

"See that tree," Tolian said, pointing to one near the wall of fire. "Neither of us can reach the bottom limb without help. But if you give me a lift up, once I am there I will reach a hand down to you. We can then climb above the fire and leap over it. When we are on the other side, it will again be each for himself."

Art hesitated. He was probably setting himself up for one of Tolian's tricks, but there seemed to be no other choice.

"All right," he agreed. "I will do as you ask."

Quickly, they ran to the tree and, as promised, Art gave Tolian a boost to reach the lowest limb. Once in the tree, however, Tolian started to climb immediately, showing that he had no intention of helping Art.

"Tolian, you would do that to me?"

Tolian laughed. "I cannot believe that you let me trick you again. When will you learn, my brother?"

"Tolian, look!" Art shouted. He pointed across to another tree where the two remaining contestants had come to the same agreement. And, like Tolian, the one who had been helped into the tree betrayed the one who had helped him and was climbing quickly.

"That's Metacoma. Would you betray me, my brother, as Metacoma has betrayed his friend? Are you just like him?"

Art knew that Tolian would not want such a comparison made.

"I am *not* like Metacoma!" Tolian insisted with a shout

of frustrated rage. Trapped by circumstances, he started back down the tree to help his brother.

Art smiled. Tolian had a degree of self-respect, and he had just played upon it, shaming Tolian into seeing that if he abandoned him, he was no better than the hated Metacoma.

"Hurry!" Tolian shouted, holding his hand down. "He is getting ahead of us!"

With Tolian's help, Art reached the bottom limb of the tree. As soon as he had a good grip, Tolian let go and scampered up quickly. He climbed above the flames, then jumped over to the other side, hitting the ground at about the same time as Metacoma. He rolled as he hit the ground to break his fall. Art, though several seconds behind the other two, got over the flames as well.

The wall of fire had been the last physical barrier the contestants had to conquer, and now nothing remained but a dash of seventy-five yards to the center of the circle and the pole from which hung the prize.

Metacoma had a slight lead on Tolian and Art, and was almost to the pole when Tolian suddenly launched his body at Metacoma's legs, bringing him down in a heap. The unsuspecting Metacoma slammed into the ground, while Tolian, who had been prepared for the impact, regained his feet as easily as if he were a cat. Now Tolian had the lead and he reached the pole first.

Tolian started up the pole. He was halfway to the top when Metacoma, having recovered quickly, shinnied up the pole, reached up, grabbed Tolian's foot, then yanked him back down. With a shout of anger and surprise, Tolian was pulled from the pole, falling nearly fifteen feet to the ground.

"I have won!" Metacoma shouted in exultation. He looked over his shoulder at Tolian, who, momentarily stunned by the fall, was struggling to his feet and shaking his head to clear it. "Stay there, Tolian!" Metacoma called down to him. "Watch me claim my prize!"

Metacoma laughed, then climbed the remaining fifteen feet. When he reached the top and stretched his hand out to snatch the prize, however, he discovered that a final obstacle had been put in the way of the contestants. Every time he reached for the vest, it began to bounce around, jerking just out of his grasp. That was because a long cord was attached to it, and standing below at the other end of the cord was a man whose job it was to make this, the final task, as difficult as all the rest.

Metacoma reached for the vest again, but managed to snatch nothing but thin air. He kept lunging for it, and once he made such a desperate grab that had he not urgently wrapped both his arms around the pole, he would have plunged to the ground. The crowd gasped with anticipation, then sighed with relief that Metacoma had regained his hold, for a fall from that high up the pole would surely have inflicted serious injury.

By now Tolian had regained his wits enough to begin climbing the pole as well. All around the circle people who had already counted him out now cheered his efforts.

For the moment Art was convinced that he was entirely out of it, for even if he attempted to climb the pole now, he would be the third one on the pole, and the farthest away from the prize. He looked over at the man who was manipulating the vest by pulling on the long cord, and saw that he had just managed to pull it out of the way of Metacoma's grasp.

Suddenly Art got an idea. Grabbing a knife from the belt of someone who was standing nearby, he ran over to the man who was manipulating the vest.

Holding on to the pole with both legs and one arm, Metacoma reached for the vest. He felt his fingers touch it.

"I've got it!" he shouted in triumph.

At that precise moment, Art made a quick slice at the cord. The cord severed and the vest dropped.

Metacoma's scream of frustrated rage was joined by Tolian's shout of surprise; then both calls were drowned out by the shouts of the villagers as they realized what had just happened.

Art was some twenty yards from where the vest fell, and he started toward it. Tolian recovered quickly, slid down the pole, then dived for the vest just as Art did. The hands of both young men wrapped around the vest simultaneously, and neither would let go.

The cheers died in the throats of the villagers. They wanted to cheer for the winner, but which one was it? Both young men had apparently reached the prize at the same time. The rules, though very lax as to what impediments the contestants could put in each other's way during the quest, were quite specific about the conclusion. Once the vest was clearly in the grasp of a contestant, the game was over and the contestant was the winner. But in whose grasp was the it?

Art and Tolian lay on their stomachs, breathing hard from exertion. Though neither would let go, they did not fight each other for possession. Instead, they just lay there to await the decision of those who would judge the contest.

Art saw that Tolian was bleeding from wounds in his forehead and lip.

"Are you hurt, Tolian?" he asked.

"No," Tolian replied. "How can I be hurt? I have won!"

Though Art did not try to take the vest from Tolian, he shook it once to emphasize that his claim of victory was every bit as strong as his stepbrother's. "Don't be so quick to declare victory," he cautioned.

Tolian looked back toward the pole where the vest had been hanging, and he saw Metacoma leaning against it, his head lowered in a posture of defeat.

"Yes, well, at least Metacoma did not win," Tolian said.

By now some of the other contestants were beginning to drag into the circle, some limping with injuries, others holding their arms or heads painfully.

"Aiyee, aiyee . . . hear me now!" Keytano shouted.

The villagers grew quiet to listen to the decision.

"There is not one winner, there are two winners," Keytano said. "Tolian and Artoor will share the prize!"

"But how can they share the prize?" one of the villagers asked. "There is only one prize."

"We will cut the vest into two pieces," Keytano said.

Suddenly Art remember a Bible story his mother had once read to him. In a dispute over who was the real mother of a baby, King Solomon offered to solve the dilemma by offering to cut the child into two pieces, giving half of the child to each mother. One mother agreed to the solution, but the other withdrew her claim, rather than see the child harmed. Solomon then awarded her the child.

Art let go of the vest and stood up.

"No," he said. "The vest should not be cut. There should be only one winner. I relinquish to my bother, Tolian."

"Aiyee! I have won!" Tolian shouted in excitement. Clutching the vest tightly, he jumped up, then began dancing and whooping with joy.

"You have done a good thing," Keytano said. "It is good that Tolian has won."

"I see you've never heard of Solomon," Art said, smiling wanly and speaking in English.

"The King in the Jesus-God book," Keytano said, also speaking in English. "Yes, I have heard of Solomon. But the woman with the child was not his daughter. Tolian is the son of my son."

"And I am the son of your son."

"You are the English son of my son. Tolian is the Shawnee son of my son. But because I am of good heart today, I will not punish you for speaking English."

Art realized then that this was the first sentence he had

spoken in English in over six months. Though he missed hearing his own language, he had to admit that the total immersion in Shawnee had helped him learn the language rather quickly.

Language wasn't the only thing Art had learned while living with the Shawnee. He knew how to make traps to capture game, he knew how to find deer by becoming a deer, he knew how to watch the birds as they went to water at night so that he could find water. He knew which plants made medicine to heal wounds and which plants would treat pain. If ever again he found himself alone in the woods, he would not starve.

Jennie's situation had improved. It wasn't that Eby was a kinder owner than Younger—Eby was every bit as despicable as her former owner had been—but Jennie rarely saw Eby because he had borrowed money and, on his note, pledged all the income she could generate until his debt was repaid. As a result Jennie was no longer relegated to doing business from the back of a wagon, but was working in Etta Claire's Visitation Salon, a first-class house of prostitution.

Etta Claire was Etta Claire Dozier, a former prostitute who, for fifteen percent of the take, provided room, food, and a convivial atmosphere for the girls.

For the first time in her life Jennie had a room of her own, complete with a vanity and mirror. She had clothes to wear and regular meals, and a real bed. If it weren't for the fact that she still had to entertain men, she would believe that life couldn't be better.

Before, Jennie had been on her own, servicing one man after another under all conditions. Here, at least, she was able to use a bed. Also there were other girls working in the house, so she wasn't expected to take care of everyone all by herself. Having other girls around helped in other ways as well. The girls taught her things she needed to know, telling her about various oils and lubricants that would make the process less painful, as well as showing her tricks that would give her more control over a man's endurance. That way if she was with someone who was extremely unpleasant, she could shorten the time he spent with her. On the other hand, if she was with someone who was gentle and she wanted to stay longer with him, she could prolong the session.

Although Saturday night was always the busiest night, Jennie was able to tolerate it because the next day was Sunday. All visitors would have to leave by six o'clock Sunday morning. Then the house would be closed for the rest of the day. That was a day of much-needed rest for all the girls, and they generally had a late breakfast, then slept, sewed, or visited. All of the girls were friendly with each other, and these times together were the closest thing to a family life Jennie had ever experienced.

Jennie's best friend was a girl named Carol. At eighteen, Carol was closest to Jennie's age, and the two had exchanged their life stories. Like Jennie, Carol had been a prostitute from a very early age. Carol had been born to a prostitute. She didn't know her father, but had gone through a succession of "uncles" until one of them raped her when she was twelve. She ran away from home when her mother didn't believe her. Since she had been raised by a prostitute, going into the business didn't seem that unusual for her.

Carol poured a cup of coffee for herself and for Jennie, then added generous amounts of cream and sugar. She brought the cup over to Jennie, who was sitting on a cushion in the window seat, looking out at the river.

"Tell me more about Art," Carol said, settling down on the window seat alongside her friend.

"I don't know no more to tell," she said. "I only know'd him for a short time."

"Is he handsome?"

"He ain't but a boy."

"And you are just a girl. Is he handsome?" Carol asked again.

Jennie laughed. "I reckon he is. Leastwise, he's goin' to make a fine-lookin' man someday."

"Maybe, when he's a fine-lookin' man, he'll come for you. He'll come for you and take you out of the life."

"He can't never come for me. You forget, I ain't just in the life. I'm a slave. I got no choice."

"Maybe he'll buy you. If he loves you, he'll buy you."

"Oh, I don't reckon he loves me none. I mean, he can't hardly do that, seein' as he's white and I'm Creole."

"But you said yourself that he stole you away from Mr. Younger."

"He done that, all right. But then we got catched, the both of us. Now, even though he's white, he's a slave, same as me."

"Have you ever been with him?" Carol asked.

"What? You mean lie with him?"

"Yes."

Jennie shook her head. "Ain't never," she said. "Been with a heap of men, but never with Art."

"How many men you reckon you've been with?" Carol asked.

"Lots of 'em. How about you?"

"Lots of 'em," Carol replied.

"Why do you reckon men like to do it so?"

"I don't know, but they surely do. And it don't seem to make no difference to them who they are with; one woman seems to be 'bout as good as another to them," Carol said.

"That's true."

"They say that if you lie with the right man, it can be good for a woman too," Carol said.

"Really? Has it ever been good for you?" Jennie asked.

Carol shook her head. "No. It ain't never been good."

"It ain't never been good for me neither."

"Maybe it would be good for you if you were with Art."

"Maybe," Jennie agreed.

Carol laughed. "See there. You are in love with him."

"Am not," Jennie said, joining in the laughter.

"Are too," Carol insisted.

"Maybe," Jennie said.

"You know what you ought to do? You ought to think of Art when you are with the other men," Carol suggested. "If you would think of Art, it might not be so bad."

It was two days later, and Jennie and Carol were sitting in the parlor waiting for the evening's business to begin, when Jennie shared something with Carol.

"It worked," she said.

"What worked?"

"What you told me to do. Whenever I'm with a man now, I think of Art."

"Oh! And do you like it now?" Carol asked.

"No, I still don't like it. But it's better."

"I wish I had someone I could think of," Carol said. "I know. I'll think of Art too."

"No, you can't," Jennie said. "He belongs to me."

Both girls laughed.

Eleven

It was the perfect place from which to launch an ambush. The river was only navigable on the east side of the island, so the flatboats would have to maneuver very carefully in order to negotiate the island.

There were two other advantages to the island. One was that it was heavily infested with old-growth timber, thus making concealment easy. The other advantage was that the island was south of the confluence of the Ohio and Mississippi, so that downstream traffic from both rivers would be passing by. That doubled the targets of opportunity.

Unlike his days on the Ohio, when Eby was primarily a front for the pirates working the river, he was now taking an active role in the venture. He no longer had an easy outlet for the goods that were stolen. That meant that the operation was much less profitable than it had been because he had to make deep discounts on the stolen goods in order to sell them. It was that lack of profitability that had forced him to get personally involved.

He had seven men with him, and two swift skiffs. Having so many people further decreased the profit from the stolen merchandise, but it also made the operation less dangerous.

Most of the flatboats would have a crew of no more than three or four men, and often, the hands were mere boys. There were always guns aboard, but rarely were the boat crews prepared for a swift attack, especially from a force of eight men. On several previous occasions the crew had abandoned the boat at the first sign of attack, thus leaving Eby and his men with nothing to do but pull the flatboat ashore and begin unloading.

At the moment, Eby was high in a tree, using a spyglass to search upriver. Below him, a few of his men were playing cards, while a couple of others were throwing their knives at a tree. One was sound asleep.

"Damn you, Philbin! I know damn well you didn't have that card!" one of the cardplayers exclaimed.

"You men shut up down there! You want to queer the whole deal for us?" Eby shouted.

Eby had no sooner finished his scolding than he heard laughter. The laughter had not come from any of his men, so he opened the telescope and began the search.

In addition to the laughter, he heard someone speaking. Then he saw the boat coming around the bend, some one thousand yards upriver.

Eby snapped the telescope shut, then slid down the tree and joined the others. He wore a smile that spread all across his face.

"Here comes one, boys, and from the way she's ridin' in the water I'd say she's a fat one."

"How many men?" Philbin asked.

"Only three."

"We got us easy pickin's, boys," Philbin said. "Easy pickin's."

Each of Eby's men was armed with two pistols and one rifle. For the next couple of minutes, they busied themselves priming, charging, and loading their weapons. Then, when all was in readiness, they moved down to the skiffs, climbed into the boats, and waited.

Eby watched as the awkward flatboat maneuvered into the mainstream. It began to drift to one side.

"Earl, get her back in the middle and keep her there," the flatboat master said. "Else we'll ground on a sandbar, then I'll have you three boys out, standin' in cold water up to your ass, pushing us off. And with the weight we're a'car-ryin', that ain't goin' to be no easy task."

"Yes, sir, Mr. Varner," the boy on the tiller said.

"Shoot the boy on the tiller first," Eby whispered to the others. "With him dead, they'll start driftin', and like as not they'll wind up on one of the sand shoals."

Two of Eby's men, the better marksmen, aimed at the tiller. They waited until Eby gave them the word.

"Now!" Eby said.

Both rifles boomed as if one, and the heavy impact of two large-caliber balls knocked the helmsman overboard. He floated away from the boat.

"Earl!" one of the other boys shouted.

"Never mind him, boys. Get your guns!" Varner shouted.

"Go!" Eby commanded, and the two skiffs pulled out into the river, then paddled hard toward the flatboat. True to Eby's prediction, the flatboat hung up on a sandbar.

Guns boomed and smoke billowed across the water as the pirates and the flatboat crew exchanged fire. The master of the flatboat went down almost immediately, and the two remaining boys were killed soon after that. By the time the two skiffs reached the boat, there was nothing left of the fight but the sight and smell of gunsmoke, now hanging in a great cloud over the river.

"Careful, boys," Eby cautioned as they climbed aboard. "Could be someone's left alive, just hidin' out."

With guns and knives drawn, the pirates climbed onto the flatboat. The master lay on his back at the stern of the boat, eyes open and looking sightlessly into the bright, blue sky. The other two crewmen, boys of no more than thirteen or fourteen, lay dead as well, one amidship, the other near the bow. The third boy, the one who had been the helmsmen, was in the water, facedown. He had drifted ashore into a growth of cypress trees, and was now hung up on one of the gnarled roots.

"All right, boys," Eby said, putting his gun away. "Looks like we're in the clear. Let's start unloading."

Eby jerked the canvas cover off the stack in the middle, then bellowed out loud.

"Bibles!" he growled angrily. "This entire boat is loaded with Bibles! What the hell are we going to do with them?"

"Maybe we can sell 'em," Philbin suggested. "I know lots of folks with Bibles."

"Look what's printed on the cover," Eby said disgustedly. "How are we going to sell them?"

"I can't read," Philbin said. "What's it say?"

Eby picked up one of the Bibles and read from the cover. "This Bible printed especially for St. Mary Catholic Church, New Orleans," he said. With a roar of frustrated anger, he threw the Bible out into the river.

"But stealing is wrong," Art told Tolian.

"When you were white, you did honor to the things that were white," Tolian said. "But now you are Shawnee, and you must do honor to the things which are Shawnee. There is great honor for the Shawnee to steal from his enemy. If you wish to become accepted as a warrior, you must steal a horse from the camp of the Osage."

"Very well," Art said. "I will go with you tonight."

Since coming to Keytano's village nearly a year ago, Art had learned a great deal about the Shawnee, including their history. He knew about their God, Moneto, a supreme being who ruled the entire universe, dispensing blessings on those who earned his favor and sorrow upon those who displeased him. He had already known about the great Shawnee leader, Tecumseh.

But he learned also that it wasn't just the whites who did battle with the Shawnee. They had been displaced from their ancestral lands by other Indian nations, forced out of Pennsylvania and Ohio into Kentucky, Indiana, and Illinois.

Now the Shawnee were scattered over a wide area, and Keytano and his band had crossed into Missouri. But here, they encountered Osage and Missouri Indians.

Keytano's group had built a village on the Castor River, in an area of the Missouri Territory that was unoccupied, either by the whites or any other Indian tribes. But even though they'd tried to find an uninhabited area, the Osage, their nearest Indian neighbors, didn't appreciate the encroachment, and often sent hunting parties to take game from areas close to the Shawnee. They did this, not due to a lack of game near their own villages, but rather as a show of possession.

Because there were many more Osage than Shawnee in Missouri now, Keytano was very careful not to provoke them into war. But from time to time, young Shawnee warriors would prove their courage by individual acts of bravery. Tolian had planned an act of bravery, and invited Art to go with him. He was going to sneak into the Osage hunting camp, steal a horse, then return.

It was much easier said than done. The nearest Osage village was three hours ride away. If Art and Tolian left just after sundown and rode hard, they would reach the Osage village in the middle of the night. They could take the horses and be back just before sunup . . . provided they weren't caught.

As planned, they reached the village at about midnight. The Osage encampment was pitched on the banks of a small stream, and Art could see, by the light of the moon dancing on the water, about a dozen lodges. He also saw a remuda of horses. The remuda was right in the center of the village, so that he and Tolian would have to pass by the lodges in order to reach it.

They tied their horses to a bush, then got down on their hands and knees and began crawling toward the village.

They had both practiced crawling great distances for several nights, and two nights ago, Art had crawled from a long distance outside their village into the wigwam of Metacoma. There, he had stolen one of Metacoma's most prized feathers, then worn it proudly the next morning for all to see.

"I took it from you as you slept last night," Art said, returning the feather to the angry Metacoma.

Now, the stealth Art and Tolian had practiced would be put to the maximum test, for if one of the sleeping Osage villagers woke up to see them, they would be killed.

A dog barked, but both Art and Tolian had come prepared. Each was wearing a sack full of bones around his neck. They opened the sacks and scattered the bones. The dogs converged on the bones, and in a moment's time, were completely absorbed in their eating.

Art and Tolian were right outside one of the lodges when a warrior came out. Art felt a quick stab of fear shoot through him, and he dropped to his stomach and lay very quietly, looking up at the warrior. Art held a knife in his hand, watching warily as the warrior relieved himself, then walked over toward the remuda for a look at the horses.

Finally, after what seemed like an eternity, the warrior went back inside. Art and Tolian lay quiet for a few moments longer, then cautiously slipped over to the remuda.

As they tried to grab a couple of the horses, the animals whinnied and stamped and snorted, and Art was afraid that someone would come out to see what was going on.

"Easy, horses," he said in English. He could speak Shawnee now, but still, in moments of stress and tension, he slipped naturally into English. "Easy, horses. We are just going to take a little trip together. Now, wouldn't you like that?"

Finally Art's soothing talk calmed the horses, and he and Tolian threw halters around two beautifully spotted ponies and began leading them out of the village.

They had nearly made it back to their own horse when they were jumped by an Osage sentry! The attack caught Art completely by surprise, and he was knocked flat. He looked up in terror to see the sentry, who was grinning from ear to ear, about to come down on him with a raised tomahawk.

But the sentry, who was much older than Art, grew careless. Intent only upon claiming coup on the would-be horse thief, he didn't notice Tolian come upon him. With a furious shout, Tolian drove his knife deep into the Osage's stomach. The Osage tried to twist away, but that was the worst thing he could do, for it caused Tolian's knife to make a fatal tear across his abdomen. The Osage fell to the ground with a death rattle in his throat.

Tolian pulled the knife out, cleaned it, then slipped it back into his scabbard. He looked at the man he had just killed, then immediately turned away and threw up.

Art remembered his own feelings when he had killed the river pirate, and he knew exactly what his friend was going through.

"Come, my brother," Art said, getting up from the ground. "We must go quickly."

Tolian stood there for a moment longer, looking down at the dead Osage sentry.

"Come," Art said again, putting his hand on Tolian's shoulder.

"Wait," Tolian said. Tolian dropped to one knee beside the Osage, grabbed the dead man's hair, put his knife to the sentry's scalp, then turned his face away as he completed the scalping.

"Now we can go," he said, holding the bloody scalp in his hand.

When they returned, they showed the horses they had stolen, and Tolian displayed the Osage's scalp. As a result of their adventure, both Tolian and Art were made warriors. That entitled them to sit in, and participate in, all future war councils. This action raised the young men's status in the eyes of the other villagers, but it created so much jealousy in Metacoma that it just widened the gulf that was already there.

"I am in your debt," Tolian told Art when the two were talking later that day.

"How are you in my debt?"

"You did not tell the others that I was weak like a woman, and that I became sick, when I killed the Osage."

Art started to tell Tolian that he too had become sick after killing for the first time, but he stopped short of saying the words. To tell Tolian that he had already killed might be construed as bragging.

"You saved my life, my brother," Art said. "You are the bravest warrior I know."

"Yes, and now your life belongs to me," Tolian replied. "I must watch out for you for all time. You will become my burden. Perhaps it would have been better to let the Osage have your scalp." Tolian laughed, and ran his hand through Art's hair.

It was being on the war council that brought to an end Art's idyllic sojourn with the Indians. Keytano called all the warriors together to hear a redcoat warrior chief.

Since Art and Tolian were very new warriors, as well as the youngest, their seats on the council were on the very last circle. This was good, because Art was far enough from the center of the circle that their visitor, a major in His Majesty's Army, did not realize that Art was white.

"To Keytano, Chief of the mighty Shawnee, I, Major Sir John Loxley, bring greetings from General Sir Edward Parkenham, on behalf of His Royal Britannic Majesty," the red-coated officer said.

Keytano translated the words for his warriors.

"As you may know," Major Loxley continued, "His

Royal Highness is presently at war with the United States. The Shawnee nation, aware of His Majesty's high regard for your people, and equally aware of the mistreatment you have received at the hands of the Americans, have been wise enough to form an alliance with England.

"I am here to call upon that alliance now, and ask that you make war against all Americans who are west of the Mississippi River. If we are successful in inflicting serious damage to this distant frontier of the United States, we shall, when we sue for peace, inherit all of the Louisiana Territory. Such territory, to be called British Louisiana, will then be closed to any further colonization, and will be preserved as a permanent sanctuary for our Shawnee friends."

As Keytano translated the last paragraph, the Indians whooped their appreciation.

"Ask the English officer what he would have us do," Techanka said.

"New Madrid, Cape Girardeau, Sainte Genevieve, and St. Louis are important towns along the river," the major replied after the question was translated for him.

"But, of those towns, St. Louis is too large, and Sainte Genevieve is nearly as large and is also quite far. That leaves Cape Girardeau or New Madrid as possible targets, and after some consideration, we have decided that you can be most effective by striking at Cape Girardeau. It is a river town of no more than five hundred, though it is becoming a river port of increasing importance."

"Are there soldiers at Cape Girardeau?" someone asked.

"Only two or three," Loxley answered. "And that makes it an even more attractive target, for New Madrid has been well fortified. Now, in return for your attacking the Americans at Cape Girardeau, we are prepared to furnish you with one hundred rifles and ten thousand rounds of ammunition."

In the entire village there were only two rifles. One of the rifles belonged to Keytano, the other to Techanka. At the British officer's offer of one hundred rifles and ten thousand rounds of ammunition, the Indians began to shout and whoop in excitement. No longer able to stay quiet in the camp, they leaped up and began dancing around, making signs as if they were already holding a rifle.

"Eeeeeyaaaa!" Tolian shouted, his excitement as great as that of anyone else.

"Understand, I cannot give you those weapons until after you have proven your loyalty to the Crown. You must make your first attack with whatever weapons you now possess. But after you have proven yourselves, I will return with the promised weapons," Loxley said. "My friends, I wish you success in your battle against our common enemy, the Americans."

After Loxley left, the Shawnee conducted war dances and sang their war chants. Then they broke up to apply their own medicine to the weapons at hand, and to invoke the blessing of Moneto on their endeavor.

Art participated as fully as any of the others in all of the war preparations, to include dancing, whooping, singing, and painting his face and body with the special symbols that gave him his personal medicine. After the ceremonies, it was time to feast. Everyone ate well, for though Loxley had held back the rifles, he had brought two pigs and three goats. When all went to bed that night, the air was redolent with the aroma of the evening's banquet.

Art lay in his blankets inside the wigwam, listening to the measured breathing and quiet snores of Tolian and his sister, Sasheen, as well as Techanka and his wife. The wigwam was warm and comfortable because of the heat that radiated from the stones that encircled the still-glowing coals. A burning ember popped, sending up a brief shower of sparks.

Art was troubled. Although he had participated in the

war dance, and had painted his body with the symbols of his own personal medicine, he did not want to go to war against the men, women, and children of Cape Girardeau. That would be like going to war against his relatives, friends, and neighbors back in Ohio, for they were not only white, as he was, they were also American.

He could refuse to join the war party when they left the next morning, but to do so would open him up to the charge of cowardice. Metacoma especially would point out to the others that Art had no stomach for war. And though Tolian would be more generous in his treatment, his private assessment of the situation wouldn't be that different.

Another popping ember from the burning wood caused Art to look back at the fire.

He gasped.

"Grandfather!" he said. "How did you . . . ?"

Keytano held up his hand, as if cautioning Art to be quiet. Keytano's deerskin breeches and shirt were bleached nearly white. The shirt was decorated with an eagle, made from colored beads. He was wearing a vest, like the one that had been the prize in the coming-of-age games. Art knew Keytano had won the vest nearly fifty years ago. Keytano was carrying a feathered staff, also a personal totem from his past.

Art had never seen Keytano dressed in such a fashion, and he wondered why he was wearing such clothes now. These weren't the clothes of someone about to go to war. This was ceremonial dress of the highest order.

"You are troubled," Keytano said. "You do not want to go to war against the Americans because you are American."

"I am . . . Shawnee," Art replied.

"Yes, you are Shawnee," Keytano agreed. "And though you told us you were English, I know that you are American. Now you are a warrior with two hearts. Both hearts are strong and both hearts should be obeyed. Your American heart tells you not to go to war against Americans and so you should not."

"But my Shawnee heart?"

"Someday you will leave the Shawnee and return to your own people," Keytano said. "Even though you will be with your own people, you will still have a Shawnee heart. If the Americans go to war against the Shawnee, then you must listen to your Shawnee heart."

"I could never make war against the Shawnee," Art said. He looked down at his hands, then held them up to examine them, as if contemplating the white skin. "Just as I cannot make war against Americans. I am pleased that you are wise and can under . . ." Art looked up, then gasped again. Keytano was gone.

"Keytano?"

"Aiiiieeeee! Aiiieeeee! Techanka! Techanka!" a woman's voice cried from outside the wigwam. Her voice was loud and piercing and it awakened everyone inside. They were just sitting up as the woman stuck her head in through the opening. It was Techanka's mother, Keytano's wife.

"Mother, what is it?" Techanka asked. "Why are you crying so?"

"It is Keytano," she said. "He is dead."

Art jumped up from his blankets. Keytano must have fallen dead just outside. He hurried outside, but there was no Keytano to be seen.

"Where is he?" Art asked, looking around.

"He is here," Keytano's wife said, pointing to her wigwam.

By now several of the others had gathered, attracted by the wailing and the commotion. Art followed Techanka into the wigwam.

Keytano was lying on a bed of fur and blankets. His eyes were open but unseeing. Techanka dropped to his knees beside his father, then reached down to close his eyes. While still touching him, Techanka began to chant the Shawnee funeral song. The funeral song expressed grief over the loss, confidence in Keytano's entering the Spirit World, and thanks to Moneto for allowing others to share in Keytano's life.

As Techanka sang, his wife and Keytano's widow began making preparations for the purification. Part of the purification called for the dressing of Keytano in his funereal clothes. Techanka's mother unwrapped a parcel, made of deer hide. This was Keytano's personal totem bundle, and inside were his clothes, clothes that were as secret and private to the individual as the contents of a medicine bag. Although the feathered staff and the vest had been seen by others, until this moment, nobody but Keytano and his wife had ever seen the breeches and shirt.

Except Art.

Art had seen it all, just a few minutes earlier, when Keytano came to visit him.

Art sneaked out of the village before light the next morning, a few hours before the attack was to take place. He'd planned to take one of the horses from the village, but changed his mind at the last minute, deciding that if he took one he would be branded a thief. He didn't know if he would ever return to the Shawnee, but if he did decide to come back, he wanted to be welcomed. He had arrived at the Shawnee village without a horse, and he would leave without one. Except for the clothes he was wearing, and the knife at his waist, Art took nothing away that he hadn't brought to the village.

He had gone about five miles when he saw a campfire. Curious as to who it might be, he approached it cautiously, until he saw that it was Major Loxley and two other British soldiers. Sneaking up as close to them as he could, he listened in on their conversation.

"Sir John, you aren't really going to give those Indians firearms, are you?" one of the men asked.

"Heavens, no," Loxley replied. "Once our victory is complete, I am to be governor of this wretched area. Do you actually think I would want a bunch of armed savages to contend with?"

"But without guns, their attack against Cape Girardeau will surely fail," one of the soldiers said. "True, there are no American soldiers there to defend the town, but nearly all of the citizen of the town are armed, and they have block-houses to retreat to in the event of an attack."

"It doesn't matter. The attack on Cape Girardeau is but a ruse. I fully expect the Indians to fail, and no doubt with a substantial loss of life."

"Loss of whose life?"

Loxley laughed. "Indian, American, it's all the same to us. The more of the blighters who are killed, the easier it will be for us to control the situation after we take over." Using a burning ember, Loxley lit his pipe. "Now, you two get back to Leftenant Whitman. Tell him to move the men into the boats so that we may proceed to Commerce. But make certain that he understands he is not to launch the attack until I am there to take command. With the Indians providing a diversion at Cape Girardeau, Commerce will fall into our hands like a ripe plum."

Both men saluted, then mounted their horses and rode off. Loxley moved over to a tree where, undoing his pants, he began to urinate. Taking advantage of Loxley's distraction, Art sneaked into the camp. The skills he had learned with the Shawnee were particularly helpful now, for he was able to pick up Loxley's rifle and pull back the hammer before Loxley even knew he was there.

When he heard the hammer being cocked, Loxley froze. "My dear sir," he said calmly, and without turning around. "You seem to have caught me in a most awkward position."

"I reckon I have," Art said.

"May I turn, sir?"

"You can turn."

Slowly, Loxley turned to face Art. "Blimey, you're but a boy," he said.

"I'm a boy that's holding a gun on you," Art replied.

"Wait a minute, I've seen you before," Loxley said, staring closely at Art. He raised his hand and pointed. "Yes, now I know. You were at the Shawnee War Council yesterday, weren't you? But you're not Shawnee, are you?"

"I'm an American," Art said.

"An American, you say? Well, it would appear, then, that we have a rather taxing situation here, don't we?"

Art didn't answer.

"Yes, indeed," Loxley said. He took a couple of puffs from his pipe and studied Art through the cloud of smoke that his action generated. "So, what are you going to do now?"

"I don't know," Art said. "I'm not sure."

"Are you familiar with the game of chess, young man?"

"No."

"Ah, it's too bad. You really should take up the game sometime. It's a wonderful game. But there is a saying we have in chess. The saying is, it is your move."

"My move?"

"Yes, dear boy. That means that whatever happens now is up to you. So, what now?"

Art hadn't really given the situation any thought beyond this moment. He wasn't sure what he should do, but somehow he knew that he had to stop the attacks on Cape Girardeau by the Indians, and on Commerce by the British.

"We're going back to the Indian village," he said. "You're going to tell them that you lied to them about the guns and ammunition you said you would give them."

"And why, pray tell, would I do that?"

"Because I'm holding a gun on you," Art said.

"Indeed you are," Loxley said. He smiled. "Fortunately

for me, but unfortunately for you, the pan in the rifle you are holding isn't primed. Whereas, the pan in this pistol is." He pulled a pistol from his belt and pointed it at Art.

Art pulled the trigger and the hammer snapped forward. There was a spark from the flintlock mechanism, but no flash in the pan and no discharge. Loxley was telling the truth.

Art looked down at the inert rifle, then out of the corner of his eye, saw that Loxley was about to pull the trigger on his pistol. Art jumped to one side just as Loxley fired. The pistol ball missed, though it came so close that he could feel the wind of its passing.

Tossing his pistol aside, Loxley pulled his sword, then smiling confidently, advanced slowly toward Art.

"It is almost heresy to put you to sword," he said as he made tiny circles with the sword point. "Only those whose names are recognized by the peerage are entitled to the blade. And you, sir, have no name." He laughed. "I know, I shall give you a name of the peerage. I will give you the name of an old archenemy of mine. I dub thee Sir Gregory of Windom Shire."

With three quick slashes of his sword, Loxley brought blood from Art's left shoulder, his forehead, then his right shoulder. When he stepped back, Art could see his own blood on the blade of the sword, and he could feel the sting of the cuts the blade had inflicted. He put his hand his forehead, touched the wound, then brought it back down to see the blood on the tips of his fingers.

"Sting a little, did it, Sir Gregory?" Now Loxley was standing sideways with his left hand on his hip, his right side and the extended sword toward Art.

"You say this fella Gregory is an enemy of yours?"

"Oh, yes, an enemy of quite long standing," Loxley said. He did a sudden thrust, which almost caught Art. Only his lightning-quick reflexes enabled him to avoid being skewered.

"Well, if Gregory is your enemy, then that's a good enough name for me," Art said.

Loxley danced toward Art, still presenting only his right side as a target. Art had drawn his knife, but it was totally inadequate against the sword. But though he couldn't counterattack, he was quick enough and dexterous enough to avoid every thrust.

Then disaster struck. While avoiding one of Loxley's increasingly closer thrusts, Art tripped and fell flat on his back. In a heartbeat Loxley was on him, with the point of his sword just over Art's chest.

"It's over, lad," Loxley said, panting from the effort of chasing Art about. "You've been quite a pest. My only regret is that you are going to die too quickly."

Loxley was just about to make the final death lunge when an arrow whistled over Art and buried itself in Loxley's chest. Loxley dropped his sword and reached up to grab the arrow. Even as he wrapped his fingers around it, however, the light faded from his eyes and he collapsed across Art's legs.

Quickly, Art scrambled out from under Loxley's body, then stood up to see Techanka and Tolian coming toward him. Behind them were at least three dozen others from the village.

"So, my brother," Tolian said. "Again I have killed another to save your life."

"Yes," Art replied.

"You left early," Techanka said. "Did you plan to attack the Americans without us?"

Art drew a deep breath, then shook his head. "No," he said. "I did not plan to attack the Americans at all."

"This I knew," Techanka said. "It came to me in a dream last night. It is good that you did not lie."

"This too is not a lie," Art said. "The red soldiers will not give you guns and ammunition. I heard them talking.

They want you to attack the town of Cape Girardeau so that they may attack another town, Commerce."

"Yes, that is a good plan. We attack one place while the red soldiers attack another," Techanka said.

"Wait a minute, you aren't still planning to attack Cape Girardeau, are you?"

"Yes."

"But why? Don't you understand what I told you? The British want your attack to fail. They want many Indians and many Americans to be killed."

"We must attack. Keytano gave his word," Techanka said. "It is not for me to break the word of Keytano."

"But many of you will be killed."

"We are not like you," Metacoma said. "We are not cowards who fear death."

Techanka held up his hand to still Metacoma. Then he looked at Art. "Go, now," he said. "You are no longer my son. You are no longer the brother of Tolian. You are no longer Shawnee."

"I am not the enemy of the Shawnee," Art said.

"Today, you are not the enemy of the Shawnee. But if we meet again, and if my people are at war with your people, we will be enemies."

Art looked toward Loxley's horse. If he had the horse, he might be able to reach Cape Girardeau before the Shawnee. Then he could at least warn them of the impending attack. But the thought came too late. By rights the horse belonged to Tolian, who had killed the major, and Tolian was already holding the animal, talking to it in soft, comforting tones. Whatever was going to happen at Cape Girardeau and Commerce was going to happen. With a sigh of frustration, Art turned and walked away.

Twelve

There was no getting around it. St. Louis just had too many people. Everywhere Art looked he saw people, moving up and down the boardwalks, crowding into the stores and overflowing the dram shops. The streets were filled too, with men on horseback as well as carriages, carts, and wagons, drawn by horses, mules, and oxen. It had rained recently, and the street was a quagmire of manure and mud.

But it was the smells that Art was having the hardest time with. Having spent just over a year living in the great outdoors with the Indians, he found the pungency of manure and rotting garbage, as well as several other unidentifiable odors, nearly overpowering. Some St. Louis citizens countered the odor by holding perfumed handkerchiefs to their nose, but most seemed adjusted to it.

The clothes Art had left home with had worn out long ago and he was now wearing buckskins; both shirt and trousers. Although most of the people he saw were wearing more traditional clothing, there were enough dressed in buckskins to keep him from being totally out of place. Only his hair was a little different from the others, as it was long and braided into pigtails. He did see several men with long hair, but no one else was wearing pigtails, so he undid his own, then shook his head, letting his hair fall freely to his shoulders.

* * *

Art had managed quite well in the woods, easily finding his way to St. Louis. He had learned from the Indians how to trap rabbit and squirrel for his meals, as well as what roots and plants he could eat. Also, as he followed the river north, he'd had an abundant supply of fish. But survival in St. Louis required a different set of skills. Here, money was more important than hunting or trapping, and Art didn't have one cent to his name.

Even as he was contemplating his lack of money, he happened across a possible remedy when he walked past a freight warehouse. Here, one wagon was being unloaded and two more were waiting to be moved up to the warehouse dock.

"I don't know where he is, Mr. Gordon," he heard one of the men say to another. "This is the third day this month he ain't showed up when he was supposed to."

Mr. Gordon, who was apparently the foreman of the warehouse, walked over to the edge of the loading dock and spat a stream of tobacco juice. He wiped his mouth with the back of his hand, then reached down into a pouch for a fresh supply.

"I'd fire James right now if I could find someone else to work in his place."

"They ain't that many people want to work unloadin' wagons," the first man said. "It's hard work."

Art turned and walked back to the dock. "Mr. Gordon?" he said.

Gordon was obviously surprised to be addressed by name by someone he had never seen before. "Who are you?" Gordon asked, pausing before he stuffed a handful of the tobacco into his mouth. "And how do you know my name?" He poked in a few of the loose ends.

"I heard this man address you by name," Art explained. "I also heard you say you would hire someone if you could find them. Well, I need a job, and I'm not afraid of hard work."

"I appreciate the offer, son, but you ain't nothin' but a boy," Gordon said. "This here is man's work."

Putting his hand on the side of the wagon and his foot on a wheel spoke, Art vaulted up into the back of the wagon. The wagon was loaded with barrels of flour. Art picked up a barrel, lifted it easily to his shoulder, then carried it over to a pile of similar barrels on the dock. He put his load down, then turned around and looked at Gordon.

"Is there anything to do any harder than what I just did?" he asked.

Gordon laughed, spitting a few pieces of tobacco as he did. "No, not that I know of," he said. "You willin' to do that all day long for a dollar?"

"Yes, sir."

"Then you got yourself a job, boy. I'm Gordon, that fella there is Tony. You do what Tony tells you to do, and you'll be all right. What's your name?"

"I'm Art."

"Art what? What's your last name?"

Art paused for a moment. His unwillingness to use his last name had caused difficulty for him back in Commerce. Many slaves did not have last names, and when he didn't give his, the sheriff was ready to believe that he was a slave. He still didn't want to use his family name, not so much to avoid being found now, for he was certain his parents had long since given up the search, but because he didn't want to take a chance on bringing any dishonor to the name. Then he remembered the name of Major Loxley's enemy. "Gregory," he said. "My name is Art Gregory. But please, call me Art."

"Art, is it?" Gordon looked over at Tony. "Tony, here's your new helper. His name is Art."

"Well, Art, grab yourself another barrel," Tony said, picking up one of his own. "We got two more wagons to do after this one."

"Yes, sir," Art said, going right to work.

Gordon stood by, watching Art and Tony at their labor for a moment or two. Then satisfied that Art was going to work out, he went on his way.

It was after dark before all the wagons were unloaded. Tony, Art's coworker, was a heavy-limbed man with broad shoulders but a prominent belly. He was bald on top of his head, but wore a full beard. A scar ran from the bottom of his left eye, down across his cheek, and into a misshapen lip. His two top front teeth were missing. Although it was relatively cool, both Tony and Art had worked up a sweat, and Tony wiped his face with a towel, then tossed the towel to Art.

"Thanks," Art said.

"You're all right, boy," Tony said. "I thought I might have to carry your load too, but you matched me lift for lift. I'm glad Mr. Gordon put you on."

"I am too," Art said.

"Come on, let's go to the Irish Tavern and get us a beer," Tony suggested.

"I'll have to get paid first," Art said. "Where do we go to get paid?"

"Paid? We don't get paid till Saturday. That's payday."

"We don't get paid today?"

"No, sir. Like I said, no pay till Saturday."

"Oh," Art said, disappointment obvious in his voice. "What day is this?"

"Tuesday, the eighteenth."

"What month?"

"What month?" Tony replied. He laughed. "Where you been, boy? It's October eighteenth, 1814."

"I sort of figured it was getting on toward fall."

Tony studied Art for a long moment. "Where you been, boy, that you don't even know what month this is?"

"I've been sort of drifting around," Art replied, not wanting to be too specific with his answer. "Here and there."

"Uh-huh. And you ain't got no money. I mean, you ain't got one dime, have you?"

"No, sir, I reckon not."

"What the hell, boy? How was you plannin' on eatin' between now and Saturday?"

"I'll get by. I can always go down to the river and catch a fish. Or I can go out into the woods. A body can never starve in the woods."

"The hell you say. You must know the woods pretty good to say that. I mean, if I suddenly found myself in the woods like that, I'd probably starve."

Art remembered his first experience in the woods. If he had not been found by Techanka and the other Shawnee that day, he would have starved.

"It is something you have to learn," Art admitted. "You can't just go out into the woods and start living off the land."

"So, you're what? Plannin' on goin' into the woods tonight, then comin' back in tomorrow to work?"

"Yes, sir, I reckon I've got to do that. I don't know any other way to get anything to eat, other than to catch it and kill it myself."

"Wait a minute," Tony said, holding up his finger. "If you really need money all that bad, let me go talk to Mr. Gordon. Perhaps we can talk him into paying you ahead of time."

"You don't have to do that," Art said.

"Yeah, I do. You're a good worker and I don't want you to up and quit. Else, I might wind up with James again."

Tony turned out to be an effective advocate for Art's cause, for two minutes later he returned with a silver dollar, which he ceremoniously presented to Art.

"Now, what do you say we get us that beer?" Tony asked.

"Do you mind if I get somethin' to eat first?"

"You can eat at the same place we get the beer," Tony said.

The Irish Tavern was run by Seamus O'Conner, a large, round-faced Irishman who wasn't opposed to delivering a homily with the whiskey, beer, and food he served in his establishment. He kept order in the place by the judicious use of a sawed-off piece of a hoe handle, and more than one drunk who began making trouble would wake up in the alley behind the Irish Tavern with a headache that wasn't entirely brought on by drink.

Art had a meal of corned beef, cabbage, and potatoes fried with onions. Tony, who had three beers while Art was eating, sat across the table from him, marveling at the young man's prodigious appetite.

"How long's it been since you et, boy?" Tony asked.

"I had me a squirrel a couple of days ago," Art said.

"A squirrel?"

Art nodded.

"You ain't been livin' in the city, have you?"

Art shook his head no.

"Where you been?"

"Like I said, I've been sort of wanderin' around the last year or so." Art wasn't ashamed of the time he spent with the Shawnee, but if they had carried through with their plans to attack Cape Girardeau, it might not be a good idea to be associated with them.

"Where is he now?" a loud voice suddenly asked. "Would someone be for tellin' me where I can find the whore's son who took the job o' James O'Leary?"

"Oh-oh," Tony said, looking toward the door.

Art, who had his back to the door, looked around. A large man, one of the biggest men Art had ever seen, was standing just inside the door, his face set in an angry scowl.

"Who is that?" Art asked.

"That would be James O'Leary," Tony replied.

At about that same moment James plowed into the room, heading for the table where the two were having their supper. James was focused entirely on the task at hand and he rushed forward, bent forward at the waist. He made no effort to go around the furnishings, but pushed through them, leaving tables and chairs overturned in his wake. Others in the saloon, not wanting to incur James's anger, jumped up and moved out of the way, giving the big man plenty of room.

"You?" he said, pointing to Art when he got closer to him. "Would it be you who took my job now?"

"I took *a* job," Art said. "It wasn't your job, because you weren't there."

"Now, he's got you there, James, m'boy," Tony said, trying to ease the situation. "You know yourself, you been absent from work more than you been there. And I don't mind tellin' you, that's made it a lot harder on me."

"I'll be hearin' no blarney from the likes of a black-heart like you," James said to Tony. "Sure'n this is between me and . . ." When James looked directly at Art, he stopped in midsentence and the expression on his face changed. It wasn't until then that he noticed just how young Art was. "Faith 'n begorrah, how old would you be now?" he asked.

"I'm old enough to do the work I was hired for," Art replied.

"Aye, lad, but the question is, would you be man enough to hold on to the job?"

"He more than held his own, James. Which is more than I can say for you when you show up drunk," Tony said.

" 'Tis not the work I'm inquirin' about now. 'Tis the lad's will to hold on to what he's got. How about it, boy? Are you man enough to fight for your job?" James asked, smiling evilly at Art. He put up his fists. "What say you we have a bit of a brawl? Just the two of us, right here, right now. Whoever wins the fight keeps the job."

"Come on, James, you got near a hundred pounds on the boy," one of the others said.

"Yeah, if you're going to fight, make it a fair fight," another added.

"Well, now, you tell me how to make it fair and I'll be glad to be doin' that. But would you be for tellin' me how the I can make it fair for a little pissant that ain't no bigger'n a pup?" James asked.

"Give him the first punch," someone said.

"Yeah, that's it. Give him the first punch," another added.

"I'll give him the first punch. He can hit me anyway he likes," James said. He stuck his chin out.

"Wait," Seamus called from behind the bar.

"And for what would I be waitin'? Pray tell me that now, Seamus O'Conner."

"Let the lad take his first punch with this," Seamus said, holding up the sawed-off length of a hoe handle.

James looked at the hoe handle, then at Art. "All right lad, I'm game. I'll give you the first blow, and you can use the club. I wouldn't want anyone to be sayin' that James O'Leary took unfair advantage of a wee lad like you. But you better make it a good one, boy, 'cause afterward I intend to mop the floor with your sorry carcass."

"Here, lad," Seamus said, putting his club in Art's hand. "It has put more than one thickheaded Irishman on the floor."

Art took the club. It was about eighteen inches long and an inch in diameter.

"I don't want to fight," Art said, handing the club back to Seamus.

"See there, Seamus?" James replied. "The lad has no stomach to fight. He wants to just walk away and let me have my job back."

"No," Art said. "I didn't say that. I plan to keep the job. I just said I don't want to fight you."

"Well, laddie, sure'n you can't have it both ways now,"

James said. He took the club from the bartender and gave it back to Art. "You'll be for givin' up the job, or for fightin' me. Now, which is it to be?"

"I . . . I reckon I'm going to have to fight you," Art said.

A wide smile spread across James's face. "Tell me, lad, would you have any family in these parts?"

"Family?" Art asked, surprised by the question.

"Aye. I'm goin' to hurt you, boy. I'm goin' to hurt you real bad, and we're going to need to know who to notify after I break you in two."

Some of the others laughed, and James turned his head toward them to acknowledge their laughter. That was the opening Art was looking for, and he did something that was totally unexpected.

Using the section of hoe handle, Art jammed the end of it hard, just below the center of James's rib cage. That well-aimed blow to the solar plexus knocked all the wind out of James. He doubled over in pain, trying, without success, to gasp for breath.

Doubled over as he was, James's head was about even with Art's waist. This gave Art the perfect leverage for a smashing blow, and raising up on his toes, he used both hands to bring the club down hard. Everyone in the tavern heard the pop of the club as it hit the back of James's head. James fell facedown, then lay on the floor, not unconscious, but still gasping for breath and now totally disoriented.

Calmly, Art went back to his supper while several others bent down to check on James. Finally, they got James over on his back, and gradually he recovered his breath. Then, groggily, he got up and staggered over to a chair, where he sat for a while, leaning forward as if trying to recover his senses.

During this time the tavern was strangely quiet, as everyone looked toward James to see what he would do, then toward Art to see how he would react. To the abject shock of everyone present, Art showed no reaction at all. He continued to eat as calmly as if absolutely nothing had happened.

After several minutes, James got up, ran his hand over the bump on the back of his head, and looked over at the table toward Art.

"Hell," James said. "Sure'n I never wanted the goddamned job in the first place." He turned and left the tavern.

"Let's hear it for the boy!" someone shouted, and the room rang with "Huzzah!"

Over the next several weeks, Art worked hard and saved his money, using only what was necessary to buy food and some clothes. He even got a haircut so that he bore little resemblance to the half-wild boy who had wandered in to St. Louis fresh from the Shawnee village.

From newspaper stories he read, Art learned that the Shawnee had attacked Cape Girardeau. Though frightening, the attack had actually had little effect, because the entire population of Cape Girardeau was able to take shelter in a blockhouse that had been constructed down by the riverfront just for that purpose. In frustration, the Indians had burned some of the buildings of the town.

The newspaper article said that it was believed that the attack was due to the result of an alliance between the Shawnee and the British. It was pointed out, however, that since Tecumseh's death, there had been little activity from the Shawnee.

It appeared that Commerce was not attacked, and for a moment Art wondered why. Then he remembered that Major Loxley had given specific instructions not to launch the attack until he was present. And since he was killed, he'd never shown up to lead it.

As Art caught up with the news that had occurred since he left home, he learned that the war with England was not going very well for America. The invasion of Canada had failed, Washington, had been captured, the White House burned, and President Madison forced to flee for his life. It was said that he even spent one night in a chicken coop.

Art didn't know much about presidents and such. His father had told him that a president was sort of like a king, except he was elected by the people. Art didn't really know anything about kings either, but he was pretty sure that no king had ever spent a night in a chicken coop.

Much of the problem, according to the newspaper, was in the government's inability to recruit soldiers. Unless their own homes were directly threatened, nobody wanted to fight. It was difficult to get men from Ohio to fight in a battle that threatened only New York, and equally difficult to get New Yorkers to defend Virginia. As a result, the British could mass their troops in any one location and, despite the fact that they were fighting on America's soil, nearly always have the numerical advantage.

One evening, after Art got off work, he was contemplating his situation as he walked toward the room he had rented. His back hurt, his hands were calloused, and every muscle in his body ached. He was growing weary of the work. It wasn't that the work was too hard, or that he thought himself too good to do that kind of labor. It was just that he had left home to seek adventure, and he could hardly call loading and unloading freight wagons a fulfillment of that quest.

Then, as he passed the high-board fence that surrounded an empty lot, he noticed that a new bill of advertising had been posted with the other flyers that cluttered the wall. He paused to read it:

MEN OF COURAGE
Gen'l Andrew Jackson of
Tennessee seeks an army of patriots.
MEN OF ADVENTURE

*You are called upon to
turn back the British despots
who have invaded our country.
Enlistments will take place at
LaClede's Landing
on Tuesday, the fifteenth Instant
whereupon a fifteen dollar signing
bonus will be paid.
You will receive a private's pay of
fifteen dollars per month,
plus all food and lodging.
JOIN NOW!
MEN OF COURAGE*

The more Art thought about that offer, the better it sounded. The fifteen-dollar bonus would just about double the amount of money he had. And if his food and lodging were to be furnished, then there would be little need to spend any of his salary.

That was the practical side of Art's consideration, but it was not what finally tipped the scales in favor of enlisting. That decision came about because Art was ready to move on. Joining the army to fight in a war seemed like a natural next step in his search for adventure.

Art didn't give notice of his intent to quit his job until the night before he did so. He felt guilty about leaving Tony without an assistant, but James had come around several times over the last few weeks, sober and contrite, and anxious to help. Indeed, James had even done some part-time work, and Mr. Gordon had told him that he would consider rehiring him if another opportunity presented itself.

Art's leaving provided that opportunity. As a result, James and Tony invited Art to have a beer with them that night, as a means of saying good-bye. Tony lifted his mug of beer in a toast.

"You were a good coworker Art. I will miss you."

"Thank you," Art said.

"And if anyone would be for askin', I will tell them I learned a good lesson from you," James said, lifting his own mug.

"Oh?" Art replied. "And what lesson would that be?"

"Just because someone is a wee little shit, that don't mean he can't pack a punch like the kick of a mule. You can bet that James O'Leary will never again give the other man a chance to take a first punch," he said. He rubbed the back of his head.

Art and the others laughed and drank, far into the night.

Thirteen

The next morning dawned cold and threatening. Art gathered the few belongings he had and threw them in a rucksack. For just a moment he looked around at the little room where he had been living, saying good-bye to it for one last time.

On his belt Art wore the knife that he had brought to St. Louis, the one that given him by Keytano. In his pocket he had fourteen dollars and thirty-five cents. On his feet were a pair of real leather boots. He put on a recently purchased wool-lined coat as a guard against the weather, then stepped out into the cold, dreary day.

A little over eighteen months ago, a young, naïve, practically helpless young boy had slipped out of his parents' home with nothing to his name but three biscuits and an apple. Since that fateful morning he had been forced to kill a man, had been robbed, beaten, and left for dead, and had nearly starved in the woods. He had lived with a band of Indians who were the sworn enemies of Americans, then arrived empty-handed in a large and hostile city.

Despite all that, he now had clothes on his back, boots on his feet, and money in his pocket, all the result of his own enterprise. He was only fourteen years old, but in any way of measuring, he would be considered a man of means.

There were nearly forty people gathered at LaClede's Landing when Art arrived. A little surprised at the number, Art looked around at the other men who had gathered in response to the recruitment poster. This gathering appeared to represent men from all stations of St. Louis life. There were businessmen in suits, and laborers in rags. There were frontiersmen, backwoodsmen, farmers, and men of color, both Indian and black. There were people of all ages, from very old to quite young. Some of those gathered here were even younger than Art.

A table and a chair were set up at the head of the group. Someone was sitting in the chair, but from this angle, Art couldn't see him very well. He could see a second man, though, for he was standing. This man was wearing a military uniform of blue and buff.

"All right, you men, gather round," the man in uniform called out. There was a shuffling of feet as those who had gathered hastened to do his bidding.

"I am Sergeant Delacroix," the man in uniform explained. "But as far as you are concerned, I am God. You will, at all times, obey me and anyone else who is put in authority over you. Is that clear?"

"Yes, sir," the men said as one.

"Now I want you all to form a line right in front of this table, then come sign your name on the paper. As soon as you sign, you will be soldiers in the United States Army."

"When do we get our fifteen dollars?" one of the men asked.

"What's your name?" Delacroix asked.

"Mitchell. Lou Mitchell."

"Well, Mitchell, you'll receive your money soon as you get on the boat."

"I got me a wife'll be needin' that money, mister. It ain't gonna do her no good, that money bein' on the boat with me."

"It's sergeant, not mister," Delacroix corrected. "And as far as your wife is concerned, she can come down to the boat to see you off 'n you can give her the money then."

Mitchell seemed satisfied with the answer and he nodded

affirmatively. Delacroix looked out over the others. "Any more questions?"

There were none.

"Then line up here at the table and commence signing, those of you who are going to sign. Anybody who ain't goin' to sign may as well leave now."

A few men left, but most of them formed a line. As they waited, they laughed and spoke excitedly to each other. Not wanting to push his way in front of anyone else, Art moved patiently to the end of the line along with several of the very young boys.

"You boys," Sergeant Delacroix called to them, making a shooing motion toward the younger bunch. "There ain't no need in you boys a'hangin' aroun' here. The U.S. Army ain't about to waste no time with babies."

Grumbling, the young boys left, but Art stayed. He no longer considered himself a young boy. Besides, he was fairly sure that the sergeant wasn't referring to him, and even if he was, he believed that if he pressed the issue, he might get away with it.

Evidently, the sergeant had other ideas.

"That means you too, boy," Sergeant Delacroix said to Art. "I got no time to be givin' you sugar titties to suck on. Get on, now, like I said. This here is for full-growed men only."

"Hold it there, Sergeant Delacroix," someone called. There was a haunting familiarity to the voice. "If this lad wants to join up with us, I'll be glad to have him."

"But, Cap'n, he's just a pup."

"He's more than a pup. How are you doing, Art? I haven't seen you in a while."

Art had begun smiling from the moment he heard the voice. The man who had been sitting at the table now stood. This was the captain, and Art was surprised to see that it was none other than Pete Harding, the boatman Art had come down the Ohio with.

"Mr. Harding," Art said happily, sticking his hand out. "It's good to see you again."

"That's *Captain* Harding to you, boy," Sergeant Delacroix corrected, putting emphasis on the word "Captain."

"Captain Harding," Art said.

"So you want to join up with us, do you?" Harding asked.

"Yes, sir, I sure do."

"Well, we'll be happy to have you," Harding said. "Sergeant, I want you to sign this young fella up. And don't be fooled by his age. I know him to be a good man."

"Very well, Cap'n, if you say so," Sergeant Delacroix replied begrudgingly. "What's your name, boy?"

"Gregory," Art said. "Art Gregory."

"Say, Mr. Delacroix," one of the others said, speaking to the sergeant.

"It's *Sergeant* Delacroix," Delacroix explained again. "If you recruits don't learn the ways of the Army, I'll make you wish you had."

"All right, Sergeant, then," the recruit said. "Oncet we sign up with you, where at is it we're a'goin'?"

"You'll be given two hours to get your affairs in order. Then you'll report back to the riverfront, where you'll be issued your equipment."

"And be give our money?" Mitchell asked, repeating his earlier concern.

Sergeant Delacroix sighed. "Yes, Mitchell, and be given your money. After that, we'll load you all onto a boat. Once we are loaded, we'll start downriver, putting in at all the ports until we find the English," Harding said.

"What do we do whenever we find them English?" someone asked.

"We fight 'em," Sergeant Delacroix answered resolutely.

"Fight 'em? You mean, with guns and sech?"

"The United States is at war with England," Sergeant

Delacroix explained patiently. "We ain't goin' to be askin' 'em to no fancy dress balls."

"What about fightin' the heathens?" another asked. "I got me a brother lives down in Cape Girardeau. The Indians attacked them last month. I'd kind'a like to get back at 'em."

"I can answer that question, Sergeant," Captain Harding said. Then, addressing the others, he began to speak.

"Men, our country, our very way of life, is in danger. If we lose to the British, we are going to have to cede most of our country back to them. Right here, where you are standing, will more'n likely become British. They've come right out and said so. In addition, the British are making all kinds of promises to the Indians, telling them they will be able to get all their land back if they turn against us. And the Indians that are Britain's biggest allies are the Shawnee. So, to answer your question, if we encounter the Shawnee, we will fight them as well."

"We're going to fight the Shawnee?" Art asked.

"Yes, we are. That is, if we run across them," Harding said. "But we aren't going to go looking for them. Our primary concern is the British."

"Your primary concern might be the British, Cap'n, but like I said, I aim to kill me a couple of them Shawnees if I can," the man who had posed the first question replied. "Fact is, if I see any of 'em while we're a floatin' down the river, I aim to shoot 'em outright."

"And you would be?" Harding asked.

"Edward David Monroe."

"Listen to me, Private Monroe," Harding said resolutely. "There will be no shooting of Indians, or anyone else, unless and until Sergeant Delacroix or I give the word. Is that clearly understood?"

"What about . . ."

"I said, is that clearly understood?" Harding repeated more forcefully than before.

"Well, yes, I reckon it is."

"That is yes, *sir,* Private," Sergeant Delacroix said. "Any time you speak to an officer, you will say 'sir.' "

"Yes, sir," Monroe said sullenly. It was clear that he didn't particularly approve of the policy of not shooting Indians, nor did he appreciate being chastised. It was equally clear that he knew there was nothing he could do about it.

It was even colder later that afternoon when twenty-two men, the total number who actually signed the recruitment papers, returned to the riverfront. Some of the men had family members with them, including Private Mitchell, the one who had been so concerned about the fifteen-dollar bonus. Once the money was passed out, Mitchell took it over to his wife, a rather mousy-looking woman, and handed it to her. He embraced her, then turned and walked quickly toward the gangplank that led onto the boat. Art noticed the tears coming down Mrs. Mitchell's face, and he looked away, not wanting to intrude on the privacy of her sadness.

Art and the other men followed Captain Harding and Sergeant Delacroix onto the boat. Longer and wider than the average flatboat, it was more like a barge, but like a flatboat, depended upon the river current for its propulsion and long steering oars for its direction.

Although there was a small cabin amidships, it was only large enough for Captain Harding and Sergeant Delacroix. Both Harding and Delacroix had their blankets thrown down inside, away from the elements. Art and the other men would be out on the deck, exposed to the weather for the entire river passage.

Upon reporting for debarkation, each man had been issued a blanket. Except for Sergeant Delacroix and Captain Harding, the men wore clothes of homespun cotton or wool.

Art continued to wear buckskins, believing that the leather did a better job of blocking out the wind than the cotton, or even the wool from which the homespun clothing was made.

Wrapping up in the issued blanket, Art found a place on the deck where he could sit with his back against the rail. That kept the wind off, and with the blanket and his wool-lined jerkin, did a passable job of keeping him warm.

The men had also been issued rifles, and as they drifted south, Sergeant Delacroix gave them their orientation on the weapon. Hefting one in his hand, he began a speech that sounded as if he had given it many times before.

"Men, this here is a government-issue, U.S. Military 1803 half-stocked, short-barreled, flintlock rifle. It fires a fifty-two-caliber lead ball weighing just over one ounce. That ball is propelled by black powder, which you will keep dry at all times. For that purpose, you have also been given a powder horn." Delacroix held up one of the powder horns to show what he was talking about. "Attached to the powder horn is a small measuring cup. One level cup of powder supplies the charge for the ball. The rifle is fired in the following manner."

Sergeant Delacroix poured a measuring cup of powder down the barrel of the rifle he was holding, then used a ramrod to drive down a wad of paper to hold the powder in place. Once the powder was in place, he dropped a ball into the end of the barrel and, again using the ramrod, drove the ball down.

"Once the ball is loaded, a small amount of powder is placed in the firing pan. Make certain that the flint is in position to cause a spark"—he checked the flint—"then draw back the hammer, raise the rifle to your shoulder, and . . ."

He completed his sentence by pulling the trigger. There was a flash, pop, and puff of smoke at the base of the barrel, followed immediately by the booming report of the charge itself. A flash of fire and a large cloud of smoke billowed out from the end of the barrel. The rifle's recoil caused Sergeant Delacroix to rock back. As a result of the burnt powder, a dark smudge now garnished his cheek. He smiled at his men as he continued his lesson.

"At a range of one hundred yards, this rifle has enough power to drive the ball one inch deep into a white oak plank. I can assure you, speaking from my own experience, it is quite powerful enough to stop any enemy."

The U.S. Military 1803 was Art's very first rifle, and though technically it belonged to the Army, it was in his hands, and that was the same thing as his owning it.

After his discourse on the rifle, Sergeant Delacroix began holding drills on board the boat as they drifted south on the current. He taught them how to stand at attention, come to present arms, right shoulder arms, port arms, and order arms.

The verbal instructions and arms drill given, Sergeant Delacroix then allowed the men to load and fire their weapons, choosing as targets trees along the bank as the boat continued its passage south.

Art learned very quickly that he was a natural at shooting. At first, Sergeant Delacroix picked only the larger trees as targets for the men, but he kept picking smaller trees and smaller still until, finally, he was pointing at saplings that were little bigger around than the thickness of a man's wrist. And yet, with every shot Art took, bits of exploding bark would mark the strike of the ball.

"You are a pretty good shot, Private," Sergeant Delacroix said begrudgingly. "Nearly as good as I am." Delacroix made no offer to demonstrate his own prowess.

"Well, I can see now that your saving my life that night was no mere accident," Captain Harding said that evening. "Sergeant Delacroix informs me that you are the best marksman in our company."

"Thank you," Art said.

"Have you ever used a rifle?"

"My father had a Kentucky long rifle," Art said. "I used to hunt squirrels with it."

"No doubt your family never went without meat when you were on the trail. By the way, your last name isn't really Gregory, is it?"

"No, sir."

"I didn't think so. Do you want to tell me what it really is?"

Art didn't answer.

"The reason I ask is, someone should know. You're about to go into battle, Art. I'm sure you know that means that you could be wounded, or even killed. Don't you think your family would like to know what happened to you?"

"I think they'd rather believe I'm alive somewhere," Art replied. "See, as long as they think that, then I am alive, leastwise in their mind."

"I suppose," Harding agreed.

"Besides which, if I ever do something to disgrace the name, I'd just as soon it be somebody else's name."

"Have you been in contact with your family since you left?"

Art didn't answer. Instead, he looked out over the edge of the boat at the riverbank, now slipping ever deeper into its shroud of evening shadows. From time to time, when he thought of his family, he realized that he did miss them. He wondered how they were getting along, and when he did remember to say his prayers, he would always include a prayer for their well-being. He tried to avoid thinking about them, though, because at this late date, he didn't want to start having second thoughts about what he had done.

"You don't want to talk about your family, do you?" Harding asked.

"No, sir, I'd as soon not."

"Well, then we will talk about something else. For example, what happened to you that night back in New Madrid? When I came back, you were gone."

"I'm not sure what happened," Art admitted. "I went outside to pee, and the next thing I knew I woke up in a wagon headed north."

"With your money gone, no doubt," Harding said.

"Yes, sir."

"I have been feeling guilty about that night ever since I left you. I don't know what got into me to cause me to just leave like that."

Art smiled. "As I recall, you wanted to go somewhere with that painted woman."

Harding laughed. "Ah, yes, Lily, her name was. A lovely young woman who is often misunderstood."

"Misunderstood?"

"There are those who would find fault with the profession she has chosen to follow, but I say she does a great service for men who sometimes find themselves in need."

"Like you were that night?"

"Yes, like I was that night," Harding said. "So, while I was satisfying my need, someone hit you over the head and robbed you. But at least you got a wagon ride all the way to St. Louis, so some good came from the evil."

Art started to tell Harding how the wagon owner had also left him for dead, but decided that Harding already felt bad enough, so he held his tongue. Then he thought to tell him of his year with the Indians, but decided this would not be the best time to do so. If they encountered Shawnee during their trip down, it would no doubt be the same village he had been staying with.

What if they did encounter Shawnee? What if a battle broke out between them? Would he have it in him to fire on his Shawnee brothers? Keytano had suggested that his white heart could not make war against his Shawnee heart. But Techanka had let him know, in no uncertain terms, that if they met again, they would meet as enemies.

* * *

Three days after leaving St. Louis, the boat put in at Cape Girardeau. They were met by a few of the merchants of Cape, anxious to sell goods and services to the Army. They were met also by a lieutenant and four soldiers, recently stationed at Cape Girardeau to defend against any repeat of the Shawnee attack.

"Any more sign of the Shawnee?" Captain Harding asked the lieutenant in charge.

"No, sir."

The lieutenant's name was William Garrison. He was a member of the regular Army and had fought against the British since the war began. He was bitter about being assigned to the wilderness of the Far West where his only adversaries were Indians.

"I doubt that those heathen cowards will attack, now that we have defenses in place," he went on. "The blockhouse is now equipped with a cannon and a swivel gun, sufficient to turn back any Indian endeavor."

"Do you have any idea where their village is?" Harding asked. "I've heard they might be on the Castor River."

"I've no idea where they are."

"You haven't sent out a scouting party to try and find them?"

"With all due respect, Captain, I have made no effort to engage the heathens. Prior to my assignment here I was fighting against the British. They are real soldiers. That is why I am happy to tell you that I have orders attaching myself to your command. I'll be going to New Orleans with you."

"General Jackson seems to think that the British troops are massing around New Orleans, getting ready to launch an attack. We are assembling whatever troops we can muster, but I'm sure that the British are going to have us outnumbered and outgunned. It will be good to have someone of your experience with me."

"Well, sir, I've been to New Orleans," one of the citizens of Cape Girardeau said. "And there ain't nothin' there but a bunch of Frenchmen, Creoles, and half-breed nigras. There ain't a damn thing there worth fightin' for, and if you ask me, they ain't nothin' going to happen there. If you want to know where all the action is, why, it's goin' to be right here, either with the heathen Indians or the swinish British. The redskins and the redcoats," he added, laughing in such a way as to suggest it wasn't the first time he had ever told the joke.

Harding laughed politely. "Redskins and redcoats," he said, turning the phrase over in his mind. "Sounds to me like they were meant for each other. It is a marriage. But the question is, was it made in heaven? Or was it made in hell?"

"A marriage?" the man asked, confused by the analogy.

"A figure of speech, sir," Captain Harding said. "Merely a figure of speech. Now, if you and the good citizens will excuse me, I must get my men rounded up. We are continuing on to New Orleans."

Fourteen

Lieutenant Garrison took over Sergeant Delacroix's duties as chief of training, and as they proceeded downriver, he continued with the instruction. His instructions included incessant drilling, which began each evening when the boat put ashore for the night.

"You know what I'm beginning to think?" Monroe mused as he was cleaning his rifle.

"No, what are you beginning to think?" Finley asked.

"I'm beginning to think we ain't never goin' to see no fightin'. All we're goin' to do is drill, sleep outside, stay wet, cold, and hungry with nothin' good to eat."

"Now, hold on there," Mitchell said. "What do you mean you ain't getting anything good to eat? Is that the thanks I get for cooking for you?" Even as Mitchell spoke, he was making corn dodgers by wrapping a paste of cornmeal, lard, and water around his ramrod, then holding the ramrod over an open fire, baking the mixture into bread. He leaned over to examine his work and, noticing that it was not quite ready, put it back into the fire.

"How much longer before they are done?" Monroe asked.

"Soon," Mitchell replied.

"Is that all we're havin' for our supper? A few corn dodgers?"

"Not a few, one," Mitchell said, holding up his finger. "One apiece."

"Damn, wouldn't some meat be good about now? Ham, or chicken, or just about anything," Monroe said. He looked around the camp. "Now where do you think Art's got off to?"

"I'll be damned," Sergeant Delacroix said. "Captain Harding, look what's coming."

Delacroix's exclamation caused Harding to look up. He saw Art coming out of the woods, a broad smile on his face, and a string of game, specifically six rabbits and three squirrels, hanging around his shoulders.

"My word," Lieutenant Garrison said. "How do you suppose Private Gregory came by those? I didn't hear any shooting, did either of you?"

"Private Gregory is a resourceful young man," Harding said.

"I wondered where he had gotten off to," Delacroix said.

"I thought perhaps the boy had deserted us," Lieutenant Garrison said.

"Oh, I knew he hadn't deserted," Delacroix said. "I was against signing him up at the beginning, but the boy has certainly proved himself to me. And now, I'm sure he has just proven himself to the men as well."

"Do you think he will share his good fortune with them?"

"Oh, I have no doubt of that," Harding said.

"Then perhaps I will go see him and make certain that we get our share," Garrison said.

"You'll do no such thing," Harding said, stopping Garrison in his tracks.

"What do you mean?" Garrison replied, surprised at Harding's comment.

"He's the one who trapped the game. Whatever disposition he makes is up to him."

"Captain, I realize that you are not a regular officer,"

Garrison said. "Perhaps, therefore, it is incumbent upon me to widen the instruction I have been giving to the men, to include you as well. We are officers, sir, you and I. And as officers, we are entitled to respect, authority, and certain, shall we say, benefits? One of those benefits is a disproportionate share of any legal booty gained by the command. In this case, the game that Private Gregory has taken."

"That might be the way of things back East," Harding said. "But it's not how it is out here. Whatever Private Gregory does with his game is up to him."

With a sullen expression on his face, Lieutenant Garrison resumed his seat on a fallen log.

Settling down by the fire, Art began skinning and cleaning the animals. Then he cut skewers and, in less than an hour, had all the meat roasting over the fires. When it was done, he took three choice pieces of the flame-broiled meat over to Captain Harding, Lieutenant Garrison, and Sergeant Delacroix.

"I thought you might like this," he said, holding out the meat.

Gratefully, they took the food.

"Won't you eat with me, Art?" Harding asked.

"Captain Harding, I'm just a private," Art said. "Lieutenant Garrison and Sergeant Delacroix already told me. Privates and officers don't socialize."

"This isn't socializing. This is business," Harding said.

"Very well, sir."

Harding smacked his lips appreciatively. "Mmm, this is very good," he said. "You've come a long way, Art. You're a woodsman, hunter, cook. And you have certainly made a believer of Delacroix. He tells me you are the best man in his company. In fact, he wants me to make you a corporal."

"I don't think I would want to be a corporal, sir," Art said. "I have enough trouble just taking care of myself."

"Taking care of yourself, huh? Like feeding the entire company?"

"Wasn't all that much," Art demurred.

"I don't agree with you," Harding said. "But I do agree with Delacroix. I've just promoted you to corporal."

Art smiled. "I don't see as I deserve it any more'n anyone else, but I appreciate it," he said.

"Cap'n Harding! Cap'n Harding!" someone shouted. "Come quick!"

"What is it?" Harding asked.

"It's Bedford and Nunlee, sir."

"Bedford and Nunlee? I put them out as sentries," Delacroix said. "What about them?"

"They're dead."

Upon hearing that, the others in the bivouac started toward the woods where Bedford and Nunlee had been last seen.

"Stay where you are!" Harding ordered. "There's no need in everyone going out to see. Corporal Gregory, take six men and investigate. The rest of you, stay alert."

"Corporal Gregory?" Monroe asked. "Did he say Corporal Gregory?"

"Good for him," Mitchell said. "He's the best of the lot, he should be a corporal."

Mitchell and Gregory were among the six men Art took with him. When they got closer, they could see two bodies lying on the ground. Several arrows were protruding from the bodies and both had been scalped.

"Shawnee," Art said.

"What?" Monroe asked.

"These arrows," Art said. "They are Techanka Shawnee."

"You can tell that just by looking at them?"

"Yes."

Suddenly there was a whir, then the thumping sound of arrows striking flesh. One of the six men went down. The remaining arrows buried themselves in the ground close by.

"Form up into two ranks!" Art shouted. Without question, the men followed his orders. "First rank, fire!"

The three men in the first rank fired. Immediately, Art began pouring powder into the barrel of his gun, readying it for a second discharge. Even as he did so, he gave orders to the second rank to fire.

Again, the sound of guns echoed back from the woods.

"Second rank, reload!" Art shouted. "First rank, fire as you are loaded!"

"Art, here come some of our men!" Mitchell shouted happily, and Art turned around to see several others coming, led by Sergeant Delacroix.

One hundred yards away, protected by a tree, Tolian drew back his bow and took a careful bead on one of the Americans. He was aiming at the one who seemed to be giving orders to the others. The American was looking back toward another group of men who were running from the camp to join them. When he looked back around, Tolian recognized him.

"Artoor!" he said under his breath. He released the tension on the bowstring. He couldn't shoot his brother, could he? Then he remembered that Techanka had said that Artoor was no longer his brother, that if they met again as enemies, they would be enemies.

"Tolian, many more have come," Techanka said. "We must go!"

"Wait," Tolian said. He drew back the bow again. It was a long shot and the arrow would need to travel far, so he pulled the bow back further. Suddenly there was a cracking sound as his bow snapped under the pressure.

"Come!" Techanka said. "We must go now!"

Disgusted with the broken bow, Tolian tossed it aside and looked again across the distance to Art.

"The Great Spirit has spared you this time," he said under his breath. "Perhaps that is as it should be. Perhaps you were not meant to die today." Tolian turned to follow the others, who ran quickly back into the woods.

"Fire!" Sergeant Delacroix shouted, and fire and smoke billowed from the ends of the barrels as several men discharged their weapons. The balls whizzed into the trees, clipping limbs and poking holes through leaves. As soon as that line fired, the second line raised their rifles to their shoulders, awaiting the order to shoot.

"Sergeant Delacroix, they're gone!" Art shouted.

"Wait!" Delacroix ordered. "Lower your weapons!"

Reluctantly, the men did so.

"Save your powder, boys, we're just shooting into empty trees."

"Two dead and one wounded," Lieutenant Garrison said angrily. "Two dead and one wounded while we still sit idly here in camp."

"And what would you propose that we do, Lieutenant Garrison?" Harding asked.

"I propose that we take the fight to the enemy," Garrison said. "Let me take ten men in pursuit of the devils."

"No," Harding said. "Our first priority is to proceed to New Orleans with as many men as we can muster. We will be extra vigilant, and if they return, we will be ready for them. But I will not take the time, nor risk the men, to hunt them down."

"If not an attack against them, then at least let me take a few men out to find them, the better to be forewarned should they attempt another adventure against us," Garrison said.

"You may take four men," Harding said. He held up a

cautionary finger. "But remember, this is only to find them. You are not to engage them."

"Yes, sir," Garrison said.

"I would recommend that you take Corporal Gregory as your second in command," Harding said. "He seems to be uncommonly at home in the woods."

"Very good, sir," Garrison replied. But as he walked away, he spoke in words that were too quiet to be overheard by anyone. "I'll be damned if I will take a snot-nosed boy as my second in command."

Acting upon his own, Garrison ordered six men to go with him. He was convinced that six men he had trained, obedient to orders, would be the equal to several times that many Indians. And he wouldn't need Corporal Gregory. Especially as Gregory seemed to exhibit total and unqualified loyalty toward Harding.

Tolian was sitting on a log eating a strip of dried horse meat when a scout reported to Techanka.

"Are they coming after us?" Techanka asked.

"Yes. Seven men."

Techanka looked surprised. "Seven? Are you certain there are only seven?"

"Yes. They walk like this," the scout said, and he held up his fingers to demonstrate that the Americans were approaching in a drill-field order.

"That is no way to go to battle," one of the Indians said. "Perhaps they are coming to talk."

"Is Artoor with them?"

"No," the scout replied.

"Then I do not believe they are coming to talk, for if they were, they would have Artoor speak for them."

"What shall we do?"

"We shall wait for them," Techanka said. "And when

they are close enough, we will kill them all and take their weapons."

"Yip, yip, yip!" Metacoma barked in excitement. "After this, we will have many stories to tell around the council fires!"

"Quiet!" Techanka cautioned. "Do you want the Americans to be frightened away by your shouts?"

Chastised, Metacoma grew quiet.

"Come," Techanka said. "We will take our positions and wait for the Americans."

The scout showed Techanka the route the approaching Americans were taking, so it was easy for Techanka to put his warriors in hiding for them. He put three behind some rocks, three more lay down on top of a little hill, and the remaining six hid in the woods. When all were in position, Techanka went up the trail for a short distance to determine if any of his warriors could be seen. He could see no one, even though he knew exactly where to look. Then, satisfied that all was in readiness, he hurried back to his own position.

He could hear the Americans before he could see them. Their steps were striking in rhythm, like the beating of a drum, and they were making a lot of noise as they came up the trail. Techanka took one last look around to make certain no one was exposed; then he crouched again and waited.

The warriors had been told not to attack until Techanka gave them the word, so he waited until the Americans were well within range. He didn't want any of the Americans to escape, and because he had more warriors and the advantage of surprise, he was sure that none would. He watched as they came into view, and he studied the faces of each of them because he wanted to know the men he killed.

The one who appeared to be the leader was a rather small man with a dark, drooping mustache. He was the one

Techanka wanted for himself, so he drew back the bow and aimed carefully.

"Aiiiyeee!" he shouted as he loosed the arrow.

His arrow buried into the chest of the leader, and his shout caused the others to shoot as well.

Only two of the other Americans were hit with the opening fusillade, leaving four who could return fire. But without leadership, all four remaining Americans fired at once, and they fired without taking aim. Afterward, they threw down their guns and turned to run.

They didn't get very far.

Fifteen

Six boats of American volunteers, one of them carrying as many as one hundred men, put ashore just south of Natchez. There, the officers of the various units met and organized themselves into a regiment, electing from among their own number the regimental, battalion, and company commanders.

Captain Harding had left St. Louis with twenty-eight men. He'd picked up five men in Cape Girardeau, including Lieutenant Garrison. At the Birds Point bivouac ten days ago, he'd lost nine men to the Indians, including Lieutenant Garrison. He arrived at Natchez with only twenty-one. His was the smallest individual unit present, but despite that, he was elected to the rank of major, and given command of a battalion of one hundred. Additional officers were elected from within the ranks of the battalion to become company commanders. Sergeant Delacroix was one who was elected, becoming a captain and assuming command of Harding's original group. Art was promoted to sergeant, while Cooper and Monroe were both promoted to the rank of corporal.

After the election, Major Harding called for a meeting of all his officers and sergeants in order to organize. Once the organization was complete, he dismissed them, though he asked Art to stay behind for a moment.

"I want to thank you for agreeing to be a sergeant," he said.

"I must confess, Major, I feel a little foolish ordering men around who are much older than I am," Art said.

"Art, you are a boy in years, that's true. But you are the equal to any man I've ever met in worth," Harding said.

"Thank you, sir," Art said. "It's gratifying to have your approval."

"Not only my approval. You have earned the respect of every man in your company."

They were silent for a moment. Then Art asked, "What's it like? Being in a battle? I mean a real battle, against soldiers and such. Not the little fight we had with the Shawnee."

"Don't know as I can answer that for you," Harding replied. "Seein' as I've never been in that kind of battle myself. But I reckon you'll do just fine."

"I hear everyone talking and bragging. Some of 'em can't wait to kill an Englishman."

"And what about you?"

"I don't feel that way," Art said. "I mean, I'll do what I have to do, but I can't say as I'm lookin' forward to killing anyone."

"That's because you've already had to do it," Harding said. "And you know it's something you do only when it absolutely has to be done. It's for sure not somethin' a body takes pleasure from doin'."

"I guess that's it," Art said. "When it comes to it, I reckon I'll do my share of killin' along with everyone else. But I don't aim to brag about it, before or after."

As they talked, Art looked around the camp. Earlier in the day the bivouac area had been alive with movement and sound, as necessary camp activities were performed and drilling and instruction continued. But it was completely dark now. More than five hundred men had crawled into their shelters, or gone to ground, and those who were still active could be seen only in silhouette against the orange, flickering glows of the many campfires. It was quiet also, except for the hushed whisper of the flowing river and a few subdued conversations.

"How is it that you were able to change so, Art?" he asked.

"I beg your pardon?"

"How'd you go from bein' a boy, not even able to take care of himself, to what you are now?"

"I had no choice, Major. I've been on my own all this time, so it was a matter of survive or die."

"I can see how that would make a man of you," Harding said. "But I am curious about one thing. Why did you enlist?"

Art chuckled. "I was loading and unloading freight wagons," he said. "I figured it was time to move on, and this seemed as good a way as any. If you don't mind my asking, why are you here? What made you give up your boat for this?"

Harding reached down into his own knapsack, then pulled out a pipe. He began filling the bowl with tobacco.

"You been following this war any?"

"No, sir, I have not."

"Not a lot of folks have," Harding said. "You would be amazed at how many people there are in this country who don't even know that we are at war with England."

"Why are we at war with them?"

"To be honest with you, I'm not sure I know why the country is at war. I know why I am."

Harding told about the fight on the Ohio River where Indians, aided by British artillery, had killed all his friends.

"I made a vow then and there to fight against them," he said. "So when I ran across Ole' Hickory, I joined up."

"Ole' Hickory?"

Harding chuckled. "That's what a lot of folks call General Andy Jackson."

"You think we'll win this war?"

"We've got to," Harding said resolutely. "If the English win, they'll be takin' over all the land west of the Mississippi River. There's a lot of land out there, and I plan to see it someday. And when I do see it, I want it to be American land I'm seein'."

"How much land do you reckon there is out there?" Art asked.

"You heard of Lewis and Clark, haven't you?"

"Aren't they the fellas that traveled all the way out to the western sea?"

Harding nodded. "The Pacific Ocean," he said. "Lewis and Clark followed the Missouri as far as they could, then struck out on foot. And according to them, there's a whole lot more land that hasn't even been looked at than we've already got. Land that goes on as far as a body can see, and then, when you get there, it goes on again, for day after day after day."

"And there is nobody out there?" Art asked.

"Nobody out there but Indians," Harding answered. "And not that many of them, I'm told. Nothing but bears and beaver, game and fish, trees and mountains."

Art's eyes sparkled in excitement. "Oh, now, wouldn't that be something to behold?"

Harding chuckled. "You've got that 'see the creature' look about you."

"If 'the creature' is out there in all that land you're talking about, then I reckon I do want to see it," Art admitted. "In fact, soon as this little fracas is over down in New Orleans, I reckon I'll just go on out there and take me a look."

"There's more to it than just going out there to take a look, son," Harding said. "There's mountains that touch the sky, deserts as big as seas, and who knows what else. It's going to be more than just a mite dangerous."

"The more you talk about it, the more interesting it sounds," Art said.

Harding laughed. "I thought you'd probably say something like that. What would you say if I told you I had the exact same idea in mind? How would you like for the two of us to go out there together?"

"You want to go too?"

"Sure. I told you a long time ago, I'm as eager to see the creature as you are." He waved his hand in the general direction of the river. "I've been up and down Old Strong near on to forty or fifty times I figure. There are no creatures hereabout that I haven't seen. I'd love to go west, at least as far as the mountains, maybe even all the way to the Pacific Ocean. What do you say? Shall we go take a look?"

"Yes!" Art replied. "Yes, I'd love that!"

The regiment to which Art now belonged was assigned to Brigadier General Humbolt's Louisiana Volunteers.

"Hey, who is this Humbolt fella?" Private Monroe asked. "I come down here to fight with General Andy Jackson . . . Ole' Hickory hisself."

"You will be fighting for General Jackson," Delacroix told him.

"That ain't what the major just told us. He said we was now a part of General Humbolt's Division."

"And Humbolt's Division is a part of General Jackson's Army," Delacroix explained patiently. He looked at the others. "Men, do yourselves and your country proud. We've been assigned to the middle of the line."

"What's that mean?" someone asked.

"It means we're a'goin' to be right in the thick of all the fightin'," another explained.

With that comment, Harding's Legion came to the realization that the drill and practice and bragging and anticipation were all over. There was no more talk of what they were going to do, it was now a matter of *doing* it.

General Jackson put his Army into position along the banks of the Rodriguez Canal. There, he built a fortified mud rampart, just over half a mile long, anchored on the right by the Mississippi River and on the left by an impassable cypress swamp. That meant there was no way the British troops could reach New Orleans without coming right through Jackson's Army.

Jackson's Army was a polyglot force consisting of units of the regular army as well as New Orleans militia, free blacks, frontiersmen such as Harding's Legion, and even a band of outlaws and pirates led by Jean Lafitte.

The British Army they were facing was one of the finest military assemblages in the world. It was led by General Sir Edward Parkenham, the thirty-seven-year-old brother-in-law of the Duke of Wellington. Parkenham, a much-decorated officer, was commanding a force of tough, proven British Regulars: the 4th, 21st, 44th, and 93rd Highlanders. These were the same regiments that had defeated Napoleon at Waterloo, and more recently burned the Capitol in Washington. This magnificent Army was augmented by the 95th and 5th West India Regiments.

On the 28th of December, Parkenham launched a strong advance against the Americans, but was repulsed. On New Year's Day Parkenham moved his artillery into position, then started a daylong artillery barrage. As the British guns opened fire, the sound of thunder rolled across the open field. Immediately thereafter, the shells came crashing in, exploding in rosy plumes of fire, smoke, and whistling death.

Although some of the regulars in Jackson's Army had undergone an artillery barrage before, this was a new and terrifying experience for most of the men. They shuddered in fear as heavy balls crashed into the cotton bale barricades behind which the American soldiers were taking shelter. Explosive shells burst inside their ranks, sending out singing pieces of shrapnel.

It was in this bombardment that Harding's Legion suffered its first casualty. Corporal Mitchell, the man who had worried so about making sure his wife got his enlistment bonus, was decapitated by one of the cannonballs. The sight of one of their own, alive and vibrant one moment and headless the next, unnerved many of the men, and some would have fled had their officers not stopped them.

Art remembered the touching scene on the riverbank between Cooper and his wife, just before they left St. Louis. He thought of Mrs. Mitchell and felt an overwhelming sense of sorrow for her loss.

Sixteen

In the chilled, predawn January darkness, American sentries and listening posts realized that something was afoot. After several days of relative quiet, they picked up a great deal of movement over on the British side. Art and the others were rousted from their bedrolls and moved quickly to the barricades. There, Harding's Legion took up its assigned position, right in the center of the line. Looking down along each side of him, Art could see the other defenders, holding their rifles and shivering in the cold, though he suspected perhaps many were shivering from fear as well.

Surprisingly, he felt no particular fear, and this allowed him to be a dispassionate observer. And what he saw was four thousand Americans, facing a British force that was nearly twice their number.

Gradually, the sky grew lighter, but an exceptionally thick fog rolled in so that, even with the coming of dawn, the Americans still couldn't see the British troops. They could hear them, though, and they listened with quickened souls as the English officers called out their commands.

"Fix bayonets!"

The order, repeated many times, was followed by the unmistakable clicking sound of bayonets being attached to the ends of the long British "Brown Bess" rifles. The rifles were so long that when the bayonets were affixed they were almost like pikes, and in the hands of trained soldiers, they made quite a formidable weapon.

Shortly after that, the Americans faced a new terror. The British began their attack with a broadside of rockets. Art had never seen anything like it before. He watched with as much fascination as fear: seeing first the flare of their launch, gleaming even through the morning mist, then the glare of their transit, and finally the projectiles themselves as they emerged, spitting fire, from the fog to explode over the heads of the Americans.

After the barrage, there followed several moments of silence. In its own way, the silence was as frightening as the whoosh and explosions of the rockets had been. Then, quietly at first, but gradually increasing in volume, they heard from the fog the muffled-jangle of equipment and the rhythmic drumming of feet. The sound grew louder, and louder still, until it was a drumming that resonated in the pounding of each waiting American's pulse.

Thump, thump, thump, thump, thump.

Suddenly there came a sound that, to some, was like the wailing of demons from hell. It was the high-pitched, haunting squeal of the bagpipes. As the noises grew louder and louder from the fog, a nervousness began to ripple up and down the American lines, and some of the soldiers began to shift about anxiously. They looked back over their shoulders several times, as if searching out the most desirable escape route. Harding noticed the unease among his troops.

"Easy, men. Easy," he said, speaking calmly. "Stand your ground now."

By now the noise of drumming feet and wailing bagpipes was nearly deafening.

"Come on!" one of the soldiers suddenly shouted. "What are you waiting for? Don't stay out there in the fog making noises!" He climbed to the top of the barricade, and would have run toward the unseen enemy if a couple of his friends hadn't grabbed him and pulled him back down.

Thump, thump, thump, thump.

Art stared into the thick mist, straining to see. For several long moments there was nothing. Then, as if apparitions were suddenly and mysteriously forming in the mist, the British Army materialized. Art saw the magnificent but intimidating sight of beautifully uniformed and well-trained soldiers in a disciplined battle-line-front formation. Their bayonets were fixed and the rifles were thrust forward.

Not until this very moment could the Americans do anything more than wait. Relieved that the opportunity for some action was here at last, Harding shouted out his orders at the top of his voice.

"Count off," Harding instructed, and the men responded.

"One!"

"Two!"

"One!"

"Two!"

They shouted throaty responses until the entire battalion was counted off.

Those who were number one would kneel and fire the first volley. Then number two would fire while number one reloaded.

"Major, we got to get outta here!" Private Monroe said. "They's more'n twice as many of them as they is of us. And with this dampness and all, it ain't all that certain our powder will explode!"

"Stay where you are," Harding said calmly. "Their powder is going to be just as wet."

"Yes, but they's a lot more of them than they is of us, and they got bayonets. We're crazy to stay here like this," Monroe insisted.

"Take it easy, Monroe," Art said.

"I don't need no wet-behind-the-ear, snot-nosed boy to tell me to take it easy," Monroe said derisively, glowering at Art.

"At least Sergeant Gregory ain't cryin' and peein' in his pants," one of the other soldiers said. "Now shut up and keep watchin' out for the British, or keep on a'yappin' and start watchin' out for me."

The last comment had the desired effect, and though Monroe was still twitching nervously, he was no longer talking about it.

"Hold your fire, men, hold your fire," Harding instructed. "Don't fire until you can clearly see their belt buckles."

The British advanced to a distance of about forty yards. At that point they halted. Then their officers' commands, loud, clear, and confident, floated across the misty distance between the two forces so that the Americans could hear the orders as well as the British soldiers for whom the orders were intended.

"Extend front!"

As if on parade, the British line extended out, fingertip to fingertip, eyeing up and down the rank in order to be properly aligned.

The officers stepped in and out of the rank, checking the alignment, here ordering one soldier to move up a step, there ordering another one to back up a bit. Only when the line was perfectly formed did the officers return to their position forward of the troops. The officers drew their sabers and held them up.

General Parkenham gave his order in a loud, clear voice.

"Forward at a double!"

The entire British line began running toward the ramparts, their bayonet-tipped rifles thrust forward. The officers ran before them, brandishing their swords.

This was a bayonet charge being made by battle-hardened and well-disciplined soldiers. Harding's Legion, as indeed most of the others of Jackson's Army, consisted of militiamen, many seeing battle for the first time. They fought back the bile of fear that rose in their throats, and they waited.

Art aimed at one of the soldiers. He held the aim for a

long moment, awaiting the order to fire. Then, capriciously, he shifted his aim to another soldier, sparing, for no particular reason, the first soldier.

Not until the British were at point-blank range did Harding give the command to his battalion.

"Fire!"

Winks of light rippled up and down the American line as first the firing pans, and then the muzzle blasts, flashed brightly. Smoke billowed out in one large, rolling cloud as the sound of gunfire rolled across the plain. Art saw his man go down.

The effect of the opening volley was devastating. In addition to the soldier Art shot, almost half of the British front rank went down under the torrent of lead. The second volley did as much damage as the first, so that when the huge cloud of gun smoke cleared away, there was nothing before the Americans but a field strewn with dead or dying British soldiers.

The British Army was stopped in its tracks, almost as if they had run into a stone wall. A few of the British soldiers fired their weapons toward the Americans, but the volume of their fire was pitifully small.

"Lord, Major, did you see that?" Delacroix asked excitedly. Delacroix was from the regular Army, and one of the few American defenders who had actually been in battle before. "We cut them down like so much wheat. They never had a ch . . ."

Delacroix stopped in midsentence when he saw that Major Harding couldn't hear him. Although the firing coming from the British lines had been weak and, for the most part, ineffective, at least one bullet had found its mark. Harding was lying on his back, dead, from a wound in his forehead.

Art saw him at the same time, and he dropped to one knee beside him.

"Major Harding!" Art said.

Delacroix, looking down at the boy and the major, shook his head sadly.

"There's nothing you can do for him now, son," Delacroix said.

Reaching down, Art closed Harding's eyes.

"Are you going to be all right?" Delacroix asked.

"Yes, sir," Art answered.

"Good man. Better get back in line, looks like they're comin' again."

Once more the English came across the field, though this time without benefit of pipe or drum, for fully ninety percent of the Highlanders, to include every piper and drummer, had been killed in the previous charges.

No longer an impressive front of redcoats and extended rifles, this was a ragged line of the desperate, brave, and foolish. The mighty yell of defiance that had issued from the throats of the attackers in the first wave was now a weak and disjointed cry from a few scattered men.

Again, the Americans fired, the volley as intense with this barrage as it had been the first time. British soldiers clutched breasts, stomachs, arms, and legs as blood seeped through their spread fingers.

Again, the line stopped, staggered, then turned and retreated back across the field.

All save one.

A single British lieutenant, screaming in rage and slashing at the air with his sword, continued toward the American ramparts even though every other man of the British Army was in retreat.

"Follow me, men, follow me!" the lieutenant shouted. Though he was now the sole target and could have easily been killed, the American defenders withheld fire, watching in morbid fascination as he used the bodies of his own dead to give him a foothold to the top of the rampart wall.

"Put them to the bayonet!" the lieutenant shouted, leaping down into the Americans, slashing out with his sword.

The Americans backed away from the sword, but not one made an effort to harm the lieutenant. Instead, everyone looked at him in awe.

Noticing his strange reception among the enemy, the British officer stopped screaming and lowered his sword. He looked behind him and, only then, realized that he and he alone had breached the rampart wall. He lowered his sword.

"Let's hear it for the lad!" someone shouted.

"Hip, hip!"

"Hooray!"

"Hip, hip!"

"Hooray!"

Half-a-dozen Americans moved toward the lieutenant. One of them took his sword, and to the young officer's surprise, they lifted him to their shoulders.

"Here's the bravest lad on the field today!" one of the Americans yelled, and once again, the Englishman was honored with cheers as he was borne on the shoulders of the men who, but moments earlier, had been his mortal enemy.

The British were unable to launch another attack because their commander, General Sir Edward Parkenham, had been killed by a bursting cannon shell. With his dying breath, Parkenham had ordered his successor to continue to press the attack. Wisely, however, the new commander had disobeyed, pulling the survivors off the bloodied field and leaving behind over two thousand of his men dead or wounded.

Only eight Americans were killed in the battle, and while most celebrated their great victory, Art could feel only sorrow over the loss of his friend, Major Harding. Harding and the other Americans who were killed were taken back to New Orleans, where they were given a military burial.

General Jackson attended the funeral, then sent word that he would like to talk to Art.

"Me?" Art asked when Delacroix took him the message. "Are you sure the general said he wanted to talk to me?"

"That's what he said."

"Why on earth would he want to talk to me?"

Delacroix shook his head. "I can't answer that question," he said. "But then, I learned a long time ago that you can't never figure out what a general has on his mind. Whatever it is, I expect you had better go see him. Generals ain't the kind of folks you want to keep waiting."

"Yes, sir," Art said.

"Here. Before you go, you ought to have this," Delacroix said, reaching out his hand. He was holding something.

"What is that?"

"It's a shoulder epaulet. Put this on your left shoulder."

"Only officers wear those."

"You are an officer," Delacroix said. "You was just made a second lieutenant."

Art held up his hand in refusal. "Captain, I expect you should give that to someone else, someone who earned it. Now that the battle is done and the danger over, I hear General Jackson is going to let everyone out who wants out. And I want out."

Delacroix snorted a half laugh. "Hell, boy, it probably ain't official. I'm not sure anyone as young as you can even be an officer. But far as I'm concerned, you earned this rank, and even if you take your discharge tomorrow, I figure you got the right to wear it for as long as you got left. I don't mind admittin' that I was wrong about you. When I first seen you back in St. Louis, I thought you was just some worrisome kid. But you sure changed my mind."

Hesitantly, Art took the epaulet. "I hope this doesn't cause any trouble with the other men."

"How do you think you got that?" he asked. "The other men elected you. Every one of them. Including, even, Corporal Monroe. Of course, part of it might be because as soon as you agree to take it, Monroe becomes a sergeant," Delacroix said, laughing.

"I'm real honored," Art said, pinning the epaulet onto his left shoulder. As he turned away from Delacroix, he was surprised to see the remaining men from the original twenty-eight who had left St. Louis together.

"Attention!" one of the men shouted, and all stood, then saluted, as Art walked by.

Awkwardly, Art returned the salute, then pulling himself up, walked by the standing men, heading for the house that had been put into service as General Jackson's headquarters.

"Thank you for coming to see me, Lieutenant," General Jackson said. He stared at Art for a long moment, a frown crossing his face.

"Damn, boy, how old are you?"

"I'm fifteen, General."

"You are fifteen and a lieutenant? That's not even . . ." He'd started to say legal, then stopped. "To hell with the regulations. I'm told that your men elected you to that position, and if they want you there, who am I to deny it? Besides, I know for a fact that Major Harding set quite a store by you. That's why he named you in his will."

"His will?" Art asked, surprised by the general's comment.

"I had all the officers make out a will and submit it to me before the battle," General Jackson said. "Were you related to Harding?"

"No, sir."

"But you knew him?"

"Yes, sir. We were friends from long before."

Was it long before? Art wondered. In terms of time, it had been only a year and a half ago since Harding had come to his rescue at Eby's cave. Only eighteen months, yet it seemed half a lifetime ago.

"Then maybe you will understand the rather strange wording of his will," General Jackson said. "He talks about something he calls the creature."

Art laughed. "Yes, sir, I know about the creature."

General Jackson stroked his chin, then looked over at one of the nearby staff officers.

"Colonel May, would you stand by, please, for the reading of the will?" General Jackson asked one of his staff officers. "Then I'll want you to witness it."

"Yes, sir," the colonel replied.

Taking a pair of spectacles from a box, then putting them on, carefully hooking them around each ear, General Jackson unfolded a document and began reading.

"To all who sees these presents, greetings. I, Peter Hamilton Harding, currently a major in General Jackson's Army of Tennessee Volunteers, and being of sound mind and body, but ever cognizant of the possibility of a premature appointment with my maker as the result of battle, do hereby make this last will and testament.

"First, I decree that any just debt owed by me shall be paid by any monies in my possession or due me."

General Jackson lifted his eyes from the reading and glanced up toward Art. "That has been taken care of," he said.

"Yes, sir."

Jackson continued reading.

"Second, all monies as may remain after the settlement of all just debt should be given to any church of the Protestant faith, said church to be selected by the regimental chaplain."

Again, Jackson looked up. "That too has been accomplished."

Reading again, Jackson continued. "And finally, I give profound regrets to my friend, Art, that I will be unable to see the creature with him. But to aid him in his own quest, I leave and bequeath my Hawken rifle and my pistol.

"Signed by Peter Hamilton Harding and witnessed by Pierre Mouchette Delacroix."

Jackson looked over at Colonel May. "Would you witness this, please, Colonel?"

Colonel May leaned over the table and affixed his signature to the place indicated by General Jackson.

"Lieutenant, you will find the rifle and pistol on a table in that room," Jackson said, pointing toward a door. "Take them and do honor to them, for they belonged to an honorable man."

"Yes, sir," Art said, feeling nearly as much pride now as sorrow.

If Art had wanted to go west to see the creature before, that desire was redoubled now. He felt a strong determination to carry out the plans he and Major Harding had made. It was no longer a drift without purpose. He felt as if he were on a mission.

top the problem with him. But to aid him in his own quest.

Seventeen

It was March 22, 1815. For the first time in several days it was warm enough, and dry enough, for Art to strip out of his coat and slicker. The sun was out and he was enjoying its warmth, not only the rays as they fell on him, but also the convection heat that radiated back from the horse.

Art had spent twenty dollars for the horse, ten for the saddle, and five for his sack of possibles. He had about ten dollars remaining, and he planned to use the last of his money in St. Louis, buying everything he might need for the trip west.

He had considered going west from New Orleans, but that would have taken him through Mexico. He had fought for the United States, so like Harding, he wanted the land he saw to be American land. The best way to do that would be to follow the trail west, as established by Lewis and Clark. That meant following the Missouri River, and to do that, he would have to leave from St. Louis.

Suddenly, and with no warning, the ground gave way beneath his horse's hooves. The horse whinnied in surprise and pain, then fell to its right front knee. Art leaped from the saddle, both to avoid being thrown, and to keep from inflicting any further injury to his mount.

It wasn't until Art hit the ground himself that he saw the problem. Recent rains had cut a channel between streams. Because the grass was high, the channel couldn't be seen, and when the horse had put its hoof down on the edge of the channel, the dirt wall had given way.

The horse stood up, but when it tried to put its weight on its right foreleg, it balked, pulling it up again sharply. Kneeling by the horse, Art picked up the leg for a closer examination.

He didn't have to search for the injury. It was a compound fracture, and the bloody stump of a bone was sticking through the skin.

"Oh," Art said, shaking his head and rubbing the wound gently. Even the softest caress brought pain, and the horse tried to pull its leg away. "Oh, Lord, I know that hurts."

Art had only owned the horse for a few months, but it had been both his beast of burden and his sole companion for the long ride. Feeling a lump in his throat and a stinging in his eyes, Art wrapped his arms around the horse's neck, embracing him. The horse looked at him with huge, brown eyes, begging the one who fed him, rubbed him down, talked to him, and cared for him, to do something to take away the hurt.

Art knew there was only one thing he could do. The stinging in his eyes gave way to tears as he loaded his pistol.

"I'm sorry, horse," he said. "There's no other way."

The horse continued to stare at him, not even looking away when Art raised his pistol and put the end of the barrel less than two inches away from the white blaze that shot down between the horse's eyes.

Art pulled the trigger. He felt something wet hit his face as the short, flat boom echoed back from the trees. The horse fell over on his side, bounced slightly, then was still.

Art ran his hand across his face, then held it out to look at it. He saw blood and brain-matter. Shutting his eyes, he turned away from the horse and walked several paces before he stopped, his gun down by his side, a small plume of smoke drifting up from the end of the barrel.

Art took several deep breaths, then turned back to the

job at hand. There was no way to salvage the saddle. Right now, it was as worthless to him as the dead horse. But he took the saddle blanket and pouches, then snaked the rifle out of its sheath. Stuffing his possibles bag down into one of the pouches, he hitched up his trousers and started walking north.

He reached New Madrid four days after his horse went down. Coming into a town that soon after losing his horse was a pleasant surprise to him. It was even better that the town was New Madrid, because that gave him a sense of where he was. There was another surprise waiting for him at New Madrid. Tied up to the bank was the steamboat *Delta Maid*.

The *Delta Maid* was one of a growing number of steamboats on the Mississippi. The *New Orleans* had inaugurated steamboat traffic on the river, commencing operation in 1811. The *Delta Maid* was one of the more recent additions to the Mississippi steamboat fleet, entering service early in 1814.

Art knew the boat, because when he was in St. Louis, loading and unloading freight wagons, he sometimes took a load to, or brought a load from, the *Delta Maid*. As a result, he knew several of the deckhands, and even the captain of the boat. He wandered down to the river's edge, then began looking out at the boat to see if he could recognize anyone. He was seen first.

"Art, how are you, boy? What are you doing in New Madrid? Last time I seen you, you was in St. Louis."

The man who hailed him was the boat's engineer, John Dewey. Dewey was near the stern of the boat, standing in the shadows of one of the huge boilers.

"Hello, Mr. Dewey," Art replied. "Yes, sir, I was in St. Louis, but I went down to New Orleans to join up with General Jackson."

"Was you there when the battle was fought?" Dewey asked. He stepped up to the boat railing and dumped the ashes from the bowl of his pipe.

"Yes, sir, I was."

"Well, good for you, boy. That was a heroic thing our soldier boys done down there. Taught them Brits a lesson they ain't likely to forget for a while."

"Mr. Dewey, you think there might be a job on the boat for me?"

"Well, now, you aimin' to be a river man, are you?" Dewey asked.

"Well, sir, I'd like to be a river man for a while anyway. My horse went down on me some way back, and I'm looking for a way to go to St. Louis."

"I could use a good man in the engine room," Dewey said. "Come on aboard, I'll talk to the captain for you."

"Thanks," Art said.

Captain Timmons was nearly a head shorter than Art. He was bald, but with a full, gray beard that reached all the way down to the beginning of a prominent belly. He wore a dark blue jacket with brass buttons and more trim across the front than Art had seen on any of the generals in the recent battle.

"Yes, I remember you, lad," Timmons said. "From what I observed of you, you were a good worker. A good worker indeed. So, 'tis a river man you want to be, eh? Well, I can't blame you. 'Tis quite a thing, being in command of this much power."

"Yes, sir," Art said.

"If you've a mind to, I'll take you on as an apprentice. A smart boy like you could be a riverboat pilot in no time."

"I appreciate the offer, Captain," Art said. "But if it's all the same, I'd rather work in the engine room."

"Here, now," Timmons said with a scowl on his face.

"The engine room, is it? You'd rather break your back and cover your face with soot than be captain of the boat? What kind of ambition is that?"

"Perhaps the lad is looking to learn the business from the bottom up, Cap'n," Dewey suggested, with a glance that told Art to go along with him. "Sure'n there's nothin' wrong with knowing the boat from stem to stern."

Captain Timmon's scowl changed to a smile. "Aye, a good point, Mr. Dewey. A good point indeed. Very well, lad, if it's a fireman's job you seek, 'tis a fireman's job you'll have. Report aboard first thing in the morning."

"Thank you," Art said.

Art stood on the boardwalk in front of the Blue Star, recalling the last time he had been here. That was nearly three years ago. He smiled. What a babe in the woods he had been then.

Hitching up his trousers, he went inside. It hadn't changed. It was still well appointed with finished furniture and gilt-edged mirrors, but somehow, it didn't make quite as big an impression on him now as it had before.

"Come in, mister, come in," the man behind the bar called. "Pick yourself out a seat. Just come in on the *Delta Maid*, did you?"

"No, sir, but I'll be leaving on the *Delta Maid*," Art said. "How have things been with you, Mr. Bellefontaine?"

Bellefontaine looked surprised at being addressed by name. "Have we ever met, boy?"

"Yes, sir, we have. But I'm a bit older and a mite taller now than I was then. I was in here sometime back with Major . . ." The rank came automatically and he stopped in midsentence, then corrected himself. "With Mr. Harding. Pete Harding."

"Glory be, yes, I do remember you, boy. Just a minute. Lily!" he shouted. "Lily, get down here."

A woman appeared on the upstairs landing. She walked up to the railing and leaned over to look down. "What is it?" she asked.

"Look who has showed up," Bellefontaine said.

Lily looked at Art, but it was obvious she didn't recognize him.

"Who is it?"

"You remember the boy who come in here with Harding that time? The boy that disappeared?"

Lily smiled broadly. "Oh, Lord, honey, was that you?" she asked, coming quickly down the stairs.

"Yes, ma'am, I reckon it was," Art replied.

Lily opened her arms wide, then pulled him to her. He could feel the softness of her full breasts under her embrace.

"Well, for crying out loud," she said. "Sit you down and tell me all about yourself. What happened to you that night? And where have you been since then. Lord, honey, you are growing into a handsome man, did you know that?"

Art blushed, and Lily laughed. "Now, ain't that cute. You're still innocent enough to blush. Damn if I'm not about half inclined to take that innocence away from you."

Art cleared his throat nervously, and Lily laughed again.

"Don't worry about it, honey. I don't do it for free, no matter how handsome the fella is. And I figure that, at this point in your life, you got better things to do. Now tell me about Pete. Where is that scoundrel, and when is he going to come see me again?"

The smile left Art's face. "I'm sorry to have to tell you this," he said. "But Pete's dead."

"Dead?" Lily gasped. Art was surprised to see her eyes fill with tears. "But when? How?"

Art told her the story of the Battle of New Orleans, playing down any role he'd had in it, telling it only from the perspective of having been an eyewitness.

Others, seeing Lily crying, came over to find out what was going on, so Art's telling was broadened to include them. He was surprised to see how many people knew and genuinely liked Pate Harding. But then, he didn't know why he should have been surprised. Harding was a very good man who had made a positive impression upon nearly everyone he'd ever met.

"Oh, uh, Mr. Bellefontaine, I owe you for a supper," he said.

"What?"

"That night I was here, I recall ordering my supper. I don't remember anything else until I woke up in a wagon, headed north. I figure you went ahead and fixed my supper anyway, and when I didn't come back, that meant you lost it. So, by rights, I should be paying for it."

Bellefontaine chuckled. "Truth to tell, I wound up getting paid twice for that supper," he said. "When you didn't show up for it, someone else bought it. Then, the next day, Harding paid for it. That was when he was out looking for you."

"Oh, honey, he turned this town upside down looking for you," Lily said. "I never saw anyone set so much store in another so fast. He was some worried about you, I'll tell you that."

"I wish there had been some way I could have let him know what happened to me," Art said. He laughed. "But to this day, I don't know myself."

"It's pretty obvious what happened to you," Bellefontaine said. "It's happened before. Someone knocked you in the head, then took your money."

"Yes, that's true. When I woke up in the wagon the next morning, I had a knot on my head and no money in my pocket."

"Uh-huh," Bellefontaine said. "And if truth be known, the fella that picked you up is more'n likely the one who hit you in the first place."

Art thought about Younger. Until this moment he hadn't considered the fact that Younger might have been responsible. As it turned out, Younger was so evil in every other way that the possibility had never dawned on Art. Now, as he considered it, he was almost positive that Younger was to blame.

"I'll be damned," Art said. "I do believe you are right."

"Well, it's not good to dwell on such things," Bellefontaine said. "Answer me this, boy. When's the last time you had a really good meal? I mean fried chicken, 'taters, beans, biscuits, maybe even a piece of pie."

Art smiled. "It's been a long time," he said. "It's been a really long time."

"Well, it ain't goin't be a very long wait till you do, 'cause I aim to whip you up just such a meal."

"I thank you, Mr. Bellefontaine, but I . . . ," Art started to tell Bellefontaine that he needed to save the money he had left in order to outfit himself for his trek west, but before he could speak, Bellefontaine interrupted him.

"I ain't goin' to be takin' no for an answer, boy," he said. "You see, this here ain't goin' to cost you one penny. It's all on the house."

"That's very nice of you," Art said. "But why would you do that?"

"Well, we could say it's because you was a friend of Pete Harding. And any friend of Pete Harding is a friend of mine," Bellefontaine said. "And that would be true. But we could also say it's because you fought down at New Orleans and I reckon that, because of what you done, this here territory is still part of America. I figure all you boys that fought down there is owed somethin'."

"Thank you," Art said.

Lily, who was still wiping the tears from her eyes, smiled through her tears and put her hand on Art's shoulder.

"Honey, I feel that way too, really I do," she said. "And I'm willin' to do somethin' I ain't never done before. I'll let you lie with me for free. Only, don't make me do it tonight. I don't intend to lie with anyone tonight. I need tonight to cry over poor, dear Pete."

"That's all right," Art said. "I understand."

Art didn't tell Lily that he wasn't going to be there tomorrow night. He was just as glad of it too. He still connected her to Harding and he felt as if it would be wrong for him to be with her. He knew that was dumb. After all, Lily was a whore and others were with her all the time. Harding also knew she was a whore and it hadn't bothered him. But somehow, Art's being with her wouldn't be the same thing.

"Lily, the boy . . ." Bellefontaine began, but Art got his attention, and with a small shake of his head, interrupted the revelation. Bellefontaine nodded his understanding.

PREACHER

The wheel was motionless now, and Art moved to join

Eighteen

Early the next morning, Art reported for work. Once on board, he walked out onto the hurricane deck of the *Delta Maid* and stood against the stern railing, then faced forward to look along the length of the boat. He could see the neat stacks of cargo and the long ricks of firewood.

Dewey told Art that his job would be to keep the boiler stoked with firewood and, when the time came, to join the other members of the crew in replenishing the supply of firewood every time they stopped.

Some distance forward of where Art was standing was the bow of the *Delta Maid*. Already, there was talk of outfitting special boats to go up and down the river, dredging a channel to facilitate faster travel by the steam-boats. But that had not yet been done, so for now the bow of those boats already plying the river were shaped like a spoon, thus allowing them to slip easily over shoals and sandbars.

The *Delta Maid* was 160 feet long, with a beam of thirty-two feet. From her lower deck to the top of the wheelhouse, she rose forty feet. It was nearly sixty feet to the running lights at the very top of the twin fluted smokestacks.

The *Delta Maid* could carry 220 tons of freight and thirty-six cabin passengers. The large paddle wheel at the stern was eighteen feet in diameter and twenty-six feet wide. The wheel was rotated by a steam engine at a rate of twenty revolutions per minute.

The wheel was motionless now, and Art turned to look down where the paddle blades met the water. A twig hung up on one of the blades for a moment, then broke loose and floated on by the keel. He had never been on a steamboat before, and he couldn't help but be a little excited over the prospect.

"Cast off the lines, fore and aft!" Captain Timmons shouted from the pilot deck, using his megaphone to amplify his orders.

"Aye, Cap'n, fore and aft!" his mate, who was down on the main deck, replied.

Captain Timmons pulled on the chain that blew the boat whistle, and its deep-throated tones could be heard on both sides of the river. Timmons put the engine in reverse, and the steam boomed out of the steam-relief pipe like the firing of a cannon. The wheel began spinning backward, and the boat pulled away from the bank, then turned with the wheel pointing downriver and the bow pointing upstream. The engine lever was slipped to full forward, and the wheel began spinning in the other direction until finally it caught hold, overcame the force of the current, and started moving the boat upstream.

They beat their way against the current, around a wide, sweeping bend, with the engine steam pipe booming as loudly as if the town of New Madrid was under a cannonading.

For the rest of the day the *Delta Maid* beat its way upriver, with the engine clattering and the paddle wheel slapping and the boat itself being enveloped in the thick smoke that belched out from the high twin stacks.

Already the boiler furnace required restoking, and Art had gone through several ricks of wood, marveling at how fast their supply of fuel was being consumed. He was told their next fueling stop would be Cape Girardeau. He couldn't help but wonder if the fuel they had on board would last even that long.

* * *

"I tole' you I heered the boat a'comin'," Eby said to the others. "Lookie there, over the top o' them trees. You can see the smoke."

Eby had eight armed men with him, nine counting himself, divided into three men each in three skiffs. They were waiting just north of a wide, sweeping bend.

"How much you reckon we're going to get offen this here boat?" Poke asked.

"I'd say more than you could get off ten flatboats," Eby replied.

"Lord, how we goin' to get all that out of here?"

"We'll scuttle the boat ag'in the sandbar," Eby explained. "Kill ever'one on board, then just take our time unloadin' it. After we get ever'thing off it, we'll burn it."

The steam pipe boomed, and Poke jumped. "What the hell? They got a cannon on that boat?"

Eby laughed. "That ain't no cannon," he said. "That's just the steam engine. It does that sometimes, makes a noise so loud you'd think it was a cannon."

"I just got a glimpse of it through the trees," one of the others said. He pointed. "There, you see it?"

"Yeah," Eby answered. "I see it. All right, boys, get in your boats and make sure your guns is primed and loaded. We'uns is about to get rich."

Art saw them when he was out on the deck, picking up another bundle of wood. Glancing toward the riverbank, he saw three boats waiting behind a fallen tree trunk. At first, he thought it was just curious; then, when he realized that there were three men in each boat, and that they were just sitting there, he got suspicious. His suspicions were confirmed when he recognized one of them as Eby, the man who had run the cave trading post back on the Ohio. He remembered that when the river pirates had attacked Harding's flatboat, one of them had mentioned Eby's name. If Eby was here with eight other men, trying not to be seen, it had to be for some foul purpose.

Putting the bundle of wood down, he went back into the engine room.

"Where's the wood?" Dewey asked.

Without a word, Art picked up his rifle, and began loading it.

"What is it, boy? What's wrong?" Dewey asked.

"I think we're about to have company," Art answered.

"River pirates?"

"Looks that way to me," Art said. His rifle loaded, he started on his pistol.

"Mule!" Dewey shouted.

"Yes, sir?" Mule answered. Mule was a free black man who worked on the boat in the same capacity as Art.

"Spread the word around, we're about to get jumped by pirates," Art said. "Tell everyone to get to their guns."

"Yes, sir!" Mule replied, springing into action.

Dewey brought the engine to all stop. As soon as he did, the speaker tube whistled. Dewey knew that it would be the captain, wondering why the engine had stopped, so he walked over to the speaker tube and yelled into it.

"Pirates ahead, Captain!" he shouted.

"There they are!" one of the crewman yelled, and Art stepped out onto the deck to see the three boats suddenly dart out. They were paddling fast, using the momentum of the current of the river to bring them to midchannel.

One of the men in one of the skiffs fired toward the steamboat. Art heard the crash of glass and when he looked up, saw that the pirate was shooting toward the wheelhouse, trying to hit the pilot and thus cause the boat to wreck. Thankfully, he'd missed the man.

Using a bale of cotton not only for cover, but also to provide a resting place for his rifle, Art fired at the pirate who had just shot, and saw him grab his chest, then fall back into the river.

That seemed to open the door, for those two single shots were followed by a rippling volley of fire as men in the skiffs and men on the boat exchanged fire with each other. The sounds of the shots, barely separated from one another, rolled back from the trees on each side of the river, thus doubling the cacophony of the battle.

The battle was brief but brutal. Realizing that they had lost the advantage, the pirates gave up the fight and started paddling hard to get away. At almost the same time, Dewey put the engine into full speed forward. The *Delta Maid* leaped forward. It was a moment before Art realized what they were doing, but once he understood, there was nothing he could do but stand by and watch.

Captain Timmons deliberately ran over one of the boats. Art rushed to the railing and saw pieces of the boat drifting away as the three men who had been in the boat were paddling hard to stay afloat. One of them slipped underwater and, caught by the severe undertow, didn't reappear. The other two swam hard for the opposite shore, chased by bullets fired at them by the angry crewmen of the *Delta Maid*.

Bullets popped into the water all around the swimmers, sending up tiny geysers as they did so. One of the two was hit and, like the unlucky man who had caught the full brunt of the collision, he went under and didn't come back up. The third man reached the sandy shore on the other side, pulled himself out of the water, then started toward the tree line.

At that moment, only Art, of all the men on board, had a rifle that was primed and ready. He raised the Hawken to his shoulder, touched his finger to the trigger, then had second thoughts. The man represented no immediate danger now, so why kill him?

Art lowered his rifle, then realized that if he didn't shoot, the others might question him. Raising his rifle, he did shoot, aiming not at the escaping pirate, but at a tree branch just above him. He pulled the trigger, there was a flash and a boom, then the tree limb exploded, just over the fleeing pirate's head.

"Ayii!!" the pirate shouted in fear, his cry of terror clearly heard by everyone on the boat.

"Good job, lad, you put the fear of God into him, that's for sure an' certain!" Dewey said, laughing.

"Too bad you ain't a better shot," one of the others said. "If you was, we would'a got 'em all."

At that moment the pirate who had made good his escape looked back toward the boat, and Art was able to see him more clearly. It was Eby.

When Eby stepped into the parlor of Etta Claire's Visitation Salon in Cape Girardeau, he was met by Etta Claire herself.

"Good evening, sir," she said. "May I get you a glass of wine while you are making up your mind which of our girls you will be visiting tonight?"

"I ain't visitin' with none of them," Eby said. "I'm Bruce Eby. I'm here to claim my girl, Jennie." He showed Etta Claire the papers proving that he owned Jennie.

"Oh, Mr. Eby," Etta Claire said. "Yes, I knew who you are, even though I've never met you. Jennie is engaged at the moment. If you will be patient for just a little longer, she'll be free, then you can go up to see her."

"I ain't here to see her. I'm here to take her out of here," Eby said.

"I've been making the deposit on a regular basis," Etta Claire said. "There is no difficulty with that, is there?"

"No, I got the money all right," Eby said.

"Then, I don't understand. If you are getting the money, then why do you want to take Jennie from here? It seems to be working out so well, and I know she is happy here."

"Happy?" Eby said. He laughed gruffly. "Woman, what the hell do I care whether or not she's happy. She's a slave. My slave. It don't make no difference to me whether she's happy or not. Now, you go upstairs and get her down here like I said. Else I'll get the sheriff on you."

"There is no need for that, Mr. Eby," Etta Claire said. "I'll bring her down to you."

"And if she's got 'ny clothes or anything that's hers, have her bring them too. We won't be comin' back."

When Etta Claire went upstairs to fetch Jennie, Eby picked up the bottle from which she had offered to pour a drink earlier. Pulling the cork with his teeth, he spat the cork out, then turned the bottle up to his lips, taking several Adam's-apple-bobbing drinks before pulling it down. Some of the wine dribbled down his chin and onto his shirt, but the shirt was so stained that it was scarcely noticeable. He ran the back of his hand across his lips, belched, then looked over toward the parlor itself, where several of the girls were looking back at him with a mixture of fright and revulsion.

"What the hell are you whores a'lookin' at?" he asked gruffly.

With a little gasp of fear, the women withdrew to the other side of the room.

"Mister, are you really going to take Jennie from us?" one of the girls asked.

"That's what I'm here for," Eby said.

"Who the hell thinks he's so important he can pull a man away from a woman before he's even finished?" a loud, angry voice said. The sound of heavy footfalls could be heard clumping down the stairs.

Eby pulled his pistol and cocked it, then held it level with the foot of the stairs.

"Where are you, you son of a bitch?" the voice declared. "Me and you are going to have . . ." At that moment the irate customer appeared at the foot of the stairs. At the same moment, he saw the pistol leveled at him and the anger left his face, to be replaced by fear. He held his hands out in front of him. "Hold it, hold it," he said.

"You goin' to make any trouble?" Eby asked.

"No, sir. Not a bit of it," the man said meekly. "Not a bit of it. You want her, you take her. She's all yours."

"Jennie!" Eby called. "Jennie, get your nigra ass down here now before I start tearin' up this place."

"Nigra?" the customer said, looking back up the stairs. "You tellin' me that girl is a nigra?"

A moment later Etta Claire and Jennie came down the stairs together. Jennie was clutching a cloth bundle. Tears were streaming down her face.

"Well, now," Eby said. "What's the cryin' about? You didn't think you'd come here to live, did you?"

Jennie didn't answer him.

"Mr. Eby, she has grown so close to the girls. Can she please tell them good-bye?" Etta Claire asked.

Eby picked up the wine bottle. "Yeah, she can tell 'em good-bye," he said. "I don't ever want it said that I'm a evil-spirited man." He drank from the bottle as, one by one, the girls came over to hug Jennie. All were crying, including Etta Claire, when Eby led her through the door.

"Mr. Eby, will I ever be comin' back here?" Jennie asked as they left the house.

"No," Eby said.

Jennie sobbed aloud.

"Ain't no sense in cryin' over it. That ain't goin' to change anything," Eby said.

Eby thought of the close call he'd had on the attempt to hold up the riverboat. Too many of his operations had taken place within fifty to sixty miles of Cape Girardeau. It was time for him to move on.

"I'm glad to see you ain't got ugly yet. Whores gets mighty ugly after a while, so iffen you're goin' to be of any use to me, I had to catch you while you was still comely."

"Yes, sir."

"Have you learned to enjoy sportin' yet?"

"Sportin'?"

"Lyin' with a man. You learned to enjoy it yet?"

"I . . . I don't enjoy it," Jennie said. "But I can do it."

Eby laughed gruffly. "Well, hell, girl, you been doin' it for what, five or six years now? I would expect you can do it. But that ain't what I ask. What I ask is, have you learned to enjoy it enough to make the man enjoy it?"

"They seem to like it."

"That's good. From time to time, maybe I'll teach you some of the things that men like," Eby said, subconsciously grabbing his crotch. "You'd like that, wouldn't you?"

In the whole time she had been with Younger, he had never been with her. She was certain it was because of Mrs. Younger, and for that she was glad. But there was no Mrs. Eby, which meant there was nothing to keep him away from her.

"I asked if you would like that," Eby repeated.

The little trick Carol had taught her, thinking of Art when she was with someone, had helped her get through some very disagreeable men. She was sure it would work with Eby as well.

"Yes, sir," she said dispiritedly. "I would like that."

"Yeah, I thought you would. Especially since I'm takin' you up to St. Louis, where you'll need to know more things. St. Louis is a fearsome big city and the men up there can't be pleased as easy as the men down here. But I figure with what I can teach you, with more men to be customers, why, you'll be makin' a lot more money in no time."

Nineteen

With a population in excess of eight thousand people, St. Louis looked particularly impressive as it was approached from the river. It spread out for some distance along the banks of the river and even back away from the river. Some of the buildings were as tall as three stories high. Art thought all of the buildings were handsome, whether they were made of brick, wood, mud, or stone. Regardless of their construction, they all glistened brightly, painted as they were by whitewash made from the limestone that was so plentiful in the area.

Even before turning toward shore, Captain Timmons signaled his presence by blowing the two-toned whistle. His whistle was answered by the firing of cannon from ashore.

Art, too recently in battle, where the firing of cannon meant more than a mere signal, jumped at the sound of the shore guns, but he recovered quickly. Sheepishly, he looked around the boat, then saw Dewey looking at him.

"Ain't nothin' to be embarrassed by, boy," Dewey said. "Only them that's actual fit in a battle knows enough to be a'feared of 'em."

Art nodded, but he didn't answer. No answer was needed.

Captain Timmons turned his boat toward the west, then ran it into the bank, putting the bow hard against the shore. A deckhand was standing at the bow, and carrying a line, he jumped down onto the riverbank as soon as the boat landed. The line was attached to a larger hawser, which he pulled off the boat, then tied around a post that was put in the ground for just that purpose.

Timmons signaled the engine room to stop the engine, and Dewey closed the throttle, then vented the steam. It was an impressive arrival.*

The landing of a steamboat was a great event in the lives of the citizens of St. Louis, and a significant number of them had come down to watch. Art's final job before reporting to the purser for his pay was to spread a tarpaulin over the remaining ricks of wood in order to keep them out of the weather. Even as he was attending to that, the gangplank went down across the front of the bow, and the stevedores came on board to begin unloading the cargo.

"Art? Art, is that you?"

Looking up toward the bald, bearded man who had called out to him, Art recognized Tony, the man he had worked with at the wagon-freight company.

"It's me, all right," Art said, smiling at his old friend.

"James! James, come look who we have here!" Tony said.

James came over and stuck out his hand. Remembering that he had once fought with James, Art was a little hesitant, but James didn't give him a chance. He grabbed his hand and pumped it enthusiastically.

"Art, m'lad, sure n' 'tis a fine thing to be seein' you. How have you been?" James asked.

"I have been fine," Art replied.

"Did you go to war?" Tony asked.

"Yes. I was at New Orleans."

---

*Although steamboats were on the Mississippi as early as 1811, the first steamboat did not actually reach St. Louis until the *Zebulon Pike* arrived at the foot of Market Street on July 27, 1817.

"Ahh, I heard we gave the English 'what for' at the Battle of New Orleans," Tony said. "It's too bad the war was already over."

"What?" Art asked, surprised by the comment. "You mean the war is over?"

"You haven't heard? The Americans and the English signed a treaty ending the war. And, as it turns out, almost a month before the fight at New Orleans."

"Before the fight at New Orleans?"

"Yes."

"Damn," Art said. "Then that means all those men died for nothing."

"All what men? I heard we didn't have but just a few kilt," Tony said.

"That's right, we only lost a few. One of them was my friend, Mr. Harding. But I was also referring to the English. They left so many of their dead on the field you could have walked nearly half a mile on them without your feet touching the ground."

"Aye, 'tis bad all right, even though the English be blackhearts, every mother's son of them," James said.

"Here, you two! You ain't bein' paid to palaver!" Mr. Gordon said, shouting at Tony and James.

"Mr. Gordon, look who is back," Tony said.

Gordon looked toward Art, then acknowledged him with a nod. "If you plannin' on comin' back to work for me, boy, keepin' them two from their labors ain't the way to do it."

"I'm sorry, Mr. Gordon."

"Boy, what about we meet later for a beer?" Tony asked. "Irish Tavern?"

"Aye, lad. Irish Tavern, same as always."

"I'll be there," Art said as his two friends went back to work.

Before going ashore, Art and the other crewmen lined up on the afterdeck to receive their pay from the purser.

Captain Timmons stood by, smoking his pipe and watching in silence, until Art stepped up to receive his pay, which was five dollars.

"Boy, a word with you," Timmons called, beckoning with his pipe.

"Aye, Cap'n?"

Timmons had a scowl on his face. "Dewey tells me you ain't at all interested in bein' a river man, that you was just using the boat as a means of getting to St. Louis."

Sheepishly, Art looked down at his feet. "Yes, sir, I have to confess that's true. I'm sorry if I misled you."

Unexpectedly, Timmons smiled. "No need to apologize," he said. "I admit, I would like to have you stay on. You're a good hand and there's no doubt in my mind but that you would make a fine river pilot if you wanted to, and set your mind to it. But I don't believe you can push a rope. If you don't want to be a pilot, there ain't nothin' I can do to change your mind."

"Being a riverboat pilot is about as noble a profession as I can think of," Art said. "But I've got a hankering to see the creature, and I made a promise to a dead friend to do just that."

Sticking his pipe back in his mouth, Timmons nodded. "Then, boy, you do that," he said. "A promise made to a dead friend is one you ought to keep." He stuck his hand out. "Good luck to you, Art. And if there's ever anything I can do for you, you just get in touch with me."

"Thanks," Art said. "I appreciate that."

Lucas Younger was one of the many who had come from the town to stand on the riverbank and watch the boat land. He was totally shocked to see that Art was one of the boat crew. Seeing the boy renewed the anger Lucas felt. After all, it was out of the goodness of his own heart that he had taken Art in. And how did Art repay him? By taking Jennie away from him, that's how. The best moneymaking scheme he ever had was gone because of this boy's interference.

I should've left you lyin' facedown in the shit and the mud behind the tavern in New Madrid, he thought. If it weren't for you, I'd still have Jennie.

As he thought of Jennie, he rubbed himself. He had never personally taken his pleasure with the young girl. He'd wanted to, but he'd held back because he knew Bess would raise hell with him.

Well, Bess was dead now, having died of the fever during the winter. She was dead, Jennie was gone, and he was left with an empty wallet, an empty bed, and no prospects. All because of Art.

Of course Younger had managed to turn a little profit on the boy, selling him to a slave hunter. It had been amazingly easy to pull it off. All he had to do was claim that Art was his slave. The burden lay with Art, then, to prove that he wasn't.

He wondered if that would work again.

"Seamus! Look who has come back to us," James called as he, Tony, and Art entered the Irish Tavern that evening. " 'Tis Art himself, a hero now he is, havin' fought the black-heart Englishmen at New Orleans."

"Welcome back, lad," Seamus said, greeting him warmly. "Find a table and it's an Irish whiskey I'll be bringin' you."

Art held his hand up. "Whiskey is still a bit too strong for my taste. Beer will do."

"Then beer 'tis, with a bit o' honey for sweetner if you need it," Seamus teased good-naturedly.

"Careful with the teasin' now, Seamus," James said. "I can tell you myself what the lad can do with a wee club."

The others laughed at James's self-deprecating humor. The three friends sat at a table in the center of the tavern, Art choosing the seat that left his back to the front door.

"So, tell us what it is like to be fightin' in a war," Tony said.

"It's noisy, frightening, noisy, cold, noisy, wet, and noisy," Art said.

"Would you be sayin' it's a bit noisy then?" James asked. The others laughed.

"Well, guns do make noise," Tony suggested.

"Yes, but it's not only the guns," said Art. "It was a big army, and when you are around that many people all the time, half of 'em are talking, the other half are singing, coughing, belching, or farting, and no one is listening. There's never a quiet moment."

"Well, that's the way of it in civilization," Tony said. "Now you take St. Louis. It's a big, noisy city."

"True," Art said. "That's why I'm leaving."

"Leaving St. Louis? Sure'n you just got here, lad. Where would you be goin', pray tell?"

"If it's your job you're worryin' about, we've already talked to Mr. Gordon. He'll put you on if you want. Without firing James," Tony said.

"I appreciate your asking for me," Art replied. "But I figure that as soon as I put together a few things I need, I'll be headin' west."

At that moment Lucas Younger entered the tavern, accompanied by the city sheriff and his deputy. Younger pointed to Art.

"There he is, Sheriff. That's my slave boy Art."

Hearing, and recognizing, Younger's voice, Art spun around quickly. He started to reach for his Hawken rifle, which was leaning against the table.

"Easy boy," Tony said quietly, reaching out to put his hand on Art's arm. "Your rifle's not primed and their pistols are."

Tony was right. Both the sheriff and his deputy were holding charged pistols.

The sheriff got a puzzled look on his face. "What do

you mean that's your slave boy?" he asked. "That boy's no nigra."

"He's Creole," Younger said. "You can't hardly tell Creoles from white folks. And he's my slave. I got the paper right here to prove it." Younger held up a sheet of paper.

"Sheriff, I'm no slave," Art said. "I don't know what that paper is, but it's wrong. And I'm not Creole, I'm white."

"White are you? Near 'bout all white folks have last names, but you don't. You two, what's his last name?" he asked Tony and James.

"He ain't never told us," James said. "But that don't make no never mind. You can look at him and tell he's white."

"My last name is Gregory," Art said. "You can check with General Jackson. I was a lieutenant in his army at New Orleans."

The sheriff laughed out loud. "You, a lieutenant? Now I know you are a'lyin', boy. Ain't no way someone as young as you would be a lieutenant."

"Read this here runaway notice," Younger said, handing another paper to the sheriff. "It'll prove I'm tellin' the truth and the boy is lyin'."

"Keep an eye on 'im, Coy," the sheriff said to his deputy. "Iffen he tries to run, shoot 'im."

"Yes, sir, Sheriff, I'll do just that," Coy replied, licking his lips and smiling at the prospect.

The sheriff began to read. "It says here a slave boy by the name of Art, so light that he could pass, escaped from his master while working in a lime pit in Sainte Genevieve." The sheriff looked over at Younger. "I thought you told me your name was Younger."

"That's right."

"This here paper says he run away from a man named Matthews."

"That's right. After the boy run away from me, I sold

him to a slave chaser. The slave chaser found him, and sold him to a man by the name of Matthews. But all that bein' said, the boy is still a slave and since Matthews ain't here to press his claim, I'm goin' to do it for 'im. Sort of a friendly arrangement between businessmen, so to speak."

The sheriff nodded, then glanced back at Art. "That true? Did you run away from Matthews?"

"Well, yes, but . . ."

"Ain't no buts to it, boy," the sheriff said. "If this be you"—he held up a piece of paper—"then you are a runaway slave. And it's my duty to take you back to your master."

"Them's my guns too," Younger said, pointing toward the table. "The pistol and the rifle, he stole 'em both from me when he run away like he done."

"Sheriff, you know he's lying now," Tony said. "If he stole them guns from Younger there, how do you suppose he still has 'em? Ain't no way this fella Matthews would let a slave boy keep guns like that."

"Ain't my job to be supposin' things like that," the sheriff replied. "Mr. Younger here is makin' all the charges. And since this boy done admitted that he run away from Matthews, well, I reckon I'll be takin' Younger's word over that of the Creole."

"I'm not Creole!" Art insisted.

"Uh-huh. And you said you wasn't no slave neither, then I got you to admit you was. All right, Mr. Younger, here he is. Now, how you goin' to hold him?"

"Don't you worry none 'bout me holdin' 'im. I got me some shackles hangin' from the saddle of my horse," Younger said. "I'll keep 'im shackled up till I get him back to his rightful owner."

"Let's go," the sheriff said, waving his pistol at Art.

"Sheriff, you're making a big mistake," Tony said. "They's too many things ain't addin' up here. I just don't believe this boy is a slave."

"Mr. Younger's got papers says he is," the sheriff said. "And the boy done admitted that he run away from Matthews down in Sainte Genevieve. 'Peers to me like that pretty much closes the case."

"Keep up, boy, keep up," Younger said, giving the shackles a jerk.

The hard yank caused Art to stumble, and he would have gone down had he not been fallen against Younger's horse. Younger was riding and Art was walking behind, pulled along by a chain that connected his shackles to the saddle of Younger's horse.

"I hear tell Matthews is a rich man," Younger said. "Ain't no tellin' what he might give me as a reward for bringin' one of his slaves back to him. What do you think, boy? You was with him. How much do you think he'll give me?"

"Whatever he gives you will be a waste of money, because I'll just run away again," Art panted. He had to pant because the brutal pace was causing him to gasp for breath.

"I reckon Mr. Matthews can break you of that. He's got hisself a big nigra with a long black snake of a whip. Slaves that runs away gets whupped by that nigra." He chuckled. "If I don't get nothin' from him but the chance to watch you get whupped, that'll be reward enough."

Art didn't answer.

"You shouldn't of come back and stole Jennie from me," he said. "You brought all this on yourself. When I let you go back in the woods, why didn't you just go your own way?"

"You didn't let me go, you tried to kill me. You left me for dead," Art gasped.

"Yeah, well, it would probably have been better for both of us if I had killed you."

Suddenly, and unexpectedly, Younger stopped his horse. "Now that I'm thinkin' on it, why am I even botherin' to take you all the way to Sainte. Genevieve? You're right, Matthews probably won't give me any money a'tall." He got down from the horse. "So, what am I going to do with you now?"

"You could let me go," Art said.

"No, I don't think I can do that. I think I'll just shoot you."

"You can't just shoot me. You won't get away with that."

"Sure I will. You're a slave, remember? There won't nothin' happen to me. All I got to say is you was tryin' to run away again." He raised his pistol, glanced at it, then laughed, an evil, cackling laugh. "But it ought to make you feel a little better to know that you're goin' to be kilt with your own pistol."

Younger pulled the hammer back and aimed at Art. Art waited until Younger was about to pull the trigger. Then, timing it just right, he swung the chain. Even though the other end of the chain was attached to the saddle, there was enough slack in it to loop around the pistol in Younger's hand. Art jerked as Younger fired. As a result, the gun barrel deflected and Younger wound up shooting himself in the stomach.

"Uhnn!" he yelled in shock and pain. He looked down at his lower abdomen and saw blood pouring from the self-inflicted wound. Dropping the pistol, he put both hands over the wound, trying to stop the bleeding. It was a futile effort, for bright red blood spilled through the gaps between his fingers. "I've . . . I've kilt myself!" he said. He looked up at Art. "You!" he said. "You!" He reached toward Art with bloody palms. Staggering toward Art, he tried to grab him, but Art stepped back and watched as Younger plopped face-down into the dirt. Younger moaned a few more times, jerked once, then was still.

Art waited another moment before he knelt beside him. Turning him over, he looked down into eyes that had already glazed over with death. Then he reached into Younger's jacket pocket and found the key to his shackles.

Two minutes later, mounted on Younger's horse and armed with his own rifle and pistol, Art turned west.

Twenty

Heading northwest from where he left Lucas Younger, Art came upon the Missouri River within a few days. Although he had never been in this part of the country before, he was now confident that he couldn't get lost. All he would have to do is follow the river, and that seemed like a simple enough task.

Shooting the turkey was easy. The bird had landed in front of him, then began pecking around in the grass as if totally unaware of Art's presence. Art could only imagine that the turkey either didn't see him, or perhaps he did see him but, never having seen a man before, didn't know enough to be frightened.

Art pulled his Hawken from its saddle sheath, hooked one leg across the saddle pommel, rested his elbow in that leg, then leaned forward to take careful aim before he fired. Nearly concurrent with the discharge of the powder and the rolling kick from the gun, feathers flew up from the turkey. The bird dropped without another twitch.

It was while Art was cleaning the bird that he came up with the idea of building an oven. He used stone and mud to make it, being careful to build it in such a way as to allow it to draw properly. After that he built a fire, and only then did he commit his turkey to the experiment.

Rather quickly, the aroma of the cooking turkey let him

know that his experiment was successful. The turkey was browning nicely, the juices sealed behind the crispy skin.

"Hello the camp!"

The hail startled Art, who had been so intent on cooking his turkey that he hadn't paid enough attention to what should have been routine camp security. He was surprised a moment later to see a tall, gaunt, bearded man come into the camp. The man was dressed in buckskin and homespun. The clothes were so gray with soil and sweat that it looked as if they had become a part of his skin.

"You campin' all by yourself, are you, young feller?" the man asked, looking around the camp.

For a moment, Art contemplated telling him that there was someone with him, but he knew better than that. No doubt, this man had already made a thorough check of the area and knew the answer to his question. If Art lied to him now, it would be a sign of weakness, a sign that he was afraid to admit that he was alone.

"I am alone," Art admitted.

"Bodie is the name," the man said, sticking out a calloused hand. "How are you called?"

"Art. Art Gregory. Call me Art."

"Art, is it? Well, you got 'ny coffee, Art?"

" 'Fraid not."

"Good, good. Then if I offer to share some of my coffee with you, maybe you'd see your way clear to share some of your turkey."

"I'd be happy to share my turkey with you, Mr. Bodie."

"Just Bodie, Art, no mister needed," Bodie said.

Bodie had ridden in on a mule, not a horse, and he went to the mule now and, reaching into his possibles bag, pulled out a coffeepot and a handful of coffee beans. Then, using the butt of his pistol, he began crushing the coffee beans.

"You headed anywhere in particular?" Bodie asked as he worked on grinding the beans.

"Just west," Art replied.

"Uh-huh. Goin' after the furs, are you?"

"Furs?"

"Beaver and sech. They pay good money for pelts back in St. Louis. Course, you don't have to go all the way to St. Louis to sell your season's take. Most o' the time you can sell 'em at Rendezvous."

"What is Rendezvous?"

Bodie laughed. "Boy, you are a green 'un, ain't you? Rendezvous is just about the most grandest thing they is. It's a place where all the trappers come together after a long winter up in the mountains. At Rendezvous they's whiskey, trade goods, and the like. Sometimes they's even women there. 'Course they's all whores, but whores is good enough iffen you been a long time without touchin' anythin' soft."

"You going to Rendezvous?"

Bodie shook his head. "This year's Rendezvous has done come 'n went. No, sir, I unloaded my furs an' now I'm headed back to St. Louis." He glanced over at Art's horse. "That's a good-lookin' horse you're a ridin'."

"Thanks," Art said.

"I guess you can see that I'm ridin' a mule."

"Yes, sir, I noticed that."

"Well, sir, they's a reason for that. You see, mules is a somewhat more surefooted critter than a horse. And that makes 'em good for use in the mountains. Fact is, it'd prob'ly be a good idea for you to trade that horse in and get yourself a mule."

"That a fact?" Art considered the situation. He was going to the mountains, so a mule might indeed be a better mount. Also, though he wasn't a slave, he was now technically a horse thief. And if caught with this particular horse, he might be tried for the crime.

Art started to say yes. After all, it seemed to him that the smart thing to do would be get rid of the horse. On the other hand, if Bodie got caught with the horse, he might be taken for the thief, and perhaps for a murderer, since only Art knew the truth of how Younger died. No matter how good a deal it might be for him, he couldn't leave Bodie holding the bag like that.

"There's somethin' you need to know 'bout how I come by this horse," Art said.

Bodie put the ground beans into water, then set the pot over the same fire that was cooking the turkey before he replied.

"You stole him, did you?"

"In a manner of speaking, yes," Art said.

"Then looks to me like you'd be anxious to get rid of him," said. "And to make it a better swap for you, I'll even throw in my trap line. If you're goin' after beaver, you're to be needin' a good trap line."

"There's more to it," Art said. He explained how Younger made the claim that he was a slave, how Younger was going to shoot him, but how he wound up shooting himself instead.

"All I was tryin' to do was get away from him," Art said. "But when I jerked the chain, somehow it caused him to shoot himself in the stomach. No one is going to believe that. Once they find his body, they are going to think I'm the one who killed him."

"Yeah, well, if you ask me, it served the son of a bitch right, killin' hisself like he done," Bodie said.

"Yes, sir. But I don't think anyone is going to believe me."

"I believe you, boy. If you wasn't tellin' me the truth, you wouldn't have to be tellin' me nothin' a'tall. You could'a just traded the horse for the mule and you'd be in the clear whilest I'd be the one ridin' the stole horse."

"Yes, sir," Art said.

"You got yourself a cup?"

"Right here," Art said, holding up his cup.

Bodie poured coffee into Art's cup, then into his own. "Her name is Rhoda," he said.

"Beg pardon?"

"The mule," Bodie said. "Her name is Rhoda. You'll be good to her?"

"You mean, after all I've told you, you'd still be willin' to trade?" Art asked.

"Well, I need me a horse," Bodie said. "And the one you're a'ridin' looks pretty good."

"What about the fact that it was Younger's horse?"

"From what you've told me about the bastard, I doubt he has too many friends who are crying over him. And since I know what to look out for, why, I reckon I can stay out of trouble. So, what do you say, boy? We goin' to trade?"

Art smiled broadly. "Yes, sir, we'll trade," he said.

"Listen, when you get up into the mountains, if you run into a couple o' ugly varmints—one is named Clyde, the other calls himself Pierre—why, you tell 'em that ole' Bodie says hello, will you?"

"Yes, sir. I'll do that."

"This be your first time in the mountains, boy?"

"Yes, sir."

"I thought so. Well, watch yourself up there. Winter comes early to the high country. Before too much longer you're goin' to be needin' to go to shelter. You any good with that there Hawken?"

"Tolerable," Art replied.

"Then I advise you to get you some meat shot, couple o' deer, an elk, maybe a bear. A bear would be nice 'cause you'd also have its skin to help you through the cold."

"Thanks for the advice."

Art and Bodie parted company the next morning, having changed mounts. Rhoda wasn't as comfortable a ride as Younger's horse had been; she had a more syncopated gait and Art had to get used to it. But she wasn't the first mule he had been around; back in Ohio his father had farmed with mules, so he knew how to work with them. And as mules go, Rhoda had an unusually gentle disposition.

Harding's description of the West had been accurate. He had said that you would travel for days to reach the horizon, only to see it continue to stretch out before you.

The plains had been impressive, with their wide-open spaces and the great herds of buffalo, along with deer and other game. But his pulse really quickened when he caught his first sight of the mountains, rising in the distant west.

At first, he thought it was a low-lying cloudbank. But after a day or two, he realized that it must be a mountain range, though certainly more magnificent in size and grandeur than anything he had ever seen before.

It took him nearly two weeks of hard traveling before he got close enough to make them out as individual mountains, rather than a featureless, purple rise in the distance. The closer he got, the higher and more formidable they became. He knew there was no way over them. He wondered if there was a way through them.

Perhaps he was too focused on the grandeur of the mountains, or maybe he was just careless, but for some reason he was nearly right on the bear before he saw it. Art had seen bears before, but he had never seen a bear the size of this one. This bear was at least twice, and maybe three times as large as any of the brown or black bears he had seen back east.

It was nearly time for it to hibernate, that is, assuming bears out here hibernated. Art didn't know whether these creatures hibernated or not. After all, he was in an area of the country he had never seen before. Here, everything was big, the mountains, the wide-open spaces, and this bear.

So far the bear had not seen Art, but that didn't mean he didn't know Art was here. Standing up on his hind legs, which gave him a height of at least eight or nine feet, the bear sniffed the air, trying to determine the source and direction of the scent he was picking up. Art had no doubt that once the bear located him, he would charge. Remembering Bodie's suggestion that a bear would be a good means of providing for the winter, as well as for his own self-preservation, Art decided to shoot it. Keeping a wary eye on it, he loaded his rifle, primed it, then pulled back on the hammer and aimed at the beast.

It was at precisely that moment that the bear saw him. Much faster than Art would have believed, the bear whirled around, came down on all fours, and started toward him. Art fired at the exact moment the bear turned to charge. As a result, the carefully aimed bullet that would have hit the bear in the heart, hit him in the side.

The grizzly roared in pain and rage as it lumbered toward Art at amazing speed. Art pulled his pistol and fired, hitting the bear in the throat. The bear slapped at the wound, as if driving away a mosquito, but it didn't stop its charge.

Art thought about running, but realized that he wouldn't be able to outrun the bear, and if the grizzly caught him from behind it would be all over. He had no choice now but to pull his knife, pray, and hope for the best.

The huge beast raised up as it reached Art. It tried to claw Art, but the bullet in its side had broken a couple of ribs, so it wasn't able to control the swipe. Art ducked under the bear's initial swipe, then stepped into the animal, thrusting his knife deep into where he thought the bear's heart was.

The grizzly made a second swipe with its other paw, and this time it connected. The long, sharp claws cut through Art's buckskin shirt and opened up four deep gashes in his shoulder and chest. Fortunately for Art, that was the bear's last effort, for even then it was dying. It fell on Art, knocking him down.

Pinned beneath the one-thousand-pound grizzly, Art

struggled to roll out from under. The struggle was difficult, not only because of the pain of his wound, but also because the loss of blood was making him feel dizzy and weak.

Then, finally free, he stood up, staggered a few steps away from it, and collapsed.

Twenty-one

When Art opened his eyes, he realized, with some surprise, that he was inside a building. He could smell smoke, and feel warmth from a fire. He could also smell something cooking.

He tried to sit up, but when he did pain and nausea overtook him, and he fell back on the bunk. He moaned.

"Bonjour, mon ami," a voice said.

Art turned his head and saw a man standing near the fireplace, in which a fire blazed. The fireplace didn't draw that well, thus accounting for the smoke Art smelled. That same smoke also filled the room with such a haze that it was difficult for him to make out the man's features.

"Who are you?" Art asked.

"I am called Pierre Garneau," the man said, speaking with a decided accent. "And you are?"

"My name is Art." Art studied his surroundings. The last thing he could remember was crawling out from under the bear. "The bear?" he said. "What happened to the bear?"

"Oh, you killed him, my young friend. It was a brave thing you did, to kill the bear with only a knife."

"I tried to shoot him, but I couldn't get the job done that way." Art looked around. "Where am I?"

"You are in the cabin of Monsieurs Pierre Garneau and Clyde Barnes."

"I've heard of you. You are Bodie's friends," Art said.

"Oui," Pierre replied, showing little surprise at Art's re-

sponse. "Monsieur Barnes and I are most curious. How is
it that you are riding Monsieur Bodie's Rhoda?"

"I traded my horse for Rhoda."

"I thought as much. Are you hungry? Do you wish to
eat?"

"Yes."

Art tried once more to sit up, but again he was overcome
by pain and nausea, so he fell back down. "I am hungry,"
he admitted. "But I don't think I can sit up."

"That is no problem. I will feed you," Pierre offered. "I
myself made this wonderful soup. I think you will like it,
and I think it will be good for you to eat."

Pierre carried a bowl of soup over, then sat on the edge
of the bed and began spoon-feeding it to Art.

"Thanks," Art said after taking his first bite. "Umm, you
are right, it is good soup. What kind is it?"

Pierre laughed. "Why it is soup from the bear you yourself killed," he said, holding another spoonful of the broth
to Art's lips.

Art studied his benefactor. Pierre looked to be in his late
forties or early fifties. He was a big man, bald, with a round
face and full beard, brown but turning to gray. His eyes
were blue, and one of them was drooping because of a scar
that started at his hairline, then came down to the eye socket
itself.

Pierre saw Art looking at the scar, and he chuckled. "My
face, it is not a pretty thing to see, no?" Pierre asked, pointing to his scar with the spoon, empty between bites.

"It's all right," Art said, not sure how to respond to the
question.

"You are a good boy not to hurt my feelings," Pierre
said.

"I . . . I didn't mean to stare," Art apologized.

"An unfriendly Sioux left this scar," Pierre explained.
"He was angry because I had no scalp for him to take."
He laughed at the self-deprecating reference to his baldness.

"Where is this cabin?" Art asked.

"It is in the mountain range called the Grand Tetons." Pierre laughed. "That is a joke, my friend. Most Americans do not know that Grand Teton means big titties." He put his hands over his chest, approximating breasts, and laughed again.

"Why would someone call mountains big titties?" Art asked.

"When you are well, look at them from a distance sometime. It looks like a woman lying down."

"Oh," Art said. He looked around the cabin. "Nice cabin," he said.

"Oui. I built this cabin myself, many years ago, when there were only a few Frenchmen and many Indians out here. At first I lived alone, then I met Monsieur Bodie. One year ago Clyde came to live with us, and this year Monsieur Bodie left, but as always I have stayed. And now you are here, so we are three again."

"Where is . . ."

"Clyde?"

"Yes."

"Clyde is collecting wood. He will be back soon, I think."

Almost as if on cue, the front door to the cabin opened and a man came in, carrying an armload of wood. This man was tall, clean-shaven except for a mustache, and with a full shock of hair that was dark brown. He was much younger than Pierre.

"Ahh, here is Monsieur Barnes," Pierre said. "Clyde, our young visitor is awake. His name is Art."

Clyde dumped the wood in the wood box, then brushed his hands together as he looked over toward Art.

"That was some deed, killin' that bear like you done," Clyde said. "Folks'll be tellin' that story for some time. Most especial you bein' someone as young as you are. How old are you anyway?"

"About sixteen, I guess," Art said. "I've sort of lost track of time."

Clyde nodded. "That'll happen to you out here. Don't happen that much to pups like you, 'cause we don't normally see folks as young as you out here. What you doin' here anyway?"

"I came to see the creature," Art said.

Clyde laughed out loud. "Come to see the creature, did you? Well, boy, that's as good an answer as any I've heard."

Finished with the soup, Pierre put the empty bowl down, then reached his hand out to touch Art's wound. Art reacted to the touch.

"Easy, *ami*," Pierre said. "Does it hurt?"

"Not too much," Art said.

Slowly, gently, Pierre pulled the bandage off the wound so he could examine it. "I've made a poultice of bear fat and pine needles," he said. "I believe that might be helping."

"Is it putrefying?" Clyde asked.

"No," Pierre replied.

"That's a good sign. If it ain't putrefying yet, it ain't likely to do it." Clyde came over to look down at Art.

"Boy, if you ever decide to become a gambler, you ought to do well by it," Clyde said. "You are one lucky fella."

"Yes, sir," Art said. "I guess what I'm luckiest about is that you two came along when you did. I'm beholdin' to you for taking me in."

"There is no need for you to be indebted to anyone," Pierre said. "You have purchased your right to be here with the food you brought."

"Food?"

"The bear," Clyde explained. "Most likely that single critter will feed the three of us for most of the winter."

"Oui," Pierre said.

"Besides which, we ain't neither one of us been back to the States in three or four years," Clyde added. "It'll be good to have someone to talk to this winter. You can fill us in on all the latest news."

"I don't keep up with the goings-on," Art admitted.

"Tell us about the war," Pierre said. "We have heard talk of a war between the United States and England. Is that so?"

"Yeah," Clyde said. "We're sort of wonderin' now if we're Americans or English."

"Or French," Pierre added.

"You are Americans," Art said. "We all are. America won the war."

"I'll be damned," Clyde said. "Beat them Brits again, did we? Well, I reckon that'll keep 'em in their place for a while."

"If the United States won it, it was, no doubt, with the help of France," Pierre said. "In the last war with England, the war you Americans call your war of independence, you won it only with the help of the French."

"I don't think the French were involved in the war this time," Art said. "If they were, I didn't hear anything about it."

"Do you know anything about the war?" Clyde asked. "Did you read or hear anything about any of the battles?"

"I know about only one battle," Art said. "And that's the Battle of New Orleans. I can tell you everything you want to know about that battle."

"And how is it you know so much about it?" Pierre asked.

"Because I fought in it," Art answered simply.

"Glory be. You? Young as you are, you fought in the war?" Clyde asked, surprised by Art's response.

"Why are you so surprised, Clyde?" Pierre asked. "Did the boy not kill a grizzly bear, armed only with a knife? Compared to that deed, I think fighting the British could not be so much."

* * *

Thanks to the attention given his wound by Pierre, Art recovered from the bear-mauling with no aftereffects. He began helping out around the cabin, preparing meals and cleaning and pressing beaver pelts. Finally, the time that Art was waiting for came. Pierre invited Art to go out with him and Clyde to help them set the traps.

When Art left the cabin to go with them, he was surprised at how cold it was. When he commented on it, Pierre reminded him that it was getting late in the fall. He also told him that the higher one went in the mountains, the colder the weather.

"How high are we?" Art asked.

Pierre shook his head. "That I cannot tell you, for I have no way of measuring such things. I know only that it is high."

Loading traps and camping gear onto their mules, for like Art, Pierre and Clyde were also riding mules, the three started out to set their trap line.

Pierre was riding in the lead, Clyde was following, and Art was bringing up the rear. The three rode for what seemed like hours, with not a word passing between them.

Art was actually enjoying the solitude, for he was coming closer than he had yet come to seeing the creature. Never had he seen such towering peaks as these, and he looked at them with wonder and appreciation, sorry only that his friend Harding hadn't lived long enough to see the mountains with him. And Pierre was right, the Grand Tetons did look like a woman lying on her back, breasts thrusting into the air. "Big titties," he said to himself, laughing at the illusion.

"I think this may be good place," Pierre said after they had been riding for several hours. When he dismounted, Clyde and Art dismounted as well. Pierre walked over to the edge of the stream and looked around. "Yes," he said.

"I was here in 1802. The beaver were many then. I think maybe they have come back to this place."

"You were here in 1802?" Art asked in surprise. "But that was before Lewis and Clark, wasn't it?"

"Lewis and Clark?" Pierre asked.

"Yes, you know, the great explorers?"

"Oh, yes, I remember them. They were nice young men. They were . . . how do you say . . . green behind the ears?"

Clyde chuckled. "Wet behind the ears," he said.

"Oui, wet behind the ears. They needed lots of help, but they were friendly enough."

"They needed help?" Art asked.

"Yes. And I did what I could to help them," Pierre said without elaboration.

"But surely they didn't need much help. They are the ones who opened the West."

Clyde laughed. "You think Lewis and Clark opened the West, do you, boy?"

"That's what I have always heard and read," Art said.

"Well, don't believe everything you hear and read," Clyde suggested. "When Mr. Lewis and Mr. Clark came West, there were already people out here, including our own Pierre Garneau. Pierre was one of their guides."

"How long have you been out here?" Art asked Pierre.

"I came out here when I was twenty-two years old," Pierre said. "That was in 1782."

Art whistled. "1782? You must've been the first one out here," he said.

Pierre laughed. "Hardly the first, my friend. And certainly not the last. Now, let us gather some traps and get to work, for we have a saying out here. *La langue n'attrape pas le castor.* That means, the tongue does not catch the beaver."

"We better get to work, Art. Else we'll have this old man to deal with," Clyde said good-naturedly.

Taking half-a-dozen traps from the back of the mule, Art threw them over his shoulder and followed his two mentors. When Pierre stepped out into the water and began wading, Art hesitated.

"What is it, boy?" Pierre asked, looking back at him. "Why do you stand there?"

"Isn't that water cold?"

"Oui, it is very cold. That's why I don't want to stand here all day."

"Then why are you standing in it?"

"You want to leave your smell for the beaver?" Clyde asked, wading out into the water behind Pierre.

"Oh, I see," Art said, understanding now that if they were careful to stay in the water, no human scent would be left. He followed the other two in the water, catching his breath sharply from the icy cold that shot up his legs when he stepped into the stream.

Pierre wandered down the stream for at least half a mile, looking for sign of fresh beaver activity. Finally, he stopped and held up his hand. Clyde and Art stopped as well.

"We will put our traps here," Pierre said. Dropping all his traps in the water, he proceeded to set them, depressing the springs by standing on them, putting one foot on each trap arm to open them up. When the traps were opened, he engaged the pan notch, holding them in the set position.

Art began setting his own traps, watching the other two in order to learn how it should be done. Once a trap was set, the trap chain was extended its full length outward to deeper water, where a trap stake was passed through the ring at the end of the chain and driven into the streambed.

Finally, the bait was placed. This was a wand of willow, cut to a length that would permit its small end to extend from the stream bank directly over the pan of the trap. Bark was scraped from the stick and castoreum was smeared on the small end of the switch, so that it hung about six inches or more above the trap. Castoreum, Art learned, was an oil taken from the glands of a beaver.

Once the trap was set, Art and the others would leave, remaining in the water until they were some distance away in order to avoid leaving their own scent to compete with that of the castoreum.

When the last trap was set, the men returned to the first group of traps. There, they found that some beavers had already been taken. They removed the beavers, then skinned them by making a slit down the belly and up each leg. After that they would cut off the feet, then peel off the skin. Once the pelt was removed from the carcass, it was scraped free of fat and flesh, the necessary first step in curing the pelts.

"Here, boy," Clyde said, lobbing off the tail of one of the beavers, and tossing it to Art. "Cook up our dinner for us."

It was the first time Art had ever eaten beaver tail, but he found it quite delicious.

The three men being hanged in St. Louis were river pirates who had terrorized the Mississippi River for several months. Their mode of operation was to wait in hiding along the banks of the river until they saw a flatboat or keelboat making its way downstream. Then they would get into a skiff, paddle quickly out to the boat, kill the unsuspecting boatmen, and take the boat's cargo.

More than fifteen boatmen had lost their lives to these same river pirates, and thousands of dollars worth of goods had been stolen. Then a group of St. Louis citizens, tired of the piracy, set a trap for them by concealing several armed men on one of the boats. The pirates were captured, brought to St. Louis, tried, and sentenced to death by hanging.

Today was the day their execution was to be carried out,

and almost two thousand people had gathered along the riverbank to watch the spectacle.

Bruce Eby, thankful that he had avoided this fate, stood in the crowd and watched as the three pirates, Moses Jones, Timothy Sneed, and Ronald Wilson, were led to the gallows. Wilson was a boy, no older than fifteen, and he was weeping and wailing entreaties to God to have mercy on his soul, and by his contrition had elicited some sympathy from the crowd of onlookers who were gathered for the execution. Moses Jones remained absolutely silent, but he glared sullenly, frighteningly at the crowd. Timothy Sneed, on the other hand, shouted taunts at them.

"Hear me, all you good people of St. Louis," Sneed called out to them. "You've come to watch ole Timothy Sneed dance a little jig at the end of a rope, have you? Well, don't be bashful. Come on up close. Hold your children up so they can get a good, close look at my ugly face. When my ghost comes callin' in the middle of the night, I want all the little children to know it's me comin' to get them!" He glared at the children, then laughed maniacally.

"Mama!" a boy yelled in a frightened voice. "Is he going to get me?"

"Yes, I'm comin' for you, sonny!" Sneed said. "I'm comin' for all of you!" he added. "No more peaceful sleep in St. Louis." Again, he laughed, a cackling, hideous laugh.

"You're an evil man, Timothy Sneed, to be frightening children in such a way," someone shouted up from the crowd.

"I may be frightenin' the children, but I'm givin' the ladies a bit of a thrill, I think. You men will all be thankin' me tonight when the ladies, still warm and twitching from watching ole Timothy's eyes pop out, will be snugglin' up to you for a little lovin'."

"Shut your evil mouth, Sneed, or I will gag you before the hanging," the sheriff warned.

Sneed laughed again. "Why would you gag me, Sheriff?

If I didn't play the fool for you at this hanging, what would be the pleasure in watching? Don't you know this is all part of the show?"

"Do you have no shame? Have you no sorrow for your wicked ways?" someone asked from the crowd.

"None!" Sneed replied.

"I do!" Wilson shouted. "I am sorely shamed that I left my poor old mother to seek my fortune. How she will grieve for me when she learns of my fate." Wilson was weeping now.

"Hell, boy, your mother's a bloody whore," Sneed sneered. "Grieve for you? She don't even remember you."

"Lord, I'm sorry for my sins!" Wilson shouted.

"Die like a man, Wilson," Sneed said. "Don't be givin' these psalm-singers your prayers."

"Leave the boy alone, Sneed. I'm thinkin' it might do us no harm to be goin' to meet the Lord with a prayer on our lips," Moses suggested.

"Ha!" Sneed replied. "It's not the Lord we'll be seein' when we open our eyes again. It'll be the face of Satan his ownself, and I'll not be goin' to see that bloody bastard with prayers. I'll be screamin' and cussin' all the way to hell. And when I get there, I plan to kick the devil right in his rosy red ass."

A gasp came from the crowd, for never had this group of God-fearing people been so close to pure evil. Some swore they could even smell sulfur.

"It's time," the sheriff said. He nodded to his deputy, and the deputy slipped a black hood over the head of each prisoner, one at a time.

Just before he put the hood over Sneed's face, Sneed happened to see Eby standing in the crowd.

"Eby, you son of a bitch!" he yelled. "I remember when you was one of us! How is it you ain't up here getting' your neck stretched?" The last part of Sneed's shout was muffled by the hood.

For a moment, Eby was frightened that perhaps someone in the crowd would connect him with Sneed's last, agonized challenge. But it quickly became obvious that Sneed's words were a mystery to the crowd.

With the hoods in place, the deputy stepped back away from the three men, then nodded at the sheriff. The sheriff pulled a handle that opened the hinged floor under the feet of the condemned.

The door fell open with a bang, and the three men fell through the hole. They dropped no more than knee-deep into the hole before the ropes arrested their fall. The ropes gave a snap as they grew taut. The hangman's knots slammed against the backs of the now-elongated necks as the three bodies made a quarter turn to the left.

Moses Jones and Ronald Wilson died instantly, and their bodies hung still. Timothy Sneed was not killed outright, and he jerked and twitched, lifting his legs and bending at the waist as if, by that action, he could find some relief. Those in the front row could hear choking sounds coming from behind the black hood, and they watched in morbid fascination as he continued his death dance.

Not until Sneed's body was as still as the others did Bruce Eby turn away. He felt a little nauseous, not because he had watched his erstwhile friends die in such a brutal way, but because he could have been one of them. It was only by luck that he'd avoided capture during his years of piracy, as it was by luck that he'd escaped death a year earlier when he and others had attempted to rob a steamboat.

He had given up piracy after the steamboat incident, and for the last few months had been living solely on the income generated by Jennie's prostitution. But though Jennie was a favorite among St. Louis's sporting gentlemen, she wasn't the only whore in town and competition was getting stiffer. It was time to do something else, and he already had his next move planned.

Twenty-two

It was a man, full-grown, who came down from the mountains three years later, riding a horse and leading a mule. His square jaw, straight nose, and steel-gray eyes staring out from under a wide-brimmed hat gave him the kind of rugged good looks that women would find handsome, if there were any women around to observe him. But for the last two years, from adolescence into young adulthood, Art had been much more apt to encounter a grizzly bear than a woman.

When he could, Art rode down the middle of a stream, thus keeping his track and scent difficult to follow. The mule behind him was packed with his share of the beaver pelts he, Pierre, and Clyde had taken over the last two years, and now he was going to Rendezvous to sell them.

This would be Art's first Rendezvous, and he was very much looking forward to it. Pierre and Clyde had told him a great deal about Rendezvous, how trappers and mountain men from all over the West would gather in one place to sell their furs and buy fresh supplies for the next year's trapping.

"They's booze there too. And gamblin'," Clyde said.

"And sometimes ladies," Pierre added.

"Whores," Clyde corrected.

"Prostitutes they may be," Pierre agreed, "but they are women nevertheless."

"What are you tellin' him about it for?" Clyde asked. "He's just a boy."

"A boy? He is bigger and stronger than either of us," Pierre said. "And I think the women might find him better-looking as well."

"Maybe so. But seein' as he's never had a woman, he's still a boy far as I'm concerned," Clyde said.

That conversation had taken place a week ago. Then, when Art announced the next morning that he would be leaving for Rendezvous before them, Clyde teased him by asking if he was going early so he could find a woman and become a man.

"I'm going because I can no longer stand the sight or smell of either of you," Art replied. It was all in good-natured fun, and though Art had already informed them that, after Rendezvous, he planned to go out on his own, the three men parted as good friends. And why not? Art knew that he owed his very life to them.

For the time being, Rendezvous on the Platte was the biggest city between the Pacific Ocean and St. Louis. Nearly a thousand people were gathered in the encampment: trappers from the mountains, fur traders from the East, Indians, explorers, mapmakers, merchants, whiskey drummers, card sharks, and whores.

Before Art left the cabin, he, Pierre, and Clyde had divided, evenly and fairly, the beaver pelts they had taken. When he arrived at Rendezvous, he was greeted by representatives from the fur traders, all wanting to make offers on his plews, as the beaver pelts were called.

"The London Fur Trading company will give you the best deal on your plews," a representative of the company said. "If you sell to anyone else, you'll regret it."

Similar offers came from half-a-dozen other traders, all anxious to take his load. Some offered "a line of credit at any merchant in Rendezvous" as their compensation.

Art sold to a dealer from St. Louis, doing so because, though the St. Louis dealer offered him less money, it was all in cash. Also, Art could remember seeing one of the company signs back in St. Louis, so he knew it was a legitimate operation.

With the money in hand, Art began wandering through the encampment grounds to see what was available.

He bought lead and powder, a new trap to replace one he lost, a new rubber slicker, and some waterproof matches. He bought some new flint, a needle and thread, a flannel shirt, and some socks. He also bought a book. When he left home, sneaking out of the house that night five years ago, the last thing he ever thought he would miss was reading. But there were times over the last couple of years when he wished he had a book, not only as a means of passing the time, but also in order to improve his reading skills.

He bought coffee, flour, and sugar. He also bought some dried peaches, thinking he might make a pie or two when he got around to it.

After he made all the necessary purchases, he began looking around the encampment to see what kind of entertainment was available. There was a tent that sold liquor, so he had a couple of beers. There were whores there too, but they were obviously whores who were no longer able to earn a living in competition with younger, more attractive whores. Every one of them was much older than he was, and all showed the ravages of their profession.

One thing that did catch his interest was a shooting contest. A hand-lettered sign offered a prize of one hundred dollars to the winner. A board was stretched across two oaken barrels, and on the board was the sign-up form for the contest. Behind the board, a man sat in a chair, paring an apple. He looked up as Art studied the entry form.

"You plannin' on enterin', mister? Or, are you just goin' to read the words offen that piece of paper there?"

"Where does the one-hundred-dollar prize come from?" Art asked.

"It comes from me," the man said.

"You are going to give one hundred dollars to the winner?"

"Yep. Crazy of me, isn't it?" the man replied. He carved

off a piece of the apple and popped it into his mouth. "But that's the kind of man I am. You think you could win?"

"I don't know," Art replied. "Maybe."

"Then you ought to enter. It would be an easy one hundred dollars for a man who can handle a rifle."

"All right," Art said. He picked up the pen and started to sign the paper.

"Huh-uh," the man behind the board said, shaking his head. "First you give me ten dollars. Then you enter."

Art took ten dollars from the roll of money he had just received for his pelts.

"Sign up, young man."

As Art signed the roster, he saw that he was the twenty-seventh man to do so. He looked at the proprietor, who was carving off another piece of the apple.

"According to this, you have already taken in two hundred seventy dollars. I don't think it will be all that hard for you to give away one hundred."

"Well, well, what do we have here, a scholar? What do you care about how much money I make, as long as you get yours?"

Art thought about it for a moment, then nodded. "All right," he said. "I won't mind taking your money."

It was early afternoon and Art was waiting, with more than three dozen other shooters, for the contest to begin. Some of the shooters were cleaning their guns; others were sighting down the barrels of their rifles at the targets they would be using. Some were just standing by calmly, and Art was in that group.

"Art? Art, do you remember me?" a woman's voice asked.

Startled to hear his name spoken by a woman, Art turned to see who had called him. He saw a young woman between eighteen and twenty. She had coal-black hair, dark eyes, and olive skin. She was pretty, though there was a tiredness about her. Suddenly Art recalled the young girl who had cared for him in Younger's wagon so long ago.

"Jennie? Jennie, is that you?" he asked.

She smiled at him. "You remembered," she said.

"Yes, of course I remembered."

Spontaneously, Jennie hugged him. He hugged her back.

"Here, now, that's goin' to cost you, mister," a gruff voice said. "I ain't in the habit of lettin' my girls give away anything for free."

Quickly, Jennie pulled away from Art, and he saw the expression of fear and resignation in her face.

"Iffen you want to spend a little time with her, all you got to do is pay me five dollars," the man said.

"Eby," Art said, recognizing the man.

Eby screwed his face up in confusion. "Do I know you, mister?"

"No," Art said. "But I know you. What have you got to do with Jennie?"

"Ahh, you know Jennie, do you? Then you know she's the kind that can please any man."

Art looked at Jennie, who glanced toward the ground. "He owns me, Art," she said.

"What about it, mister?" Eby said. "Do you want her, or not?"

"Yeah," Art said. "I want her."

Eby smiled. "That'll be five dollars."

"No," Art said. "I don't want her five dollars worth, I want to buy her from you."

Eby took in a deep breath, then let it out in a long sigh. "Well, now, I don't know nothin' 'bout that. She's made me a lot of money. I don't know if I could sell her or not."

"You bought her, didn't you?"

"Yes, I bought her."

"Then you can sell her. How much?"

"One thousand dollars," Eby said without blinking an eye.

"One thousand dollars?" Art gasped.

Eby chuckled. "Well, if you can't afford her, maybe you'd better just take five dollars worth."

"No," Art said. "I reckon not."

"On the other hand, you could come back next year. I 'spec she'll be a lot older and a lot uglier then. You might be able to afford her next year."

Art looked at Jennie. For just a moment, there had been a look of anticipation and joy in her face. When she realized that her salvation was not to be, the joy had left. "I'm sorry," he said.

"Shooters, to your marks!" someone called.

Looking away from Jennie so he wouldn't have to see the disappointment mirrored there, Art picked up his rifle and walked over to the line behind which the shooters were told to stand.

Those who weren't in the shooting contest gathered round to watch those who were. There were a few favorites, men who had participated in previous shooting contests, and the onlookers began placing bets on them.

The first three rounds eliminated all but the more serious of the shooters. Now there were only ten participants left, and many were surprised to see the new young man still there.

"All right, boys, from now on it gets serious," the organizer said. "I'm putting a row of bottles on that cart there, then moving it down another one hundred yards. The bottles will be your target, but you got to call the one you're a'shootin' at before you make your shot."

As Art looked up and down the line of competitors, he saw that one of them was Eby. He wondered if anyone but him knew who Eby was, that he was a river pirate and, probably, a murderer.

Eby had the first shot. "Third from the right," he said. He aimed, fired, and the third bottle from the right exploded in a shower of glass.

This round eliminated four more, the following round eliminated two, and the round after that eliminated two. Now, only Art and Eby remained. A series of shots left them tied.

"Move the targets back another one hundred yards," the organizer ordered, and two men repositioned the cart.

By now all other activity in the Rendezvous had come to a complete halt. Everyone had come to see the shooting demonstration. Only two bottles were put up, and Eby had the first shot.

"The one on the left," Eby said quietly. He lifted the rifle to his shoulder, aimed, then fired. The bottle was cut in two by the bullet, the neck of it collapsing onto the rubble.

"All right, boy, it's your turn," the organizer said.

Art raised his rifle and aimed.

"Boy, before you shoot, how 'bout a little bet?" Eby said.

Art lowered his rifle. "What sort of bet?"

"I'll bet you five hundred dollars you miss."

Five hundred dollars was all the money Art had left. If he missed, he would leave here totally broke. Plus, he would have lost the shooting contest, so he wouldn't even have that money.

On the other hand, he had already bought and paid for everything he needed for another winter's trapping.

"Ahh, go ahead and shoot," Eby said. "I'll be content with just beating you."

"I'll take the bet," Art said.

"Let's see the color of your money."

Art took the money from his pocket, then held it until Eby also took out a sum of money. Both men handed their money over to the organizer, who counted and verified that both had put in the requisite amount.

"It's here," the organizer said.

"All right, boy, it's all up to you now," Eby said.

Once again, Art raised his rifle and took aim. He took a breath, let half of it out . . .

"Don't get nervous now," Eby said, purposely trying to make him nervous.

Art let the air out, lowered his rifle, looked over at Eby, then raised the rifle and aimed again. There was a moment of silence, then Art squeezed the trigger. There was a flash in the pan, a puff of smoke from the end of the rifle, and a loud boom. The bottle that was his target shattered. Like the other bottle, the neck remained, though only about half as much of this neck remained as had been left behind from the first bottle.

The crowd applauded as the organizer handed the money over to Art. "Looks like you won your bet, but the outcome of the shooting match is still undecided," he said. "Gentlemen, shall we go on? Or shall we declare it a tie?"

"We go on," Eby said angrily. "Put two more bottles up."

"Wait," Art said.

Eby smiled. "Givin' up, are you?"

"No," Art said. He pointed toward the cart. "We didn't finish them off. The necks of both bottles are still standing. I say we use them as our targets."

"Are you crazy? You can barely see them from here. How are we going to shoot at them?"

"I don't know about you, but I plan to use my rifle," Art said.

The others laughed, and their laughter further incensed Eby.

"What about it, Eby?" the organizer asked. "Shall we go on?"

Once more, Eby looked toward the cart. Then he saw that the neck from his bottle was considerably higher than the neck from Art's bottle. He nodded. "All right," he said. He raised his rifle, paused, then lowered it. "Only this time he goes first."

Art nodded, and raised his own rifle. "The one on the right," he said.

"No!" Eby shouted quickly. "You have to finish off the target you started. "You have to shoot at the one on the left."

"I thought we could call our own targets," Art replied.

"You can. And you already did. Like you said, we didn't finish them off. You called the bottle on the left. That's the one you've got to finish."

"I think Eby's right," one of the spectators said.

"All right," the organizer agreed. "Your target is what remains of the bottle on the left."

"A hunnert dollars he don't do it," someone said.

"Who you goin' to get to take that bet?" another asked. "Ain't no way he can do it."

"What about you, mister?" Eby asked. "You want to bet whether or not you hit it?"

"No, I'll keep my money," Art said.

"Tell you what. You wanted the girl a while ago. I'll bet her against a thousand dollars you don't hit it."

Art looked over at Jennie and saw, once more, a flash of hope in her face.

Could he hit it? It was a mighty small target and it was a long way off. He had never made a shot quite like this.

He knew he was a fool for taking the bet, but he used the same rationale he had used before. If he missed, he still had everything it would take to trap for a year. And Jennie would certainly be no worse off. On the other hand, if he hit it, she would be free.

"I don't want the girl to come to me. I want you to set her free."

"You hit that sawed-off piece of a bottleneck on the left there, and I'll set her free," Eby promised.

"All right, Eby. You've got a bet."

Everyone expected to wait for a long moment while Art aimed, but to their surprise he lifted the rifle, aimed, and fired in one smooth, continuous motion. The bottle neck shattered. The reaction from the crowd was spontaneous.

"Did you see that?"

"Hurrah for the boy!"

"Who would'a thought . . ."

"Look out!"

The last was a warning from someone who noticed that, while everyone else was cheering and applauding, Eby had raised his rifle and was aiming it, not at the target, but at Art. He came back on the hammer.

There was a loud bang, followed by a cloud of smoke. When the smoke rolled away, Eby was lying on his back with a large bullet wound in his chest. Turning quickly, Art saw Clyde Barnes.

"Mr. Barnes! Where did you come from?" Art asked.

"I decided to come on in early as well," Clyde said as he held his still-smoking rifle. "I couldn't let you have all the fun."

"Ever'one seen it," the organizer of the shooting match said. "Eby was about to shoot the boy, when this fella shot him. We ain't got no judge nor law out here, but I say it was justifiable killin'."

"Here, here!" another shouted.

"Anyone say any different?"

There were no dissenters.

"Then let's get that piece of trash buried and get on with the Rendezvous. Oh, by the way," the organizer said, looking over toward Jennie. "I reckon we also heard the bet. Girl, you're free."

Jennie smiled as the others applauded, though some got the distinct impression that she would just as soon have belonged to the young man who had come so gallantly to her rescue.

Art took his winnings, then turned to Jennie.

"Where will you go now?" he asked.

"I could stay with you," Jennie offered.

Art smiled. "Don't think the offer isn't tempting," he said. He shook his head. "But it wouldn't work. I'm not ready to leave the mountains yet. And I don't think you'd get on well here." He gave her one hundred dollars.

"What is this for?" she asked.

"I figure you can get back to civilization with one of the traders here," Art said. "But once you get back, you'll have to find some way to support yourself. Until you do, you'll need some money to live on."

"Thanks," Jennie said, taking the money.

"You have any idea where you'll be going?"

Jennie smiled. "You mean so you can find me if you ever come back?"

"Something like that," Art agreed.

"I'll be at Etta Claire's Visitation House in Cape Girardeau," she said.

"What is that? A hotel?"

Jennie laughed. "Something like that," she said.

When Art saw Clyde watching them, he introduced Jennie to him, telling how he had met her many years ago. "I tried to free her then," he said. "I stole her, but we got caught. This is the first time I've seen her since."

"You've changed, Art," Jennie said. "I called you a boy once. Now you're a man."

"Not quite a man," Art said.

"What do you . . . ?" Jennie started to ask. Then she smiled as she understood what he was saying. "Well, maybe we can do something about that," she suggested.

That night, Art left Jennie's tent, his passage into manhood complete.

For a sneak preview of William W. Johnstone's
next novel

The Last Gunfighter: SHOWDOWN
(coming from Pinnacle Books in March 2002)

just turn the page. . . .

The town had grown quite a bit—it had been no more than a wide spot in the road the last time Frank Morgan had ridden through. About ten years back, he thought with a smile. He didn't remember the name of the town.

Still not much to it, Frank thought, looking down at the buildings from a hill. But maybe there's a barbershop with a bathhouse. Hard winter was fast approaching, and Frank was out of supplies and needed a bath, a rest, and a meal he didn't have to fix himself. He looked down at Dog, sitting a few yards away.

"And you need a good bath too, Dog," he told the cur.

Dog wagged his tail without much enthusiasm at the mention of the word "bath."

A few weeks had passed without incident since Frank left the valley of contention and the twin towns of Heaven and Hell. But peaceful times were coming to a close, and events were now in motion that would forever change the life of the gunfighter known as The Drifter.

They were events that Frank could not alter even had he known about them. Events that had taken place in a private men's club in New York City, a club to which only the very wealthy could belong.

Frank had intended to head southwest when he left the valley, but instead he headed northwest. Why he didn't know; he just did. He rode slowly toward the town, passing a weather-beaten sign that read: SOUTH RAVEN.

Frank shook his head at the name. "I wonder where North Raven is."

It took Frank about a minute to ride the entire length of the town, passing a general store, a saloon, a leather and gun shop, a barbershop/bathhouse/undertaker's combination, a small cafe, a stage office/telegraph office, and several other stores, and finally reining up in front of the livery stable.

Frank swung wearily down from the saddle. An old man walked out of the shadows of the livery, sized up Frank for a few seconds, and said, "Howdy, boy. You look plumb tuckered out."

"I am," Frank replied.

"Come a ways, have you?"

"A good piece, for a fact. Did I miss the hotel coming in?"

The old man chuckled. "Ain't nary. But they's rooms for hire over the saloon."

"Where's North Raven?"

"You're funny, boy, you know that? There ain't no North Raven. Never has been. Town is named for the local doctor. He's from the South. That's how the town got its name."

"What part of the South?"

"Alabama. Raven was a doctor in the Confederate Army. I think he was a colonel."

"There were a lot of them, for a fact."

"You was a Rebel?"

"I was."

"I was on the other side. That make a difference to you?"

"Not a bit. War's over."

"We'll get along then. I hate a sore loser. You want me to take care of your horse?"

"And my dog. I'll stable them and feed them."

"You don't think I can do that?"

"I don't want you kicked or bitten."

"I'll shore keep that in mind. Them animals got names?"

"Horse and Dog."

The liveryman smiled. "That ain't very original."

"It suits them."

"I reckon so. You look sort of familiar to me, boy. You been here 'fore?"

"Can't say I have. But I appreciate you calling me 'boy.' "

"I'm older than dirt, boy. Everybody's younger than me." He stared hard at Frank for a few seconds. "I've seen you 'fore. I know I have. It'll come to me."

"Let me know when it does. Is there anyone in town who does laundry?"

"The Widder Barlow. The barber'll get your stuff to her."

"All right. My gear will be safe here?"

"Shore will. I got a room with a lock on the door."

"The cafe serve good food?"

"Best in town," the liveryman said with a wide smile.

"It's the *only* cafe in town," Frank reminded him.

"That's why it's the best!"

Frank smiled and led Horse into the big barn, Dog following along. Dog would stay in the stall with Horse. Frank left his saddle in the storeroom, and walked across the street to the barbershop. He arranged for the washerwoman to launder his trail-worn clothes, and then took a long soapy bath in a tub of hot water. He dressed in his last clean set of long-handle underwear and clean but slightly wrinkled jeans and shirt, and then got a shave and a haircut. He stepped out onto the boardwalk smelling and feeling a lot better, and walked over to the cafe for some lunch.

"Beef stew, hot bread, and apple pie," the waitress told him. "It's all we got, but it's good and there's plenty of it."

"Sounds good to me," Frank told her. "And keep my coffee cup filled, please."

Frank ate two full bowls of the very good stew and drank several cups of coffee before his hunger was appeased. He walked across the street and signed for a room, then went into the bar for another cup of coffee and to listen to the local gossip, if any. The patrons fell silent when he entered, everyone giving him the once-over. Frank ignored them, and took a table in the rear of the room and ordered a pot of coffee.

"I know who you are," a man said from across the room.

Frank sipped his coffee and offered no reply to the statement.

"What are you talkin' about, Ned?" another patron asked.

"The gunfighter who just walked in," Ned said.

"What gunfighter?"

"Frank Morgan."

"Frank Morgan! Here in South Raven? You're crazy, Ned."

"That's him what just walked in, Mark," Ned stated. "Sittin' over yonder drinkin' coffee."

Frank took another sip of the strong coffee and remained silent.

"Is that true, mister?" Mark asked. "Are you Frank Morgan?"

"Yes," Frank said quietly.

"Oh, my God!" another patron blurted out as the front door opened, letting in a burst of cool air. "He's here to kill someone."

"I don't think so," the old liveryman said, stepping into the saloon. "Seems like a right nice feller to me." He walked to the bar and ordered a beer. "Your name come to me, Mr. Morgan. I knowed it would."

Frank lifted his coffee cup in acknowledgment.

"I seen Doc Raven right after you stored your stuff. Told him 'bout you. I reckon he'll be along any time now."

"Why are you here in our town, Frank Morgan?" another bar patron asked.

"To spend a couple of days resting my horse," Frank said. "To eat a meal I didn't cook and to get my clothes washed. Is that all right with you men?"

"Shore suits me," the liveryman said.

"You're not lookin' to kill no one?" Mark asked.

"No."

"By God, it is you," a man said, stepping into the saloon from a side door. "I thought old Bob was seeing things."

"Told you it was him, Doc," the liveryman said. "Dr. Raven, Mr. Morgan."

Frank nodded at the man. "Do I know you?"

"No," the doctor replied. "But I've seen your picture dozens of times and read a couple of books about you."

"Don't believe everything you read," Frank told him. "According to those books, I've killed about a thousand white men, been wounded fifty times, been in gunfights all over the world, and been received in royal courts and knighted by kings and queens."

The doctor laughed. "And you're still a young man."

"I'm forty-five, Doc. And feel every year of it."

Dr. Raven walked over and sat down at the table with Frank. "Coffee," he called to the barkeep. He looked at Frank. "You're very relaxed, Mr. Morgan."

"The name is Frank, Doc. And why shouldn't I be relaxed?"

"You're not aware of what's been planned back East?"

"No. Something that concerns me?"

"I would certainly say so. It's been in the works for . . . I'd guess six months, at least. Probably longer than that. You're about to become the prey in what some are calling the ultimate hunt."

Frank's eyes narrowed for a few seconds; that was the only betrayal of his inner emotions. "You want to explain that? And also, how did you find out about it?"

"I have a doctor friend in New York City. We went to college together; graduated just in time to serve in opposing sides during the Northern aggression against the South. He wrote me months ago asking if I knew you. Of course I told him I didn't. In his next letter, which was not long in coming, he told me about a group of wealthy sportsmen who had each put up thousands of dollars for this hunt. To be blunt, the money goes to the man who kills you."

"The authorities haven't stepped in to stop this . . . nonsense?"

"Obviously not. The so-called sportsmen are on their way West as we speak."

"The West is a big place, Doc. How do they propose to find me?"

"I understand the group has hired private detectives to do just that."

Frank hottened up his coffee and sugared it. "Doc, this is the damnest thing I ever heard of. Hell, it's *illegal.*"

"Of course it is. But you're a known gunfighter. In the minds of many people, the world would be a better place without you in it."

Frank sighed heavily. "This is going to bring out every two-bit gunslinger west of the Mississippi."

"Well, we have a couple of gunfighters right here in this community. They'll be in town later on today, you can bet on that."

"You know that for sure?"

"It's Friday, Frank. And they always come in for drinks on Friday."

"Ranch hands?"

"They occasionally hire on to some ranch, when they're not stealing cattle or horses."

"I'm surprised anyone will hire them."

"Oh, they're careful not to steal from any of the ranchers in this area. But they've already heard about the other money being offered for your head."

"I think everyone in the West has heard of that," Frank said sourly. Then he took a sip of coffee and smiled. "But no one's collected it yet."

"Obviously," Doc Raven replied. "But don't sell these

two men short, Frank. I'm told they're fast and good shots to boot."

"Young?"

"Midtwenties."

"The worst age. They're full of piss and vinegar and think they're ten feet tall and bulletproof."

"That's an interesting way of putting it, but accurate, I would say."

"Doc, if I could have one wish granted me by the Almighty, it would be that I could live out the rest of my years in peace and never have another gunfight. And that's the God's truth."

Doc Raven stared into Frank's pale eyes for a few seconds. He took in the dark brown hair, peppered with gray. The thick wrists and big hands. "I believe that, Frank. But it doesn't change anything."

"No, it doesn't. Doc, do you have a marshal here?"

Doc Raven smiled. "No. We had one, but he died several years ago. Not much goes on here, Frank. It's a very peaceful town."

"If you want it to remain peaceful, then I'd better move on, Doc."

"Nonsense. You're welcome to stay here for as long as you like."

"The mayor and town council might have something to say about that."

"I'm the mayor, Frank. And we don't have a town council."

"Interesting. How about a bank?"

"A small one, located in the stage office."

"Do you own it too?"

Raven laughed. "As a matter of fact I do. Would you like to open an account?"

"Not really. I have ample funds with me."

The doctor pushed back his chair and stood up. "Enjoy

your stay in South Raven, Frank. I've got to see about a patient. We'll visit again soon."

"I'm sure."

The doctor walked out of the saloon and into the crisp fall air of southern Idaho. Frank poured another cup of coffee and rolled a cigarette.

THE FIRST MOUNTAIN MAN SERIES BY
WILLIAM W. JOHNSTONE

__**The First Mountain Man**
0-8217-5510-2 $4.99US/$6.50CAN

__**Blood on the Divide**
0-8217-5511-0 $4.99US/$6.50CAN

__**Absaroka Ambush**
0-8217-5538-2 $4.99US/$6.50CAN

__**Forty Guns West**
0-7860-1534-9 $5.99US/$7.99CAN

__**Cheyenne Challenge**
0-8217-5607-9 $4.99US/$6.50CAN

__**Preacher and the Mountain Caesar**
0-8217-6585-X $5.99US/$7.99CAN

__**Blackfoot Messiah**
0-8217-6611-2 $5.99US/$7.99CAN

__**Preacher**
0-7860-1441-5 $5.99US/$7.99CAN

__**Preacher's Peace**
0-7860-1442-3 $5.99US/$7.99CAN

Available Wherever Books Are Sold!

Visit our website at www.kensingtonbooks.com